Frank O'Connor (pseudonym of Michael O'Donovan) was born in Cork in 1903. His childhood and adolescence in Cork, much of it spent in poverty, is reflected both in his classic autobiography *An Only Child* (1961) and the novels *The Saint and Mary Kate* (1932) and *Dutch Interior* (1940; reprinted by Blackstaff Press in 1990). He fought on the republican side in the Irish Civil War (1922–3) and was imprisoned in Gormanstown during this time. The political turmoil of that period is described in his first volume of short stories, *Guests of the Nation* (1931) and his biography of Michael Collins, *The Big Fellow* (1937). Active in the Irish literary revival of the 1930s and 1940s, he was a director of the Abbey Theatre and poetry editor of *The Bell*. Frustrated by official censorship of his work, he left Ireland in 1950 to accept invitations to teach in the United States, where his short stories won great critical acclaim. At the time of his death in 1966, O'Connor's reputation was assured and his work continues to have an enduring influence on modern literature and Irish life.

The
Saint
and
Mary Kate

FRANK O'CONNOR

**THE
BLACKSTAFF
PRESS**

BELFAST

U.S. DISTRIBUTOR
DUFOUR EDITIONS
CHESTER SPRINGS,
PA 19425-0449
(215) 458-5005

First published in 1932 by
Macmillan and Company Limited
This Blackstaff Press edition is a photolithographic facsimile
of the first edition printed by R. & R. Clark Limited, Edinburgh

This edition published in 1990 by
The Blackstaff Press Limited
3 Galway Park, Dundonald, Belfast BT16 0AN, Northern Ireland
with the assistance of
The Arts Council of Northern Ireland

Printed by The Guernsey Press Company Limited

British Library Cataloguing in Publication Data
O'Connor, Frank *1903–1966*
The Saint and Mary Kate.
I. Title
823.912 [F]
ISBN 0-85640-445-4

TO MY MOTHER

Let nothing disturb thee,
Nothing affright thee,
Everything passes,
God is unchanging.
He who has patience,
Everything comes to him;
He who has God,
He lacks for nothing—
God, only, suffices.
St. Teresa

I

MARY KATE'S mother was going away to Dublin.

For weeks this had been dinned into the child's mind by all her acquaintances, normal and grown-up. About her head hovered a sort of halo like that which had crowned young Doyler's head when her father died. Her mother was going away. 'And what will you do when your mother is gone?' a neighbour would ask jovially, and Mary Kate, who was nothing if not respectable, replied that she would cwy. That she should cwy seemed to be the accepted thing, though in her heart of hearts she looked forward to her freedom and had no intention of cwying. Neither had she any illusions about what she would do. She knew quite well that she might do what she pleased so far as Auntie Dinah was concerned, because Auntie Dinah seemed incapable of thinking child for more than three minutes on end. Whatever her thoughts were they only very remotely concerned Mary Kate. The child knew that when Auntie Dinah's logic faltered or her glance wandered for an instant—plop!— suddenly and inexplicably she had been shot out from the warmth of memory into the icy abysses of nonentity, as if a trap-door had sprung open under her feet.

Her aunt did not worry if she was out. Mary Kate

felt if she remained out for a week her aunt would never notice. So when excursions were mooted among the older girls and someone asked, 'Will *you* come, Mary Kate?' or when a dare was thrown at her—'I dare and double-dare you to do that'—Mary Kate would reply earnestly and with perfect confidence, 'I will when me ma goes to Dublin.' And this always created an impression.

The older girls were rather pleased to take her round. 'Mary Kate's old one is going to Dublin,' they told one another gravely. It sounded as if they were saying 'to America'.

'Mary Kate's old fellow is in Dublin,' they added. This was a pretty tough nut for the child to crack. Other girls all had an old fellow or old fellows, that was clear; young Doyler had an old fellow who went down the Big Hole and would not come back; this was not quite so clear, but it was an event witnessed by her own two eyes, and as such could not be denied. What, though, was an old fellow in Dublin like? Accordingly, there were conversations of this sort:

'Auntie Dinah, what's me old fellow?'

'Your old fellow's on the railway.'

'What's "on the railway"?'

Conversation was temporarily short-circuited.

'Auntie Dinah?'

'Well, bandylegs?'

'Is me old fellow like Mr. Vaughan?'

'No, he isn't.'

'Is he like Doyler's old fellow?'

'Listen to that one!' her aunt appealed despairingly to an invisible audience.

'Is he?'

'Oh, he is, he is, breeches and all! Will you be quiet?'

'Auntie Dinah, have he a habit?'

'He have; a dozen, all bad.'

Her aunt's attention was fading. Clearly she had not caught the dramatic implication of the word 'habit'. Mary Kate raised her voice.

'Have he cangles?'

'He have.'

'Have he' (a moment of meditation and a shout)— 'have he a coffin?'

And then—the trap-door.

But from the remarks of Big People she began to recognise that the neighbours approved as much as she her mother's going to Dublin. Over things as they were now hung a cloud. Apparently an old fellow in Dublin was not all that it might be: it was half way between Blind Drunk (a regrettable interlude) and Herring for Dinner (which was a misfortune that carried a taint of reproach). Anyhow, it was an omission to be repaired at the earliest possible moment.

Many times she heard the question, 'I suppose yourself will be going up soon, Mary Kate?' Many times she was asked which she would rather, stay here or go to Dublin, and learned that politeness required a preference for her present home, which would be rewarded by a pat on the head and a 'That's my good little girl!' But other remarks were made in her hearing which were not so lightly to be disposed of.

'Isn't it about time she went back to her husband, the vagabond?'

'Indeed and indeed it is. After her five or is it six year?'

'Believe you me, if he was another man he'd put her hair in the grass.'

Remarks like these spoke unmistakable venom against her mother, but they passed lightly through Mary Kate's mind. She was not one to bear malice.

Many visitors appeared in her mother's attic, all coming as much to make a survey of the position as to present a neighbourly instalment of farewell. The McCormicks lived at the very top of the huge old tenement that was known locally as the Dolls' House.

"Twill be hard and difficult enough on you now, God help us!' sniffed Doyler's mother, half pitying, half in judgment. "Tis no easy thing getting used to a man and you your own boss all these long years. Men are a fright, the dear knows! Fidgeting and cobbling and daubing whenever they get a hammer or an old paint-brush; nosing round and dirting everything; coming in with the wet smell off them in winter; and in summer—with respects to you, ma'am —a stink of perspiration that would turn your stomach. . . . I dare say now he takes his drop?'

'Oh my, no!' Babe McCormick exclaimed in her loftiest tone.

'Look at that now! Well, well, some people have all the luck.'

'I never as much as seen him with the sign of drink on him.'

'You never seen much of him any other way either, ma'am, by all we hear.'

'Well, I hope I know my own husband better than most people!'

'I hope so, indeed, ma'am; but all the same 'tis a fright the way men do change. Is it six years now since you seen him last? Well, I wonder you'd be able to stop without him that long!'

'Oh, after all, he couldn't expect me to go until he made a home for me.'

'Indeed you're right, ma'am. He could not. And you that was always used to a good one.'

Another visitor came in. This time it was Babe's oldest crony, Bridie Daly, more often called Dona Nobis, a very pious maiden lady of rather more than medium height; thin and sallow, with but one tooth left in her head. She had an air of immense and righteous understanding, faintly touched with humour, and stood primly by the door, her hands folded before her canvas apron.

'We were saying,' Mrs. Doyle went on respectfully, 'what a terrible toff Babe's husband must be, Miss Daly.'

Dona Nobis sniffed, looked suspiciously about her, and turned to Babe.

'You're taking the plunge?'

'Oh, yes, I'm taking it,' Babe sniggered.

'Is it he gave you the bag?' Dona Nobis asked, bending short-sightedly to Babe's brand-new travel-ling-case of polished leather.

'It is.'

''Tis a nice bag,' Dona Nobis remarked sadly.

''Tis a beautiful bag!' exclaimed Babe indignantly. 'It must have cost him a mint of money.'

'It isn't a bad bag,' Bridie added, pursing her thick purple lips. She disapproved of commendation that outstripped her own.

'Well, 'tis a great thing to have money,' remarked Mrs. Doyle.

'Was it Canon Whalen done it?' Dona Nobis rapped out.

'Canon Whalen?' Babe's eye flashed the newcomer a withering look. 'What have Canon Whalen to do with it?'

'Oh, I seen him pass up the stairs, that's all.'

'I didn't lay my eyes on Canon Whalen this three weeks.'

'I thought I heard the child say,' Mrs. Doyle began feebly, for Babe was a noted prevaricator, 'it was up here he came.'

'Maybe it was,' replied Babe shortly. 'If he came I didn't see him.' Then with a toss of her head, ''Tis a queer thing to say priest nor minister can't come to see a woman without rising all the gossips of the neighbourhood.'

Dona Nobis laughed dryly, a pleasant, girlish laugh. But her mouth was ugly, the heavy lips exposing one yellow tooth that protruded from her bare gum like the prow of a ship.

'Oh, my good girl, believe you me, believe you me, for all the care I care you might have Saint Peter and Paul's presbytery in with you.' She nodded her head and smiled—a palpable hit.

Babe flushed. 'Now I wasn't referring to you, Bridie.'

'And for the matter of that'—Bridie's voice grew still more unctuous—'the Lord Bishop of Cork and the whole Cork diocese.'

'Now you're taking me up wrong,' the other woman protested.

Bridie's voice grew into a deeper calm, and her palms sketched a priestly *Ite, missa est*.

'And after that, Mrs. McCormick, for your information you might have the Holy Office, the Pope of Rome, and the whole college of cardinals.'

She tossed her greying head, clapped her hands lightly to mark the period, and strode smiling out of the room.

As the day fixed for her departure drew nearer Babe went out less and less, and if she went out at all it was after dark. She didn't, as she said to Dona Nobis, want people to be pulling her up and gossiping about it for hours with her. 'Oh, no, Babe,' replied Bridie, 'them were people you only wanted to know when you needed the loan of a drop of milk or a pinch of sugar.'

To the end of her life Mary Kate would best remember her mother as she was on those early winter evenings, standing under the wall lamp before the cracked mirror, puffing powder on to her bright, pretty, girlish face. Mary Kate would demand a kiss merely to be enveloped in the soft clothes and heavenly odour by which she identified her rough and slattern mother. Then another dab of powder to detach herself afresh from contact with Mary Kate, a hoisting of skirts and pulling up of stockings, one stiff marionette-like whirl under Dinah's piercing eyes, and she was off down the stairs.

At last she caught a slight cold and ceased going out at all by night; so she remained at home in the attic, regulating her trousseau, as the neighbours said. Mary Kate's father was a toff all right; everyone admitted that; nothing was too good for her mother—travelling-bags and warm overcoats, dresses, shoes, boxes of silk stockings, and a marvellous selection of underwear, the faintest of faint pinks and palest of spring-sky blues.

But alas for Babe! Her cold grew worse. She began to get shiverings and acute pains in the back from which she took to her bed. The room stunk of the odorous liniment with which Dinah rubbed her. It was just her rotten luck, she remarked bitterly, on the verge of tears. God knew she was the sort of unfortunate creature, if she took it into her head to have a day's outing in Crosshaven it would be sure to rain bucketfuls, and if she didn't go, as soon as the last train had departed the sun would be splitting the flags.

The landing was all for her going, cold or no cold. The change, they said, would be certain to do her good, and besides her husband was just the sort of simple young man that would make provision for her illness and have nurses and what not else for her if she got really bad. The alternative to this was the appalling misery of being ill in the Dolls' House. This was just what Babe thought herself. Whatever else she wanted, she did not want to be ill there. So she hurriedly sat up in bed to write to her husband and fix an earlier date for her departure.

Everyone in the tenement came to say good-bye the evening before she went. She was to leave by an early train, which started at a quarter to eight. She received her visitors lying down but looking otherwise well and happy. Nick had arranged that she was to travel second class and was bringing a car to the station to meet her. Her bags—three spick-and-span leather ones—were standing by the door. She was just a little pensive; it was all so strange going out like this into the world and leaving everything familiar behind.

Mary Kate was very solemn that night as she was rolled into her cot by a far-away-eyed Auntie Dinah. She told herself it was the last night her mother would be with her, the very last, last, last night. She would never again see her lying in that corner—never again. But it was queer how little this meant to her. She was genuinely shocked by her own callousness, for it has been said that Mary Kate even at this early age was nothing if not respectable.

Auntie Dinah undressed, lowered the lamp, and blew it out, and the long shallow window began to bloom and flicker mysteriously in the darkness. It was the stars that were emerging from it like delicate white moths. Mary Kate thought of them as flying towards her, hundreds of them, their fine white wings a-tremble. They came closer and closer, and she drew the clothes about her in delicious excitement. But to her disappointment they remained outside, beating against the window-pane. She must really think of her mother.

By closing her eyes tightly she succeeded in getting two tiny tears to spring from the corners of them. Then she rubbed hard with her fists until her eyes were sore and as many as five tears were squeezed out. These she carefully gathered and preserved in the hem of her nightdress in order to prove to herself by its ultimate wetness that she had done all a little girl could decently be asked to do. But by some strange ill-luck just when she began to labour with the sixth she remembered a girl who had promised to take her down the quays when her mother went to Dublin, and all at once the quays, long magical miles of quays, appeared before her eyes just as the others described them, with mountains of timber for hide-and-go-seek, great flocks of sea-birds and pigeons, all fluttering wildly about in search of scattered grain, and big, big, big ships (at each successive whispered 'big' her mind soared up and up), and black sailormen and bearded sailormen that chewed tobacco, and these last you had to dodge, or if you didn't—so the girls said—they'd put a spit in your eye and choke you.

And on this ecstatic vision she fell fast asleep.

II

AWAKENED suddenly by a moan, she opened her eyes
and looked about her. The lamp was lighted and standing beside the bed in which her Auntie Dinah sat up,
apparently talking at great length to herself. Her face
looked so white and drawn that Mary Kate thought it
was she who was ill, but then she heard in her mother's
familiar tone the same little gasp of pain. She remembered with consternation that last evening her aunt
had not rubbed her mother's back as she was used
to do; and now no doubt her mother would die, and
Auntie Dinah would never forgive herself.

You gathered as much, because each time Babe
moaned Auntie Dinah, startled as it were from a
momentary somnolence, would toss back one of the
stiff black shiny pigtails that framed her face, and at
the same instant a perfect torrent of speech would pour
from her lips. After a while Mary Kate gathered that
the torrent was in fact a very urgent entreaty addressed
to something or somebody who appeared to be standing
immediately behind her own head. This, she felt, was
distinctly uncomfortable. Such a passionate, one-sided
conversation with somebody at her poll, just where the
wall most usually was, gave Mary Kate the creeps.

Even more creepy was the way this torrent was
launched forth in a sudden spurt of demonic energy

by the merest sigh from her mother, and then grew fainter and thinner until it dried up altogether. Then Auntie Dinah, who while it lasted had not as much as glanced at the sister lying on the pillow beside her, but had kept her eyes fixed rigidly upon the wall in front, would automatically twirl her bright, birdlike head and ask hopefully, 'Are you better now, Babe?'

'I am not better,' Babe would reply, gritting her teeth.

'Stick it,' her sister counselled. 'Stick it whatever happens. Oh, for the love of the good God, stick it until morning!'

And then that quick rustle of clothes and that little cry of pain, and Auntie Dinah tossed her pigtails back distractedly and spread her hands out in supplication to the invisible being at the head of Mary Kate's cot, gabbling the while.

'Oh, Sacred Heart of Jesus! Good, kind, Sacred Heart, have pity on me poor sinners now and at the hour of my death amen. If anything happens her, Sacred Heart, I warn you 'twill be the death of me. I know no more than the man in the moon what'll become of me. Now I beseech thee, sweet Heart of Jesus, don't let her give another screech, because I swear to you if she do me misfortunate head will fly off me. There's a pain inside it now you'd think 'twas a mowing machine. . . . And she going to Dublin in the morning, and her bags packed and her ticket bought and everything. . . . I tell you again it isn't right. Thou canst not do things like that. . . . Six candles I promise if only she gets her train; six candles and a novena of masses. I'm sure she's going to start off again in a minute. She's getting ready. I know it.

I can feel it coming. Stop her! Stop her, do, I beg of you!'

But no one seemed inclined to interfere, and in a few moments Babe cried out again, only more loudly; she was lying on her side, and her mouth was buried in the pillow.

'Oh! oh! oh! oh!' the torrent burst out, 'I know I'm a wicked sinner, but really this is too much of a cross to put on me. Maybe 'tis because I didn't go to mass? Now you know quite well I hadn't the clothes to go to mass, but still in all, I promise you faithfully I'll go to mass for the rest of my life; not twelve o'clock mass either, but eight o'clock, seven o'clock mass, to mortify my sinful flesh. Never again will you see me coming up ten minutes late, and standing outside the door and running away after the last gospel. And never again will I say a word against the Vincent de Pauls, not even that old jade of hell Maggie Counihan, though she'd break the heart in a saint with her screwing and scrounging and scraping. Sweet Sacred Heart —and you, Holy Mother, I always had such a real liking for—I'll promise anything at all you care to mention if only——'

'Oh, shut up! shut up!' Babe cried bitterly, and her fist thumped feebly on the pillow. But the effort was too much for her, for in a moment a little scream burst from her as she writhed helplessly on the bed.

The scream seemed to act like an electric shock on Auntie Dinah. It blew her headlong, pigtails mounting behind her, nightdress in a parachute about her thighs, out of the warm nest of pillow and mattress to the bare boards by Mary Kate's bed. It seemed to the startled child that she had been shot through the air,

legs foremost, across bed and bedrail, and that only
by the mercy of heaven had she alighted standing.
Mary Kate, simulating sleep, closed one eye and
watched her. Her face was working in an extraordinary fashion, the mouth twitching and snickering and
the chin appearing and disappearing under the stress
of emotion. Two great tears that seemed also to have
been shot out of her by the shock trickled slowly down
her cheeks, making paths for a stream of them. Her
whole body worked, but in particular her arms,
which performed helpless windmill gestures before
her. Fascinated, Mary Kate watched the twirling of
the fingers.

'I bubububuseech thee—I bubububuseech thee
all' (her manner of address was becoming confused)
'just this one night. A couple of hours. I'm naturally
good—all I want is the chance. I feel certain I'm
going off my head. They warned me of it. Bububu-
besides, there was me old fellow going dotty like
that . . .'

'Go down for Maggie Vaughan,' hissed a despairing voice from the bed.

'Oh, listen to her! Just listen to her for one minute,
do!' Dinah went on. 'Sweet Sacred Heart, you can see
yourself how 'tis taking her. She's going queer too
with all this trouble, and, mind you, you'll be responsible.'

'Do what I tell you, you idiot,' cried Babe in a rage.

'Stick it, Babe girl,' stuttered Dinah over her
shoulder. 'I'll talk to them now.'

'If you don't go down for her I'll get up and go
myself. It's no use, I tell you! It's no use! I can't stick
it any longer.'

'What are you saying?' Dinah turned on her in stupefaction, almost sobered by surprise. 'Are you going mad? Don't you know well enough you have to stick it, and you going to Dublin in the morning?'

'Stick it? I'll scream the house down if you don't call her this instant.'

Dinah hovered unsteadily about the doorway, looking back at her sister in the bed. Her mouth spread suddenly across the whole width of her face, and a dry 'ha-ha-ha-ha' gurgled in her throat and came down her nose in a long thin wail. Her teeth chattering, she picked up an old shawl and drew it tightly about her.

'Then 'tis all up?' she asked, sobbing and trembling.

'Do what you're told, you fool!' cried Babe.

'But aren't you feeling better now?'

Babe did not even answer, Auntie Dinah gave a little whinnying cry, and Mary Kate heard her bare feet pattering down the stairs. She drew a long deep breath. The form on the bed tossed and writhed with a low moan that seemed to Mary Kate more like crying.

In five or six minutes Mrs. Vaughan came up, followed by Dinah. She was a very tall, fat, fair-haired, big-boned countrywoman, absurdly youthful and handsome for her age. The whole room seemed to rock beneath her weight, and glasses and cups started a delirious dance of relief as she walked in on tiptoe, one hand clutching an old coat across her breasts, her eyes puckered in their generously-fleshed rose-bud sockets.

'Wisha, for the love of Almighty God!' she whispered in her sharp East Cork lilt. 'You foolish and misguided woman! Show me!' Then she raised her eyes to heaven and gave a kindly little croak. "'Tis it, 'tis it, as sure as you're there, 'tis it! Now, amn't I the roaring damned idiot didn't see nor suspect it all this time? Wait till I put a bit of clothes on me.' She made a dive for the door, then stormed about and peered again. 'Where's that misfortunate child till I take her with me? Light the fire, Dinah, you cross-eyed gazebo!'

She chuckled gamely and Mary Kate felt herself being whirled up in two mighty, soft, warm arms and wrapped as in a summer cloud against the fat breast of the young countrywoman, who carried her downstairs as lightly and effortlessly as if she were a pat of butter.

The child had an astonishing first impression of the bedroom she was rushed into. A lighted candle illumined the red, red-nosed, red-moustachioed countenance of Mr. Vaughan, whose left arm was stretched out from under the bed-clothes rocking a converted orange-box in which an infant was softly mewling, his right supporting the stub of a pipe. Outside the range of the light was another bed in which three boys were sitting up, and, half screened from it by a bit of bagging, a trestle on which lay a young girl.

'Here, bad cess to you, take that in for a substitute,' cackled Mrs. Vaughan, thrusting Mary Kate into the glowing hollow where her own body had rested.

'Well, blasht me!' grumbled her husband philosophically, 'as if I hadn't enough of me own.'

'Wait till I get an old skirt and petticoat on,' said his wife breathlessly.

'Women,' he said, 'they're the cross of a man's life! The cross and bane of a man's life,' he shouted, turning and puffing his warm, pipe-laden breath on to Mary Kate's face. 'Aren't they, girleen?' He began to bang the cradle with amusement.

'Isn't that one asleep yet?' asked Mrs. Vaughan excitedly. She gave the cradle two or three great jolts that should have been sufficient to stun the occupant. Stunned or asleep, it suddenly stopped crying. Mr. Vaughan transferred the pipe to his left hand and put the other about Mary Kate's slight and trembling frame.

'Mammie, what is it, mammie?' four voices insisted in chorus.

'Go to sleep! Go to sleep!' said Mrs. Vaughan. 'If ye don't I'll bate blazes out of ye.'

'Are you comfortable there, girleen?' asked Mr. Vaughan, giving Mary Kate a squeeze.

'I'm lovely, sir,' she replied breathlessly.

'Daddie, daddie,' another chorus began, 'take me in too.'

''Tis that, I suppose?' he asked his wife.

'Divil been in it, but 'tis all that,' she replied, grunting contentedly as she bent her great matronly frame and tugged at her stockings.

'Well, well, well, well,' he commented, 'don't that bate all you ever heard of?'

He nodded gravely three times to no one in particular, turned and looked at Mary Kate, nodded again and gave her another great squeeze. She adored his red nose and face and ears and his acrid, smoky breath. Never in all her life had she been happier than she was beside him, ecstatically breathing in the heavy smell of his shirt under the armpit. She surmised that heaven must be like this, and that God the

Father wore a smelly grey army shirt whenever He retired to rest. She hoped He would have an armpit to spare for her.

Mrs. Vaughan bent suddenly across him in the bed and said fiercely into his right ear, ''Tis the hand of the Lord and nothing else.'

He knew the phrase had been maturing in her mind for some time and nodded appreciation.

'It bates all I ever heard of or read of,' he said with materialistic finality. He took three or four savage pulls from his pipe to redden it afresh and then lashed a spit almost to the door.

'You'd get half a crown for it if you sent it to the jokes in *Jackson's Weekly*,' he commented.

'I'm better be going,' said his wife determinedly, sticking a pin in her hair.

Then quite frankly he chuckled, a very doubtful, discreet little chuckle.

''Pon me sowl,' he explained, 'they'd say you made it up.'

She went out. A few minutes later Mr. Vaughan laughed. It was like the premonitory rumble of an earthquake. There was a deathly silence broken only by the gabble of children in the outer darkness, a gabble to which Mary Kate paid no more attention than if it had been taking place in Timbuctoo. All the eyes and ears she possessed were needed for her new idol. And then she felt the solid wall of his chest tremble and heave beside her. He put out his pipe on the ledge of the cradle and coughed to clear his lungs. He gurgled. The laughter seemed to well up from deep down within him as if only now was the whole flood of it answering the superficial disturbance of its crust of bone and sinew. The children fell silent and then broke out with a renewed babel of questions.

He moved his head and shoulders helplessly from side to side in the bed, displacing Mary Kate as if she were a little boat running in the swell of a steamer. He drew his hairy wrist across his streaming eyes. 'Ooohooohooo,' he rumbled, as if he were choking. Every spring of the bed creaked jovially in answer. 'Oohoohoo,' and he began to cough again. He rolled over in the bed and faced Mary Kate, who was perturbed but adoring. 'Be damn!' he exploded suddenly in her face, and, withdrawing his arm, sat up straight in bed and propped his face on his hands, his fingers delightedly tickling the cracked skin behind his ears.

'Daddie, daddie, what is it, daddie?' the chorus insisted.

'Dublin,' he coughed suddenly. 'Dublin—in the morning!'

There was a running up and down stairs, there were cries, whisperings, and protests. Then someone knocked at the door. It was Mrs. Doyle. She looked pale and cross.

'What is it at all, Mr. Vaughan?' she asked, putting her head through the door.

'Come in, come in, Mrs. Doyle,' he said gaily, and lay back cuddling Mary Kate again; 'herself is upstairs doing the good Samaritan.'

'Is it the McCormicks?' she asked, entering inch by inch.

''Tis of course the McCormicks. 'Tis the way she've changed her mind.'

'Who? Is it Babe?'

''Tisn't to Dublin she's going at all, but the Isle of Man.'

'The Isle of Man?'

He nodded, pressing Mary Kate to join in the joke.

'Shut that door, ma'am, and whisper here to me,' he said at last.

She did so very gingerly, and gingerly, with proper regard for her reputation as a respectable widow woman, approached the bed. As his fiery moustache touched her ear she recoiled. Then she clapped her hands slowly and solemnly. Speech left her for a moment; she could only shake her head pendulum-wise while her lips moved silently as in prayer.

'I'll send it to the papers,' exclaimed Mr. Vaughan triumphantly, thumping his knee.

Two other women came in. He seemed to revel in the glory of his deserted nuptial couch and greeted them all as old friends. The last to enter was Dona Nobis. At the door Mrs. Doyle whispered the fatal words to her. She appeared stupefied for a moment. Then she pulled at the sleeves of her coat, pushing them up to the elbow.

'Where is she?' she called so loudly that the others instantly shooed her to silence. 'Where is she, the monster, till I paste her?'

The idea of this set Mr. Vaughan off again.

'Paste her!' he stuttered. 'Paste her! Begod, 'tis better than a play, this house is. Do you know what? Do you know what I say? They'll charge it in with the rent, that's what they'll do. They'll rise the rent on us all.'

'The Lord,' chanted Dona Nobis, in an awe-inspiring monotone, 'the Lord will strike that woman down. He will strike her down and turn her into a pillar of salt as He turned the sinful woman in the Scriptures. And He will strike this house as He struck Sodom and Gomorrah. Believe me, not one stone will He leave on top of another. He will destroy it by fire and flood, and everyone in it He will destroy, from the oldest to the youngest.'

She pointed a menacing finger at the bed where the three boys were lying. They immediately set up a wail.

'Daddie, daddie, what's up with that one, daddie?'

It was full daylight before Mrs. Vaughan came downstairs again. The little group of women whispered at length, shivering in the cold greyness. Mr. Vaughan blew out the candle. Mary Kate fell asleep in the warmth and fragrance of his armpit. The other children too were tired, and dozed. The women went away one by one. Then a cart passed along the quay, rattling loudly across the cobbles. Mrs. Vaughan began to undress, tossing skirt and cardigan anywhere and whispering excitedly at intervals. She stood before the alarm-clock in her nightdress, scratching herself sleepily and peering short-sightedly at the dial.

''Tisn't as if you hadn't to be out at all hours,' she complained crossly. 'That vagabond up there wouldn't suffer for it if you missed a quarter.'

'A quarter?' he chuckled mildly. 'I wouldn't have missed that if I had to miss a week.'

She climbed helplessly into the bed beside him, the springs complaining under her soft powerful limbs. Amicably he patted her bare posteriors, causing her to gurgle with pleasure and threaten him in whispers. Did he want to wake Mary Kate? Then she lay back with a sigh of relief and adjusted her long legs so that her feet protruded as in stocks through the rails of the bedstead. She breathed noisily in great contented gusts. He touched her with his foot.

'You're cold,' he commented.

'I'm perished.'

He laid his feet gently against her calves to warm her.

'And 'tis a son she have instead of a husband this blessed and holy day,' he resumed.

'Ah, the vagabond!' she sighed. Then she bent across Mary Kate's unconscious form and whispered fiercely into his ear, 'Mind you, Will, as I said before I say again—the hand of God descended on her in the night.'

He knew she was happy now. She had the phrase right, and he wouldn't hear the end of it for a week. Women were like that. Still he did not begrudge her her little pleasure. She was a grand stook of a woman, God bless her! as big and fat and soft and fresh and healthy as a cock of hay.

III

'THE Hand of God,' said Mrs. Vaughan. 'Sodom and Gomorrah,' retorted Dona Nobis. But the more general illumination was 'Pride goeth before a fall'.

If, as the landings said, Babe McCormick had been satisfied to bear her child like a normal woman she would have found a good deal of sympathy, for the landings had never been known to let down a girl in trouble. But what no decent man or woman could or would stomach was 'put-on', and Babe, God forgive her, had so much 'put-on' that she would tempt a saint to beat her. So it was that in strict justice her escapade, instead of being hushed up, and referred to, if at all, only in whispers, became a symbol and a moral. When a girl was turning flighty they said 'she was going to Dublin by an early train'.

Mary Kate grew up feeling that a fierce limelight was being focussed on her mother, a light that showed up clearly all the flaws and cracks in that poor, vain, trivial character of hers. She grew up cruelly wise. She knew things about her mother that she should never have known, and knew them at an age when she should have been unaware that such things existed. And she suffered acutely from the thought of what a father's sympathy and affection would have meant to her in the crisis of growing-up.

23

Never after the calamity of her mother's 'trip to Dublin' was she left without the longing for a father all her own. On the next night when she was put to bed by her Auntie Dinah she wept bitterly and inconsolably. Beyond a brief to-do and a lengthy scolding neither mother nor aunt had tried to comfort her. They thought she was jealous! But if they had questioned her she could not have explained her emotion. What could she have said? That turn or twist as she might, she felt Mr. Vaughan's protecting arm about her? That when she closed her eyes it was his wine-red, pimply, scarlet-nosed, crimson-eared, flaming-moustachioed countenance which haunted her imagination, swaying hither and thither before her eyelids like a red balloon against the light? Worse, far worse—because most difficult to explain to Big People—that she could not rid her nostrils of the smell that hung about his armpit and his heavy grey army shirt? All this monstrous desire she explained with many tears to God Who hung above the head of her cot, and begged Him to send her without further delay a father who smoked a pipe and smelt like Mr. Vaughan, or, as an alternative, to take the four Vaughan children back to heaven and allow her to be adopted in their place.

At any rate it is quite certain that for weeks afterwards Mary Kate was going through all the phases of extreme infatuation. Mr. Vaughan was never out of her mind; at one moment she dogged his steps; at another she avoided him. When he took her up in his arms and kissed her she was in the seventh heaven of delight. If he went by without noticing her sitting by the top of the stairs in wait for him, she took a sort of gloomy Byronic pride in his indifference, and trailed about with dark brows and hanging head, treating the other children with superior scorn and thinking her own dark thoughts; of how he would weep for her when she suddenly disappeared from home or was picked out dead from under a car. On several evenings she wandered down the lane and waited for him in Sheares's Street, and the climax came when she hung round the factory in which he worked for an hour and a half, to pick him up as it were by accident. This led to a sharp warning from Mrs. Vaughan that she must never again go so far from home, and for days that good woman went round telling everyone what a useless stick Dinah Matthews was, and thanking God for his mercy that Bill happened to be coming out of work at that particular moment and sighted the child before she got lost. 'I assure you, woman,' she used to say, turning her eyes to heaven, 'when I heard where he found her my heart stood still. If he was half a minute later the dear knows but she'd be picked out of the river.'

Out of the river! How little she knew her Mary Kate! Possibly, if she had been able to understand them, her children would have enlightened her about the state of Mary Kate's mind; for with them, especially with Maisie, the eldest, in anything that concerned their father she was as jealous as a cat; yet while a Vaughan child was to be played with, she despised the whole wide world beside.

There was one dreadful moment when she thought it was all up. Maisie and she had been discussing whom they would marry when they were grown. Maisie was determined on marrying a soldier; she did not know any soldiers at that time, so she could not say who he would be, but Mary Kate knew well whom she wanted to marry, and could not keep it to herself.

She immediately became an object of derision. The matter was referred to every child in the tenement, and Mary Kate, growing every minute more harassed and tearful, found herself beaten to the wall. Whoever heard of the like? Sure, wasn't Maisie's father married to Maisie's mother already? Mary Kate didn't know, and anyway it made no difference. And then in spite of tears and protests Maisie rushed into the Vaughan apartment. Mary Kate put her two hands before her eyes.

'What's that?' she heard Mr. Vaughan say, his voice coming from inside the room as from a cloud. 'Mary Kate says she's going to marry me? Of course she is. Who else would she marry?'

Mary Kate thrilled with delight.

'But, daddie, sure, aren't you married to me mother?'

'Ah, your mother won't mind! Run away now and don't be bothering me!'

'There now,' hissed Mary Kate to the crestfallen Maisie, 'there now! What did I tell you?'

It is possibly a tragedy that her idol did not know what was churning about in Mary Kate's pretty head (for everyone had begun to recognise that she had inherited more than her mother's share of good looks). Yet how could he? And even if he had, how could his clumsy adult wits have followed the intricate dance required of him if he were to pursue in word and gesture the patterns which Mary Kate's intensity of longing created. As we grow older our loves become simpler —that Nature has decreed; we fill up in our minds the mighty chasms that yawn between the moment of tenderness and the moment of indifference. But for the child love has all the agonising peaks and abysses of a graph; there is no such thing as character; there is no good nor bad nor even power of choice; there are only the many it need not love and the one it must.

But if Mary Kate's passion for Mr. Vaughan made her critical of her mother, at least she grew more tolerant of her aunt. Or rather grew up more tolerant of her. For as she got older her aunt's attitude to her also insensibly changed. Auntie Dinah was one of those ageless people who have never been less than fifteen or more than twenty, and who find it impossible ever to be really nonsensical. Consequently, of all women born she was probably least fitted to make friends with a child. She must be understood straightway or not at all, for she had no patience and would not attempt to explain herself. But when the child grasped even the most obvious point in her quite uncontrollable flow of speech Auntie Dinah's attention was held. The child had ceased to be a local nuisance and become a possible audience, and though understanding did not come quickly and would never come completely; though after talking sensibly to Mary Kate for five minutes the older woman would suddenly launch her afresh on to the icy seas of nonentity, there was a faint but tightening bond between them.

Dinah was a character extravagant to the last degree. She liked talking—when she was appreciated. She hated working whether or not she was appreciated. And it was her misfortune, her 'cross' as she called it, to be possessed of a terrific energy which at all times left her open to the machinations of designing housewives. Hold a sweeping brush before Dinah's eyes and she shuddered, but force it into her hands and show her something to do with it and she became a whirlwind. So that when once she had worked at a house she was never again free from the persecution of its mistress. There were a dozen of the breed, 'gad-flies' Dinah called them, and from these gadflies of domesticity she was always in flight. But they were pertinacious. The height of the stairs did not frighten them; they panted and stewed and sniffed their way up that mount of smells, and stood in the doorway, fat and lean, tall and tiny, all with the same ingratiat-ing, sad, housewifely smile, all with the same story.

'Oh, Miss Matthews, Miss Matthews, the trouble we've had since last you were with us! Really, it does seem as if that house would never be clean again. Our new girl—you wouldn't believe what a wretched, help-less good-for-nothing that girl is, Miss Matthews.' And so on.

And Auntie Dinah, putting up her two hands before her face as though to shield herself from contact with such baseness, would cry in a tiny, bird-like voice, 'Oh'm! Fancy that'm!' Her whole share of the con-versation was carried out in ejaculations and nods and excuses. It was incredible, the number of excuses she concocted in order to avoid a task, and as she talked she never rested, but fluttered helplessly round like a bird with a broken wing, or a slattern geisha from some provincial opera; hopping and nodding and gesticulating, her hands flitting to and fro about her. 'Yes'm. No'm. You see'm. It's like this'm.' And excuse would follow excuse, one contradicting another; and the bonds would tighten and tighten about her, and it was as if the circle in which the poor broken-winged bird hopped grew narrower and narrower and its panic more extreme, until at last it was tight-caught, panting, and crushed in spirit. And then Dinah would smile!

It was tragic, that smile of Dinah's, that last deceitful glow which seemed to say: This and only this was what she had always been seeking; that if life was not so difficult for a poor girl she would ask nothing better of her days on earth than to scour and dust and polish in that one house of all others. 'It's so kind of you'm,' was all she could bring out, adding to the helm of the conqueror the plume of magnanimity.

Bowing, nodding, skipping, smiling, ejaculating, obsequious Dinah escorted her visitor to the door. Then with one hand on the handle, the other to her left cheek, she would slowly close the door three-quarters of the way, and fixing her dazed and despairing eyes upon a spot on the threshold where she still imagined she could see the impress of the tyrant's heel, she would gather all her vital strength into one supreme gesture and spit three times upon the accursed spot. She would spit three times and then she would dance on it. Her voice, rising from a faint, almost inaudible whisper when her visitor had descended to the next landing, would reach a poignant fortissimo when she judged her to be near the hall— not too close for hearing, yet not too far for cursing.

'Divil melt you!' she would begin in a hoarse whisper. 'That you might break your scraggy neck before you reach the hall door! That something would trip you and send you out of this world before you can do the people in it any more harm! You and your charity, and your half a rasher of bacon for breakfast and your grandeur the whole world knows you haven't paid for yet! That I may live to see you choked with your own soap-suds, you screech-owl from God-knows-where, you and your pasty-faced, big-bottomed, thick-headed, rickety, cross-eyed, snub-nosed monument of a husband! That I may live to see you hopping on two crutches for fear one wouldn't be enough to keep you from what everyone knows you were brought up to; for whoever had a good word to say for your old rag-and-bone merchant of a mother, with her stall in the market and her fancy-man Jackie Rinolds that married her for charity? Oh, that I might see you limping and moaning and begging at every street corner! That you might put out your dirty paw to me for a penny till I put a spit in it!'

And so on, at the rate of a house afire. By the time the poor woman who was being 'read' (this was Auntie Dinah's technical term for the ceremony) had reached the footpath, cursing lost its power and Auntie Dinah was off on another tack. Step by step she retraced the conversation to its source. Every word uttered by the absent woman was recalled, and mimicked with an astounding art that was compounded in equal parts of realism and slapstick. That Auntie Dinah, who during this interview had had her whole soul turned inside out with fear and rage, should have been able to remember the words that were used was surprising enough, but that every trace of a mannerism down to a nervous fumbling with gloves and rings or a frightened sniff at the combination of odours that was the atmosphere of Dinah's garret should have been recorded in her 'take-offs' was little short of

miraculous. For her sister's benefit Dinah would
launch into the 'servants-of-the-day' speech, snap-
ping distractedly at the little finger of her right hand
as she did so. Then becoming aware of some minute
inaccuracy, she would suddenly pull herself up, 'No,
no, no. What am I dreaming of? 'Tisn't that at all,'
and begin all over again. Then when Babe, admitting
the portrait, laughed, she would laugh too, capering
wildly about the room in the full glory of achievement.
By the time the performance was repeated—and it
was repeated a dozen times before Dinah grew tired of
it—it was word-perfect and gesture-perfect, a masterly
ten-minute skit which threw the landings into hysterics.

Beside her distaste for work for which she had such
a regrettable aptitude, cleanliness in any shape or
form caused Dinah mortal anguish. She disliked hot
water, she hated cold, she abominated soap, and would
run a mile from the sight of a scrubbing-brush. In all
this she differed considerably from Babe, who had at
least the nodding acquaintance with toilet formalities
made necessary by her occasional week-ends in hotels,
and was so neat in public that she might, except for
her laziness, have been quite a good housewife in
private.

But Babe lay in bed until all hours; twelve or one
was as early as she would rise except on what were
called 'field days', when it was necessary to replenish
the larder, and Dinah unassisted could produce no
more than a bone for soup or a pig's foot. Occasionally
her conscience would prick her and she would shout
at Dinah, who sat with her feet baking comfortably in
the ashes while her battered old boots smouldered and
sent up a bitter but pleasant odour to heaven.

'Di, give Mary Kate's face a wipe for the love of God!'

'Eh, give us a chance, will you? What do you think we are?'

'I know 'tis all hours and the child's face not washed yet!'

'Why the blazes don't you get up and wash it yourself, then? Think I'm going to be let in for all the work in this house? Anyway, look at me! I'm not washed at all, and I'm not complaining, am I?

But there were mornings when sleepy, good-natured Canon Whalen would walk in and fly into such a rage at the dirt and laziness and squalor that he would raise his stick and thrash Babe in the bed until she bawled; when for a whole week he would come in regularly to inspect the children, and Dinah, with long muttered imprecations, would wash them and herself—herself last, since this was the peak point of her grief and indignation. She would stand white with passion in front of the cracked mirror, a well-squeezed wash-cloth in her hand, and as she applied it compassionately to certain chosen spots on her cheeks and forehead her face would crumple and writhe with loathing, both of water and priests.

'God knows,' she said, drawing in her breath with a hissing sound as the wash-cloth discovered some sensitive spot, 'you wouldn't wonder the English are all Protestants! It just shows you what a sensible race they are and that they don't keep their tongue in their cheek. Everyone knows an Irishman would be afraid to open his mouth about the goings-on of the priests, though the whole world knows them to be a lazy lot of schemers and skinflints. But no one need ever say

Dinah Matthews, for all she's only a simple poor girl without much education, didn't say out plain and straight what they are, because I'm saying it now, and I'm not afraid like some people that the priests will turn me into a goat. Let them try it! That's all I say! Let me see them at it!'

This last jab was intended for Babe, who, otherwise quite progressive and modernist, did in her heart believe that a priest might at any moment turn her into a goat, and in an unguarded moment had admitted it to Dinah. Still when Canon Whalen came it was 'Yes, father,' and 'No, father,' with Dinah, and she hopped and fluttered about him in a tremble of panic until he begged of her for goodness' sake to keep her feet where they were put.

And so for a whole week, or two and three weeks at a time, Babe would be flogged into devotion and even get inspired by it. Every morning she would be up and out to eight o'clock mass, and sit right in front of the church before the High Altar, so that any priest who knew her might see her. But with time Canon Whalen's zeal would moderate and Babe's fervour would moderate, and again she would stay in bed until the afternoon, and again go out at night, to the great scandal of the womenfolk and the sardonic delight of the men.

IV

IF Mary Kate was not altogether happy in her home life she soon realised that Auntie Dinah was no happier, a realisation which served to strengthen her in her will to get free.

It happened like this.

It was no unusual thing for Babe's 'young men', as these, old and young, were euphemistically called, to take her away to Glengariff or Killarney for weekends or even for an occasional 'rest-cure'. Whether the proximity of mountain, lake, and sea tended to inspire more passionate and less mercenary considerations in Babe is a matter for doubt. At any rate, she never commented to Dinah upon anything more poetic than an expensive dinner, the cut of a skirt, or the price of a car.

To Dinah these absences of her sister were inexpressibly boring. All day long she moped, hopping about with her air of a broken wing, her face unwashed, her hair in a tangle, a filthy old raincoat tied about her throat, her ungainly feet flip-flopping from landing to landing and lane to lane as she sought for company. She invented requests to secure admittance; in some ways she was sensitive and this was one, so that in a morning's stroll she might collect under her raincoat a dozen excuses for a short conversation:

pinches of tea, spoons of sugar, drops of milk, morsels
of dripping, all of which, when she reached her attic
again, she would consign to the flames in gleeful
extravagance, only to discover that one at least of
these offerings would be required for her mid-day
meal. Then with the same childish inconsequence she
would steal off and borrow afresh.

Usually she was not an unwelcome guest. She
parodied strangers for the natives, the natives for one
another, and pushed far enough would not hesitate
to give free character sketches of Babe's 'young men'.
These, naturally, were most in demand, since the neighbours could be expected to draw no more than a slight,
malicious pleasure from the picturing of folk they
knew; but Babe's 'young men' were a world apart,
like the characters they read of in Miss Braddon's
novels or in penny novelettes.

'He thinks, if you please,' commented Dinah of one
young man from Oxford who was staying with Babe
in Killarney, 'the scenery is so original and elevating,
and the lakes and the boats and the Eagle's Nest or
whatever they calls it, is all so full of mermaids—I
dunno is that the name he have for them; but, anyway,
all so full of mermaids and things they used to believe
in long ago that he says, my dear, every well you
come to you ought to kneel down and say a little
prayer to whatever gazebo might be in it. I'm not
speaking of holy wells at all, my dear, but any old well
if it was only a hole in the wall! Now, I beseech you,
wouldn't I look fine popping down on my two bended
knees at every turn of the road? Thanks be to God,
they'd put me up in the madhouse before I got back!
And do you know what he wanted a little girl down

there to do? To take off every stitch she had on and let him take a picture of her—with respects to you, ma'am—in her pelt! He wouldn't say that before our Babe, of course' (in passing, we may remark that he had, and that the little girl was a figment of Babe's imagination), 'but she heard it after him. Now isn't it surprising if the police knew that they wouldn't lock him up? In her pelt! So's he could write a book about it after, and say this was a mermaid he seen himself with his own two looking eyes in Killarney. And, of course, he'd make millions and millions of money on account of everyone wanting to have a look at the girl in her pelt. I always heard it, and now I know 'tis true, them English is all queer.'

But though scandals like these filled Dinah's days very happily they did not make the evenings more cheerful. Several times Mary Kate saw her dress up in some fragments of Babe's discarded finery and was called upon to admire the result. She was enthusiastic, and this served to encourage Dinah, who one evening astonished her by dressing up in full and proceeding to redden her lips and cheeks with great liberality. Mary Kate was enchanted. She had never seen her aunt look so well, nor indeed had she ever seen as much red on any one before. A profusion of powder applied over this Indian war-paint completed what in her eyes was a transfiguration.

'God knows,' said Auntie Dinah reverently, survey-ing herself in the cracked mirror, 'how bad I am! Maybe if some of the bloody beauties was dressed up in old rags like mine and had as much rotten dirty work forced on them by scabby old jades like Maggie Counihan of the Vincent de Pauls, with her God-speed-the-plough air, they wouldn't look half as well as me.'

'I think you're nicer than any of them,' said Mary Kate with loyal conviction.

'To be sure I am,' replied Auntie Dinah to the glass.

'I think you're nicer than me ma even,' added Mary Kate, withholding nothing, as her way was when roused.

'Do you now?' asked her aunt. 'Ah, I wouldn't say I was as nice as her.'

'I think you are, anyway,' affirmed Mary Kate.

''Deed, I don't suppose there's much to choose between us, Mary Kate. After all, isn't she my own sister, and wouldn't any one with two eyes in their head recognise me out of her?'

'Are you going walking now, Auntie Dinah?' asked Mary Kate.

Dinah giggled and shook all over, fluttering helplessly to the centre of the room and posing with an umbrella in her hand before she made a sudden fresh swoop upon the mirror. She portrayed on a lower plane all the anguish of the artistic nature, which continually images a life more abounding than its own and always dreads to approach it.

'I wonder,' she asked breathlessly, 'is me kisser too red?'

'It give you a grand colour,' said Mary Kate.

'It do,' admitted Auntie Dinah, 'it do. But I'd never have the face to go down the quay like that. Isn't it cruel I haven't someone to go out with, Mary Kate?'

'Wouldn't you go out with Mrs. Vaughan?'

'Ah, sure, that old show wouldn't come, and anyway she's married.'

'Isn't there any one else?'

'There's that old idiot Dona Nobis,' reflected her aunt. 'I was thinking of her. I wonder would she come. If I had her out once—just once—with me I'd soon get into the thing on me own. I needn't do anything at all, only walk along, and if a fellow smiled at me I could give him a wink, and to-morrow night then I could sort of be passing the same place and he could be passing the same place and maybe he'd stop and speak to me.'

'Can't you go down and try her?' asked Mary Kate.

'God direct me! I suppose I'm better.'

She tiptoed to the door and then swung round on Mary Kate, growing green under the lily and rose of her complexion.

'Go out you, Mary Kate, like a decent child, and see is there e'er a one looking!'

Mary Kate tiptoed to the landing and, bending over, signalled to her aunt that the coast was clear. Dinah replied with furious silent gestures that directed her ever forward. On tiptoe she went down the stairs and on tiptoe her aunt followed, one hand upon the banister, the other drawing down the brim of Babe's wide summer hat over her rouged and powdered cheeks as though this might have served for a disguise. Steps started in every room, and at each sound Dinah would hiss silence at her childish vanguard, who moved with exaggerated caution a flight below. At last Mary Kate reached the door of Dona Nobis's room, and Dinah, abandoning all caution, gathered up the skirts of an unnecessarily long white dress and scampered down the remaining steps. As she flung

open the door and tumbled in, Mary Kate saw the
upturned whites of her eyes and heard her whispered
cry, 'Jesus, Mary, and Joseph!'

Inside Dona Nobis was reading a book of meditations and looked up from over her glasses in her stern
old-maidenly way. Her sight was bad, and she had to
look for some time at Dinah before she realised who
was there.

''Tis me, Bridie,' brought out Dinah at last, giggling and blushing furiously. 'I come down so that
you could have a look at me grandeur.'

'My, my, my!' breathed Dona Nobis, her meditations resolving gradually into a normal woman's
passion for dress. 'Is that Babe's get-up you fecked?
Here, turn round until I have a look at you.'

Dinah swung on her heels with a perfect parody of
Babe's familiar final twirl.

''Tis a bit long,' said Dona Nobis. 'But you have a
grand colour. Were you walking?'

Dinah drew a long breath of relief. The rouge had
not penetrated her companion's myopia.

'No,' she said glibly; 'I was washing.'

'Thanks be to God!' added Dona Nobis with pro-
fane humour.

'Will you come for a bit of a walk?'

'Well, I wasn't thinking of it, but if you're going I
might as well go with you.'

'We can go up the Mardyke.'

Dona Nobis put on her hat. She had succeeded in
doing up her tiny crop of grey hair in a tall pyramid
that was faintly reminiscent of an eighteenth-century
toilet, and one saw her always, when she wore a hat
instead of a shawl, with this article of dress seemingly

lifted off her head at a rakish angle. She then put on her coat and took an umbrella from the corner.

'You won't want the brolly,' said Dinah.

'When I'm dressed I don't go without it,' replied Dona Nobis severely.

They went downstairs, Dinah hiding behind. At the door she grabbed Dona Nobis by the arm and dragged her down the steps and along the quay at a rate that annoyed her companion, talking all the time in a very loud voice. She had seen a few women gossiping outside. Dona Nobis was astonished, because the talk seemed to have no sense in it. Neither had it—it was entirely a projection of Dinah's excited nerves.

At last Dona Nobis pulled up and shook off Dinah's arm.

'Now listen here to me, young woman,' she said impatiently, 'I'm not going to be dragged along like this at the rate of a mile a minute not for anybody in the world. I'm a respectable middle-aged woman and not a whipster of fifteen.'

Dinah groaned. It seemed to her that everyone she passed stopped and stared at her. She expected that at any moment a train of children would attach itself to her white dress.

'Tis so bitter cold, Bridie,' she said despairingly.

'Cold? Did you say cold? And the sun splitting the flags! Cold, you yahoo? The sweat is dripping off me.'

But the trip was already doomed to failure. It was the desire to get away from the slums and into respectable country—if it was not Nemesis in person—that induced Dinah to suggest their going up Wyse's Hill, instead of along the Mardyke. And it was certainly Nemesis who arranged that a belated coalman should be flogging his horse up Wyse's Hill just as they appeared. And it was the nine-and-ninety disasters that the horse should refuse to go. For Dona Nobis had a passionate affection for animals, and though the lane-dwellers did not know it, all those visits from 'cruelty' (as the inspector was called), concerning cats with the mange and dogs with sores and hens that were only skin and bone, were all her doing. And now to her horror Dinah knew the reason for the umbrella. Like Moses' rod, it scented of its own accord, but it scented blood, not water. It began to dance in Dona Nobis's hand. She stood on the edge of the footpath, leaning over the iron railings, while an agonised Dinah tried by whispered cajolery to draw her away.

'Ahaha!' chanted Dona Nobis, 'don't imagine I didn't see you beating that defenceless animal, you brute! You strike him again and I'll go straight down and report you to the police.'

The man looked up at her for a moment, the darkness of his countenance seeming to express doubt rather than wrath; then he lifted the reins and gave the horse another blow, trying at the same time to push the cart forward.

'Oh!' bawled Dona Nobis, 'if only I had you where that poor horse is now I'd teach you kindness to animals.'

The driver looked up again, but this time as though he had been shot.

'Are you addressing me, you saucer-eyed old mer?' he demanded with frozen dignity.

'If I had you here I'd break my umbrella on your thick head,' retorted Dona Nobis.

The man pushed his cap back upon his poll, revealing a narrow fringe of rosy forehead, then he spat upon his hands and rubbed them reflectively together. Anything, he seemed to be saying, that would give him a lawful respite from his thankless job. There was very little face to be seen beneath the coal dust, but what there was glowed very red. He left the horse and strode over to the footpath. Then he glowered up at Dona Nobis swung over the railings and Dinah shivering behind her.

'When did you take to the preaching, sister?' he asked with grateful irony.

'Coward!' spat Dona Nobis. 'Coward! Dirty, objectionable, worthless little coward!'

Four or five people had gathered at a respectable distance and others were appearing with alarming rapidity. The man did not hasten the climax nor did his irony wilt under the abuse. He raised his eyes fervently to heaven, two lurid torches of red and white, and clasped his hands as if in prayer.

'And did you join the Holy Marys at last, sister?' he asked unctuously. 'Begod, then, let me remark, woman, that you're the greatest miracle since the penitent thief. 'Tis a historic day for Holy Ireland when we have Flossie Conway selling tracts in Patrick Street and yourself and the girls joining "cruelty".'

As Flossie Conway was a notorious old bawd who had developed religious mania late in life, the implication was obvious and went straight to the heart of Dona Nobis. She grew quite pale.

'You're a witness, Dinah Matthews,' she screamed; 'you're a witness to what that blackguard said about me! Remember his words, because you'll repeat them

elsewhere! . . . Very well,' she added grimly, pointing
the umbrella at a spot between his rolling eyes, 'oh,
very, very well. You'll answer for this before a court
of law. Don't think you'll escape me, you savage, you
defamer of women. I'll identify you! I'll identify your
hangman's gizzard among a million, and I'll make
you answer for your words.'

The little crowd drew closer. The coalman clearly
felt that he was more on trial now than he would ever
be before a court of law. He guffawed and pointed
with his whip, first at Dona Nobis then at the terror-
stricken Dinah.

'Listen to her, ye people of Cork!' he proclaimed
dramatically. 'Listen to her, the old coadjutor, and then
cast one lingering glance at the thing of hell that's
shivering behind her. Look at that, and tell me is she
coloured like a Christian or painted like a railway
signal? Them are the ones that talk about kindness to
animals. Them are the ones that abuse a poor man
that's working until nine o'clock at night! I tell ye,'
he shouted with ferocious energy, 'on the likes of them
even a misfortunate horse would turn his backside!'

It was clear to everyone that a dreadful change
had come over Dona Nobis at the word 'painted'. As
the coalman concluded she turned on her heel and
walked away downhill, her head in the air. Dinah
followed at a run. The giggling crowd broke to let
them pass. It was true that Dona Nobis by her air
seemed to disown Dinah, but Dinah refused to be dis-
owned. She trotted after Dona Nobis with the fidelity
of a frightened puppy. In a few minutes they had
crossed the bridge and were bearing down upon the
Dolls' House. The coalman was still holding forth to

an amused audience about the class of people that
were behind 'cruelty'.

But it was the sequel that showed Mary Kate how
unhappy her aunt really was. Dona Nobis's wrath was
as nothing to Babe's when the former repeated the
scandal. There were violent scenes in the attic. Babe
swung out of Dinah's hair, and Dinah wept and
screamed. 'A low, dirty, despicable creature,' was only
one of the things that Babe called her. And her moral
indignation did not stop at this, for she called upon
Canon Whalen to interfere and yet another scene took
place. It was useless for Dinah to protest that she
meant no harm and only thought she'd like to have a
boy of her own. She wanted to be married, she said.
She wanted to get out of the attic and have a home of
her own. Canon Whalen did not believe her. No one
believed her. She was beaten and lectured into tears
and submission. Only some words that she said, sniffing and hiding her head before the priest, stuck in the
child's mind.

'When the poor woman in Sunday's Well flung herself out of the window and was picked up dead no one
said a word to her.' Her finger was lifted at Babe, who
immediately struck her fiercely on the mouth and
effectively reduced her to silence.

Mary Kate was twelve when this occurred, and she
never forgot it.

V

HER passion for Mr. Vaughan died a hard but natural death.

One night about a year after her brother's appearance in this vale of tears Mr. Vaughan was late in coming to his tea. It was a Friday evening, an evening when his hours were fairly regular, that is to say, when he might be expected home from the factory between seven and eight o'clock. As eight struck from Shandon, Mrs. Vaughan took up her position at the door of the Dolls' House, a tall, shining, matronly woman, her fair hair sending out stray locks in the light breeze that blew along the quay, her little army of children, among them Mary Kate, clustered about her knees. No one passed without speaking to her and offering some consoling suggestion or other to account for his being late, and each suggestion she accepted with the same artless confidence; but at heart neither she nor her comforters believed in any of those suggestions.

As Shandon struck the quarter she despatched the children all in different directions to search for the truant. It fell to Mary Kate's lot to find him, leaning against a railing in Sheares's Street. He was examining the grass inside the railing. He was also very drunk—she knew the signs of that well enough. So being wise in the ways of drunken men, she doubled back to the tenement and warned Mrs. Vaughan.

The tall country woman was like a creature distracted. Followed at a run by Mary Kate, she strode off down the lane, her fair hair tossed, her blue apron flapping about her, talking aloud in a long, distressed monotone. When she saw her husband she gave a little scream and ran to him. He greeted her dazedly, without recognition, but allowed himself to be propelled in the direction of home. Once or twice he swore vehemently, and stood to conduct a belated argument with an invisible opponent, but she pushed and dragged him away. Knots of people gathered at the doorways to see them pass; three or four women trailed them, offering advice and assistance, and to these Mrs. Vaughan confided in a loud voice that it was queer the way people stared, as though it was a thing wouldn't happen anybody to have a bottle of stout taken and be overcome by the heat. To which her husband replied by wildly waving his right arm and offering to fight the best bloody man that ever came out of the Barrack Stream, or Blackpool for the matter of that.

Help had to be called to cart him bodily up the stairs and fling him headlong on the bed. The children had gathered and began to cry. This made him very cross, and he told them all to be off out of the house before he slit their so-and-so throats, themselves and their harlot of a mother. Mrs. Vaughan managed to get the sight-seers out of the room, and then sat upon a little stool by the fire and wept bitterly. It was the dinner, she said between her sobs, the bit of dinner made her cry.

'There he is,' she cried, 'and the week's wages spent, and to-morrow I must dip into the stocking that I was putting by to contrive a little house of my own, and now I'll never have house nor garden either, but spend my days in this stinking hole. Oh, child, child, when I thinks of my little home in Killeagh, and the hens and the pigs and the bit of garden, I could cry down tears of blood! Seven years I've rotted here and slaved here, and seven years he's promising me he's off it now for good and all.'

She continued in this strain while her husband slept, and Mary Kate, who was a ready learner, began to realise that behind all the love of women for men lies a secret sorrow. Over this she brooded as darkness fell, and she sat closer to Mrs. Vaughan's skirts, as though to warm her, and trembled at the thought of the ugliness that is in life. Then the man on the bed (who had somehow ceased to be Mr. Vaughan) woke up and got violently sick on the floor, ignoring the basin which was already set for him. After that he rose and ordered them all out of the room again. When his wife begged him to be quiet he rushed for a razor and slashed at her with it. She screamed and fell into hysterics. Dona Nobis and one or two other women came and dragged her out and with her the children. 'Dirt and no man', was what Dona Nobis called him, but it was surprising what little effect it had on him. They all slept together on the floor of Dona Nobis's room.

So Mary Kate's heart was emptied of its first great love. After a month or so her idol was his own self again, but Mary Kate knew that the stocking was no more and that everything in the house that could be pawned was gone. And though Mrs. Vaughan became hopeful once more, and once more began to save up her pennies, Mary Kate knew that she might as well have thrown them into the river outside her window. Never as long as she lived would she see the little home she dreamed of.

It would be absurd to pretend that Mary Kate went to school. She frequently saw the inside of the school, but no amount of custom could make it endurable to her, and, being extremely intelligent, she passed for the most stupid girl in the class, which was another cause for her dislike of it. So when she had to go she went, but never otherwise; and in this attitude she was encouraged by mother and aunt, who had got along pretty well so far on the minimum of book learning. Mary Kate's school was the Dolls' House, and in this she studied earnestly.

When she was a few months short of fifteen she met the lad who was to take Mr. Vaughan's place in her affections. He was about eight months older than she, a good-looking, well-built boy whom she had often seen playing hurley on the quays when a bobby was not looking, or enjoying a game of handball against the side wall of the Dolls' House, infuriating the people who lived behind it by banishing the ball on to their tea tables. His name was Phil. His mother was a charwoman. She had high hopes of him, and at the expense to herself of six days' crushing toil in every week succeeded in keeping him at his books instead of letting him work as a messenger boy. She was a reserved and timid creature, very devout and very hardy. In the Dolls' House and along the quay, where clocks are a rarity and undependable at that, she was known as 'Five to Nine'.

Now it is a noteworthy fact that though Mary Kate, who was by long chalks the prettiest child in the Marsh, and Phil, who if not the handsomest was not the ugliest and was certainly very clever, though these lived in the same smelly tenement, the sun of his glory had not yet shone for her, nor had Phil, so far as one can discover, ever bothered his head about her good looks. And Phil, it must be admitted, had at that time an eye for good looks.

Then one day Mary Kate came in from school with her young brother who had endured his painful initiation into the mysteries of culture. Her mother was sitting over the fire reading a novel, and Auntie Dinah gave the two children their dinner of tripe. Those were good times in the McCormick family. A mysterious benefactor had turned up whose age and appearance were occasionally referred to with chaste and caustic humour by Dinah.

'Maggie Dinan is laid up these three days I hear,' she said to her sister.

'Is that Phil Dinan's old one?' asked Mary Kate.

''Tis. Five to Nine.'

'More fool she to be working herself off her feet,' said Babe severely.

'She'd get just as much thanks in the long run if she took her ease,' finished Dinah.

Neither knew how those two sentences, which so perfectly expressed their own philosophy, were to decide the fate of the child who was devouring her tripe with great attention to the saucepan, which might still produce a helping if her luck were in. There was silence for a few moments, then Mary Kate put down her fork and said, 'I don't see why.'

Mother and aunt looked at her curiously. Lately she had taken to contradicting them like this out of pure wilfulness, and when they were not irritated it amused them.

'Well, bright girl, if you don't you don't, and that's enough about it,' said Dinah.

'She have to work to keep Phil at school,' said Mary Kate obstinately.

'And who asked her to keep Phil at school?' Dinah looked up at her with challenge in her eyes.

'Listen to the studious girl talking!' commented her mother.

'That's different,' Mary Kate replied calmly. 'I'm no good at school, and I'll never be any good at school, and for all the use it is to me I might as well stop at home.'

'That's consoling, anyway,' said her aunt.

'But if I was,' added the youthful lawgiver, resuming her interrupted meal, ''twould pay ye to keep me there.'

'Well, for the love of heaven!' exclaimed her mother.

But the spirit of contradiction had entered into Mary Kate. As soon as dinner was over she went downstairs to the first landing and knocked discreetly at one of the doors. A startled voice bade her enter. She went in. Mrs. Dinan was sitting up in bed with her eyes on the door. Clearly she was not accustomed to visitors.

Mary Kate was shocked when she saw her. Somehow she had noticed no change in the little charwoman recently, and now within a day or two she seemed to have wasted to nothing. She recognised Mary Kate, and a glance, half hostility, half suspicion, warned the

child that she was one with those people who seemed
to hold her responsible for her mother's misdeeds.
Mary Kate could never remember that a stranger
might look on her in this way and was always slightly
grieved when she noticed it.

'I heard you were sick and I thought you might
want me to do a message,' she blurted out.

'No, thank ye,' the sick woman said coldly, but with
an air of surprise, 'there's nothing I need. But thank
you all the same.'

'I knew Phil wouldn't be in for another hour. And
I'd like to do any little turn for you.'

''Tis very good of you,' Mrs. Dinan replied, her
coldness giving way to confusion. 'I don't think there's
anything.'

'Could I clean up for you?' asked Mary Kate insis-
tently. 'I'll wash that cup and saucer if you like.' And
expectantly she laid hold of an unwashed cup and
saucer which stood beside the bed.

Mrs. Dinan lay back with a groan. The strain of
sitting up vanquished her feelings of dislike more
readily than the child's frank and pretty face, for with
the pain came the knowledge that now she needed
somebody to be attentive to her; and though she would
not have admitted any supernatural intervention in
Mary Kate's visit, she could not forget that for the
past three days she had been wishing that she had
had a daughter. She had not wanted that cup and
saucer washed up in a hurry, but the child's persist-
ence made it seem a matter of life and death. Besides,
she had been alone so long that any human voice was
welcome.

'You're a good child,' she said; 'I wish you would.'

Mary Kate washed the cup and saucer. She then offered to tidy the room, and in an unlucky moment Mrs. Dinan let her. For Mary Kate was as clever with a sweeping brush as with a pen, which was not at all, and Mrs. Dinan had to direct her from the bed while she sweated in her quite genuine efforts to do things in a proper way. Fortunately she was not sensitive about her incompetence, and took her instructions with an infectious smile. When she had finished she went deliberately across to the little sideboard where the newly washed cup and saucer were standing. She held them out to Mrs. Dinan.

'I suppose they're not done properly either?' she asked.

The sick woman looked at them severely. Inside they were clean enough. On the outside they were almost untouched.

'Ah, they'll do,' she exclaimed.

Mary Kate burst into a ringing laugh. It almost coaxed a smile to the bluey lips of the little charwoman.

'Well, amn't I the divil?' she cried, and shrugged her shoulders despairingly. But again she broke into her gay laugh.

She dawdled, dusting and arranging things. She was there when Phil came home, and promptly disappeared, promising to look in again that evening. She said nothing to her mother, but about her heart there was a warm feeling of contentment—contentment not so much that she had helped Mrs. Dinan, but that she had successfully defied an authority that deep down in herself she despised.

She did look into the Dinans' that evening just as

dusk was falling and began to wish that she had never done so. For she was acutely sensitive to suffering, and this time she saw Mrs. Dinan in its grasp. The doctor had ordered her into hospital weeks ago, but she had refused to leave Phil and her work. When Mary Kate asked how long she had been in this condition she said for months.

'Then you ought to be ashamed of yourself,' said Mary Kate bluntly, 'didn't go into hospital long ago and get rid of it.'

'Ah, you don't know what you're saying, child,' exclaimed the sick woman bitterly. 'How would we live?'

To this Mary Kate had no reply. Mrs. Dinan turned her face to the wall and said in a broken voice words that would always remain in Mary Kate's mind as expressing the agony of millions of her kind, 'We stop on our feet when we can, for when the likes of us go down we go down for ever.'

'Don't talk like that, ma,' the boy said pitiably. His anguish went to Mary Kate's heart. 'You'll be all right in a day or two, with the help of God.'

'No, child,' she added after a moment's silence, 'I know I oughtn't to have said that. We must trust in the Sacred Heart.'

The room was almost in darkness except for the shadowy beauty of the river and the trees on the opposite bank flattened greyly like pressed flowers against the window-pane. Mary Kate rose and Phil rose with her. She was going to the chemist's for a bottle of castor-oil for the sick woman (it was characteristic of Phil's mother that, knowing his shyness, she had suffered for three days rather than

ask him to get it). He accompanied Mary Kate, a
head and shoulders above her, but gawkily miserable
and looking to her silence for comfort as though she
were an elder sister. After she had stalked in and
purchased the medicine he suggested that they should
visit the altar of the Sacred Heart in the Friars'
church in Liberty Street.

They knelt and prayed together, he in a cold sweat
of anguish, she in awakening childish dread of what
sorrows life might have in store for herself. The church
was dimly lit, but a smoky constellation of candles
flared before the statue of Saint Anthony round which
the greatest number of worshippers had gathered.
There was an intense and brooding silence that was
not disturbed by the occasional flip-flap of an old
boot-sole, and it seemed to the girl that the whole
wide church with its dimness and consoling poverty
(that half assured her its God was indeed the God of
the poor) was filled with the faint susurration of
moving lips, a momentful of sorrow cupped from the
day-long stream of sorrow that flowed endlessly into
this humble church of the outcast, the abandoned, the
oppressed, and flowed seaward away into the bound-
less memory of God.

She felt chastened by the experience, chastened
and yet exalted. When she came out of the dark
church the sky seemed brighter and the bustle of life
in streets and lanes gayer, as though holiday had come
into the air with the fall of night. A star flickered
busily above the dark roofs. The dusty old tree beside
the doorway shook itself out in the wind and Saint
Francis from his pedestal raised a hand in blessing
over the two children. Phil too seemed to be more

hopeful. He said maybe with the help of God the bottle of castor-oil would do his mother good, and Mary Kate said there was no doubt of that.

Then he opened his heart to her. He told her, stumbling over every sentence, of his fear lest anything should happen his mother, and of the things he had offered up to God that she might be spared to him. Every morning he went to Mass and Holy Communion at the Franciscan church; and it was hard enough for him to get up, for though he did not like to let his mother know, he got very little sleep at night, and lay awake listening to her groans. She cried worse at night, he said, and that was because she thought he was asleep.

'I'd go with you myself if I could get up,' said Mary Kate suddenly.

'Yes,' admitted Phil. 'It isn't easy.'

'But if you gave me a knock I might go all right.'

'That would be grand,' he said simply.

'We could make a novena of masses together for her.'

'I'll give you a knock up in the morning so,' he said gratefully.

Next morning at twenty minutes to eight a tap came to the McCormicks' door. Mary Kate, who had been waiting for it, answered with a whispered 'All right' and listened to the footsteps padding lightly downstairs again. Then she jumped up and began to dress. Her mother tossed irritably in the bed and blinked up at her.

'What ails you?' she demanded.

'I'm going to mass,' Mary Kate answered boldly.

Her aunt seemed to be stirred awake by mere dislike of the word, and cast a cold and disapproving eye at her over the faded scarlet lettering of her flour-bag sheet.

'What's that you say?' she asked, frowning and yawning.

'She's going to mass,' said Babe.

'Notions, my dear!' exclaimed Dinah.

'Oh, notions is no word for it,' said her sister.

VI

NEXT evening when Mary Kate went to see Mrs.
Dinan she was lying back in bed, looking tired but
radiant. There was no need to ask ill-bred questions.

'I drank the whole bottle,' said the invalid triumphantly, and Mary Kate gasped. The chemist had
distinctly told her there were a half-dozen doses in it.

'I was thinking I'd get up for a bit to-morrow,' said
Mrs. Dinan.

'The doctor wouldn't like you to be doing that,' said
Mary Kate.

'Ah, doctors!' There was a lofty contempt in Mrs.
Dinan's tone. 'They don't know what they do be talking about half their time.'

Mary Kate cleaned up for her, rather more satis-
factorily than on the previous evening. Now that Mrs.
Dinan was nearly all right again there was no necessity to call a second time—surely she wouldn't be
wanting a second bottle!

On the following morning she was roused again by
Phil's gentle tap on the attic door. She did not jump
out of bed quite so quickly as on the previous day, but
suddenly remembering the contemptuous way her
mother and aunt had spoken she gave a sigh and
proceeded to dress. Her mother again cocked a cross
and drowsy eye at her. How long was she going to

stick it? she asked. Mary Kate's heart hardened. Oh, well, she'd let her see!

'I'm making a novena,' she replied stubbornly.

'What for?' asked her mother, with a yawn.

Mary Kate looked away and smiled as she yanked up the shoulder slip of her combinations.

'For a good husband.'

Her mother laughed sarcastically and nudged Auntie Dinah.

'Did ye hear that, Di? Mary Kate is making a novena for a good husband.'

'Good hunting to her,' said Dinah drowsily.

''Tis about time you began one yourself, Auntie Dinah.'

That was one for Dinah.

'Who was it knocked you up?' asked her mother.

'A boy,' said Mary Kate incommunicatively.

'What boy?'

'Phil Dinan.'

The two women giggled.

'So that's the good husband!' exclaimed Auntie Dinah.

'I wouldn't be seen dead with him,' said Mary Kate with finality. And from the door she fired her parting shot. 'No man ever I seen around here would be worth marrying. That's the reason I'm making the novena.'

She chased down the stairs. Once outside the house she was glad she had got up. There was a feeling of freshness, of buoyancy, in the summer morning air. She could understand why it was that people who went to early mass every day had equable tempers and became pleasing to God. There was a sort of holiness in the air, and the stillness of the lanes was like contemplation within the mind, calm and virginal. She began trying to make up a song about it and hummed it between her teeth. 'All young girls should be up in the morning early, for the morning is like a young girl, but the evening is like an old woman. I love the young girl and I hate the old woman. The girl's soul is clean, but the woman's soul is dirty and cracked like old ware; evening is cold with sticky cold like a corpse, but morning is cold with healthy cold like my hands, like my feet, like my forehead, like the wind in my hair, like the wind in my hair.'

There was no rhyme nor rhythm to the song, and no tune that you could call a tune, but Mary Kate did not mind that. She was no precocious singer who would preserve every tittle she wrote, but a quite genuine poet whose poems flowed out from her so fast that it would have been impossible in twenty lifetimes to get them all within the bonds of metre and set them down in print. She had made hundreds of poems as good as that and still they kept coming.

Another was beginning as she tiptoed up the aisle of the church. Mass had just started, and she saw Phil's head in the front row. She tried to say the prayers in the mass-book, but somehow her thoughts were drifting back to her poem. She hadn't said all she wanted to say; that was what was wrong. She should have said that in her heart she wanted it to be always morning, without mother, without aunt, without brother (a brother whom she disliked with all the arrogant respectability of her soul); she should have said they all belonged to some soiled evening world. And they did! She knew that she was not one of them, and nothing made her happier than to dream that they had kidnapped her, long ago, as a baby, and that one day her real father and mother would come and claim her, and it would be proved that all the time her home should have been a court or a great castle among the woods. She felt no bitterness against them for having kidnapped her; she would tell her father nothing of what they had done to her, but praise them and have them dismissed with gold and jewels, or maybe choose them a little cottage not far from the castle where she would visit them and bring them presents.

She woke to find her thoughts miles away. Then she pinched her thigh savagely and tried to find her place in the mass-book.

The truth is, as the more acute of my readers may already have recognised, that Mary Kate was not really devout at all. She had prayed hard for Mrs. Dinan to get better, and her prayer had been answered; whenever she or any one she cared for was in trouble again she would again turn to God for help, but on what she would have called the 'in-betweens' of piety she found it impossible to concentrate. She intended to continue going to early mass, but whatever reason she gave herself for doing so, it was really the desire to get away into this morning world of her fancy that was stirring in her. Already her thoughts were drifting again from the prayer-book; already the church was growing a picture on her mind; a little yellow island of candles, and dark shawls and vestments, red and blue, and boys' smooth faces set in a sea of morning light, and outside on every hand clean, tall, contemplative houses, cold to the touch, and creamy, high, blue-ribbed heavens. So, though she reproached herself, she was happy, and though she felt she was offending God, she was praising Him like any fresh wind that blew about a corner or any little dazzle of light the clouds let slip.

She waited for Phil outside the church; the congregation emptied itself out, but still no Phil appeared, so she tiptoed back and touched him on the shoulder, smiling in anticipation of his start. She was conscience-stricken when she saw his white face upturned to hers; she had imagined it so thankful, and instead it was so dreary, so sharp with the concentration of prayer. He blessed himself and followed her out. And now she could scarcely believe in the pool of dazzling summer light outside the cool porch, the shadows of the dancing leaves, and the dreamy, chocolate-coloured Saint Francis.

'How is she?' she asked, as they stepped into the warmth (she was trembling, almost afraid to ask).

'She's dying, Mary Kate,' he said, suddenly sniffing back tears. '. . . I'm afraid,' he added, to ward off the evil eye.

He did not see how hard it hit her. 'It was all my fault,' this was how she thought of it. 'I promised God to make a novena for her, and my second mass was a bad mass. I never thought of her and I never thought of God. And He did it to show me what a vain, wicked thing I am!'—'But, surely, she was sick before that?' a portion of her mind asked comfortingly; to which the first portion answered remorselessly that she wasn't in His eyes; for before Mary Kate had gone to bed for the night He had already looked into her vain soul and seen there no gratitude for his mercies, no promise of regeneration. It was as well that Phil, unlike God, could not see into her thoughts at that moment.

'Mary Kate . . .' he went on. She heard him now call her by her name for the first time and looked up gratefully, to see that he was crying.

'I wanted,' he said, breaking down completely, 'I wanted her to live until I had a good job and could pay her back, and now she'll die—I know she will—she'll die, and I won't want to do anything after. Oh, all the plans she used to make, Mary Kate! All the things she wanted to do when I was grown up and earning lots of money. We were going to have a big house on the South Mall with three servants and a woman to come in and do the washing—and she was so good, Mary Kate, she even used to think of all the nice things she'd give the poor woman, and how much she'd pay her, more than ever she got while she was working; and she was going to give her all my clothes when they were a bit worn for her son, because she thought she'd like to have a woman that would have an only son of her own, so that they could talk about him. She used to talk about that for hours, Mary Kate, and when I went to school I used to wake up and find myself thinking of her out working for a shilling or one and threepence; and I worked, I worked like no one else did, Mary Kate, ever!'

Mary Kate's soul was enduring a crisis of repentance such as she had never known in her life before. As Phil spoke she thought of Mrs. Vaughan and the little cottage she would never see, and it seemed to her that the whole world must be full of dreams like that. And to think that Mrs. Dinan would be deprived for

ever, for all eternity (she understood now the meaning
of those awful words), of her beautiful home on the
South Mall with its three servants and charwoman
because of her own rudeness to God. It would be terrible if Phil knew of the remorse that was now gnawing
at her.

The bright summer morning lay shattered to pieces
about her. The beauty of trees and river seemed to
mock at her, and the entrance to the Dolls' House,
with its decaying flight of steps and its lovely half-
destroyed portico, looked like the entrance to some
under-world of the imagination such as one passes in
dreams. The stench that came to her out of the coldness and damp of its jaws was the stench of corruption.
Phil was still crying quietly and growing ever more
frightened as he drew nearer the place where his
mother lay dying. She wanted him to go to school, he
told Mary Kate, but though he did not wish to dis-
obey her he could not go. Yesterday had been a tor-
ture; between the book and his eyes the image of his
mother's face had floated continually, and twice the
master had caught him crying at the ruined mask it
presented to his imagination. And he hadn't been able
to explain. He had to leave the class-room. Nor would
his mother understand. She wanted him all the time
to be at his books, even at home, even when she was
in pain. Everything she ever dreamed of seemed to
her to be in those tattered old books in which she
could not read.

Mary Kate could bear it no more.

'I'll come in after school and see if I can do anything,' she muttered, and ran upstairs.

Dinah was just stirring, and noticed the child's dark

set face. Over her breakfast the storm of weeping broke. Neither mother nor aunt could understand it, and both joined in thumping her vigorously on the back and shoulders to rouse her from it. Then Billy, her young brother, began to bawl too, as a protest against so much attention diverted from himself, and she desisted. She had not shed all her tears, not by any means.

'If that's the way early mass affects you,' her mother pronounced unsympathetically, ''twould be better for you to stop at home.'

'Begod, if she expected to get a husband after the second one,' giggled Dinah, giving Billy a vicious dig, 'she's impatient.'

All day the cloud brooded over Mary Kate's mind. Reluctantly, when her dinner was over, she turned to go into the Dinans' room. She noticed a startling change even within twenty-four hours; the little charwoman's eyes seemed to stand out stark and glittering from her head, her temples and cheeks had fallen in, her nostrils had shrunk, and her chin looked more pointed. It was astonishing to see how disease was bleaching all life from her face. Mary Kate, in shame, kept her own averted. She hardly spoke to Phil, who was sitting by the window, silent, half looking out at the bright river and summer-laden trees, yet wholly occupied in watching his mother's face. He had been walking round all day 'on the lang', and though he had not spoken to her about it, he had known the moment he set foot inside the door that she knew he had not been to school.

As Mary Kate was taking out Mrs. Dinan's cup to wash it she turned to Phil.

'Didn't you have your dinner yet?' she asked.

He made a sign of deprecation.

'I'll have a cup of tea in a minute,' he said.

'I'll wet it for you.'

If she could have seen herself as she said this she would have been astonished. There were two sculptors at work in that little room, death and life, and life with a touch had flicked into her lovely girlish face the terrible responsibility of womanhood. It was no more than a touch, but it altered her appearance completely. A moment and it had disappeared again under his thumb, but life the sculptor knew just how that look must be.

As she put the tea things on the table she swung round on him again.

'Haven't you any butter?' she asked.

'It doesn't matter,' he said. 'I'll get it later on.'

'I'll go for it.'

He made a slight, helpless gesture with his hands, and at that moment a shrill, fierce wail burst from the woman in the bed, a wail of spiritual, not of physical, anguish. Her face was contorted with pain. It was the first time in her life that this boy of hers had ever needed anything when she was too ill to earn it for him. As he listened the sweat stood out visibly on Phil's forehead in shining beads and his fists clenched convulsively. Mary Kate put the teapot back on the hob.

'I'll get it in a minute,' she said. 'Don't touch that.'

She rushed upstairs, her whole body stiff with purpose. Dinah looked round sharply as she tumbled in.

'Give us a bit of butter for Mrs. Dinan,' she said breathlessly.

'For what?' asked Dinah.

'They haven't it, and they haven't any money.'

'For the love of Moses!' exclaimed her aunt roughly. 'As if I'd enough for our own tea.'

The child did not bandy words with her. As before, she rushed downstairs and burst in upon Mrs. Vaughan.

'Mrs. Vaughan, Mrs. Vaughan, Mrs. Vaughan!' she said, 'give us a bit of butter for the love of God. It's Mrs. Dinan is sick and they haven't a ha'penny in the house.'

Mrs. Vaughan looked down at her, her round, red, handsome face a picture of dismay.

'Lord, child,' she said, 'you give me a fright! Is it butter you want?' She fumbled at her improvised larder, a worried look tightening her forehead. 'How much will I give you?' she asked.

'Give me all you can spare,' said Mary Kate boldly. 'Maybe I'll be able to pay you back. I don't know what they're going to do for something to eat. They'll starve before to-morrow if they don't get money somewhere.'

'Oh, God love us! God love us!' exclaimed Mrs. Vaughan, measuring the pat of butter with her knife. 'And the poor little woman sick and all! Well,' she added warningly, setting her teeth to make a clean break in her little store, 'it might be our own case to-morrow, Peg Vaughan.'

Mary Kate took down the butter to Phil, who obediently had not touched his food. No one said anything. Phil was very red, and Mary Kate, having poured out his tea, left him alone with his mother. She stood on the landing, thinking. She was happier now.

The terrible burden had been lifted from her mind and it was full of her secret responsibility.

There was something she wanted to know, something she could not ask her mother or aunt, and she wondered where to apply for information. Mrs. Vaughan she ruled out; Mrs. Vaughan had never had recourse to these quarters. She thought of Dona Nobis. Yes, she would be the proper person.

Poor Dona Nobis, whose wide knowledge of theology and church Latin was of no avail in the practical affairs of life, was always getting into swamps, and though she had a tiny pension which about paid her rent, she was for ever running to pawns or charitable organisations for a shilling or two to eke it out. Mary Kate knocked at her door and heard a mild, 'Come in if you're good-looking.'

There was nothing to be seen in her room but a bed, a table, a chair, a stool, and a lot of holy pictures and books, as well as a heap of yellow-backed penny novelettes. Bridie adored novelettes and swapped them with Mary Kate's mother. There were three statues on the kitchen table, and Bridie was sitting with one elbow resting on it. She was reading; the cheap glasses, tied with twine, raked perilously into her ash-grey hair; her forehead, whether from eye strain or a fell anatomical perversity, a mere bulge above eyebrows that seemed on the point of disappearing into her hair. Her jaws, that had known no teeth for many a year, were a load upon her sunken cheeks.

Very pale and thoughtful, she glanced up at the child over her glasses like some old reverend mother. She breathed sour old-maidish sanctity as her room

breathed old-maidish cleanliness. The laundry was
sent home for the week and she was taking her ease
until nightfall.

'There's something I wanted to ask you, Bridie,
love,' said Mary Kate coaxingly, feeling the table
behind her with her hands and lifting herself on to it.

'What is it, girl?'

'Where'll I get charity money?'

'Are you sure,' asked Bridie good-naturedly, removing her glasses, 'some of mine wouldn't do you?
Sure, you know I'd always be glad to lend you a
pound or two when I have it.'

'All jokes aside, Bride. Phil's mother is dying, and
they haven't the price of a loaf of bread in the house.'

'Is that the boy Dinan?'

''Tis.'

'And is she as bad as that?'

'Ah, God, you wouldn't know the creature, Bride!'

'You mean she wouldn't know me, child. She was
very reserved in herself so far as I was concerned, I
always thought.'

'Sure, that's the worst of it,' sighed Mary Kate. 'It
would go to your heart the way she is, without a soul
to do a hand's turn for her, and she as simple as a
child, not knowing where to look for it. If it was me
Auntie Dinah now——'

'Not making you a saucy answer, Mary Kate, your
Auntie Dinah was always a fine maker-out, and by the
same token that saucepan she have on me didn't come
back yet.'

'I know. I'll bring it down myself.'

'Not that I'm for stopping you if you thought you
could do a kind turn.'

'Who would I see, Bride?' asked Mary Kate eagerly.

'Well, you might go to one of the priests, though indeed I never got much from them myself. If I was you I'd see Mr. Etchingham from Montenotte. He's a gentleman, anyway, and knows how to speak to a lady, even if his father did drink himself to death.'

'And you won't tell me ma I did?'

'Now why would I tell your ma, child?'

But Mary Kate was growing artful.

'She's out with me because I'm going to early mass every morning.'

The lever worked beautifully.

'And right you are to go to mass, child. Never mind what your mother says, but do what your own conscience directs you. I always said the people who go to mass on Sundays and don't see their God for the other six days of the week are the people who'd never go at all if they had their way.'

Mary Kate took her leave, satisfied that Dona Nobis would hold her peace. As the door closed behind her she suddenly heard the latter call her name. She pushed back her head.

'Oh, Mary Kate,' Dona Nobis added casually, returning to her book and without looking up, 'you could tell that Mrs. Dinan, or whatever her name is, if there was any little thing she wanted I'd be glad to do it for her.'

VII

NEXT evening after school Mary Kate inquired her way up the long road to Mr. Etchingham's in Montenotte. From this she was directed back to his city office. She was horribly frightened when the tall, loose-limbed young man with the finicking moustache came out to her. By the odour of whiskey that enveloped him she judged that he would not be the last of his family to drink himself to death.

She stuttered atrociously. But he was jolly and shouted in an affectedly laney strain to put her at her ease; he knew her mother and aunt—many's the pound that pair had of him, and she could tell them they weren't getting any more. But Mary Kate in trepidation explained that she did not want her mother or aunt to know she had called on him.

'I wouldn't come at all,' she added sullenly, 'but there's nothing for the boy's dinner.'

'So 'tis the boy you're interested in?'

'If you don't believe what I'm telling you, can't you come and see?' she asked.

'What's your name?'

'Mary Kate.'

'Well, Mary Kate, I believe every word you're telling me, and to prove it to you there's two half-crowns for yourself. You're the only good-looking girl that ever came out of that quarter, for you can tell them from me, that of all the ugly, bandy-legged streels the Lord put into this world, the women in the Marsh are the worst. Do you hear that?'

'Eh, how bad they are!' Mary Kate murmured airily. 'I could never see myself why fellows give themselves a crick in the neck looking after girls.'

When she reached home Phil was sitting by the bed, watching his mother's face. She had dropped into a sort of coma; her mouth hung wide open and a little foam had gathered at the corners. Her breathing was loud and unrestful.

'I brought that,' said Mary Kate, holding out the money. He looked at it dully, without understanding.

'Had she anything to eat?' she asked impatiently.

'Nothing since this morning. . . . There's nothing in the house,' he added.

'I'll send Dona Nobis out for something,' she said, and went across the landing to Bridie's room. Bridie was ironing and singing hymns in time to the swish of her iron. She took the half-crowns and put on an old shawl.

'I'll get a bone and make a drop of soup,' she said. 'Have they any bread?'

'No. There isn't a thing in the house.'

'Oh, Lord!' said Dona Nobis, her face falling. Already her conscience was accusing her of being unneighbourly. 'Isn't she a queer woman,' she asked dryly, 'wouldn't ask for the loan of a thing?'

Mary Kate went back to Phil. He had fallen asleep, his two arms folded upon the bed and his face sideways on them. She did not rouse him, but put the kettle on to boil. Dona Nobis came in and they worked

quietly, in whispers. When tea was made, Mary Kate
shook him gently. He woke, moaning drowsily, and
looked up in a frightened way at Dona Nobis, who
smiled at him with extravagant tenderness, her great
yellow tooth exposed like the prow of a ship. There
was a suggestion of benevolent cannibalism about that
kindly woman's mouth. He ate greedily.

'I'll tell you what now,' said Dona Nobis at last,
'the two of ye go for a nice little walk and I'll look
after your mother while you're away. And to-night you
can sleep in my room and I'll take a spell with her.
'Tisn't right you should be up all the time and you
with your work to do.'

'She won't be easy,' he protested.

'She'll be easy enough when she know you're next
door,' replied Dona Nobis comfortingly.

So he and Mary Kate went for a walk together.
His mother was still in the stupor when they left, and
Dona Nobis said she would not rouse her till she had a
sup of broth for her to take. The two children scarcely
spoke as they wandered together up the Mardyke Walk
under the long avenue of trees, into the Lee fields, and
along the bank of the wide river at its shallowest.

'That's a nice woman,' said Phil at one point, as
though he had been making up his mind about it all
along.

'She is so.'

'Why do they call her Dona Nobis?'

'A hymn she do be all the time singing—the *Agnus
Dei* I think it is.'

'I know,' he interrupted, '*Agnus Dei qui tollis
peccata mundi*. So that's how she got her name, *Dona
nobis pacem*?'

'That's it.'

'That's a queer sort of hymn for a woman like her to be singing.'

'Oh, she is a bit dotty,' Mary Kate answered lightly.

'I don't mean that,' he protested. 'But it's so queer!'

She had the impression that he was trying to tell her something, because the words seemed to be sweated out of him, but what it was she did not grasp. She was surprised at the way Dona Nobis, after five or six minutes of silent moving about the room, had fixed herself in his mind.

The river was moving sluggishly between its low banks. Elm trees dipped themselves in the water. Convolvulus sprang up about the old alders. Swallows skated across the dark and wrinkled surface of the river. The valley of the city was well behind them. They returned under a canopy of white and shining mist.

As they were coming back he tried in a harassed and shy way to thank her for the money. He was very foolish about it—did he imagine the half-crowns were her own, Mary Kate wondered. Anyway, he seemed to know little about money.

He wanted to go to work. His mother was bitterly opposed to it, but somebody would have to go out and earn for them both. He was afraid he was fit for nothing but to be a messenger boy, though his ambition was to be a carpenter. Mary Kate thought this a very queer ambition for a boy who was so well educated, but she did not say so, for there was a tradition of respect in the Marsh for a man who 'had a trade', and could, as the saying had it, 'go anywhere'.

Dona Nobis had shifted her quarters into the

Dinans' room when they returned. Phil reluctantly retired to hers, at his mother's request carrying his school satchel, though with neither the intention nor the power to study. He was tired, but knew he could not sleep. Once or twice he went across the landing on his stocking vamps and listened at his mother's door. He could hear nothing. Bridie's room was too strange to sleep in, so he lit a candle and sat for a long time before the table, looking fixedly at the little group of statues with their fierce and wayward shadows, and letting the strangeness of his surroundings sink into his mind.

It was strange not to be seeing the river; he rose and looked out; no river, only a blank of dirty grey wall and the purple roofs above it. Below him the yard; he watched the men and women pass in and out on their nightly calls. Gulls from the river skated greyly on motionless wings into the geometrical pattern of blue sky that the dark buildings made, and fluttered out again as from a cage. Stars prinked it. The floor squeaked under his feet. Cats called. Voices seemed to wake and die away slowly in the crazy shell of the house like waves sounding in a sea-shell. A cradle rattled to and fro above his head. Shandon chimed across the river. Death was a queer, awful thing; death was all this and more; death dragged you out of them all— the nightly call to the yard, the squeaking floors, the cradles, the gulls, the river, and Shandon; it collected all the bits of you that were in all these things, and when everything was there, when not a particle of you was left in the whole of life or time, it destroyed all of you in an instant.

To the dying every moment must be as the gathering of faggots for a fire; you would hear a voice say terribly as Shandon chimed, 'I bring the last chime'; and when a gull flew into sight against the night sky, 'I bring the last seabird'; or when a star shone out, 'I bring the last star'; and the dying creature recognised that all these were portions of himself that would be destroyed in the final destruction when death put a match to the fire. He shivered at the thought. The room was cold. He was tempted to turn into bed and try to snatch an hour's sleep, but he knew he would not sleep with all this coming before his eyes, before his mind.

Almost unconsciously he opened a booklet that lay before him. 'The Wooing of Angelina' he read, and a picture faced him of a man and a woman kissing. He shivered again, but now the trembling continued and shook him from head to foot. He took down a prayer-book from Dona Nobis's collection, which lay well away from the heap of novelettes. He tried to forget himself in that. Almost casually his finger flicked open the prayers for the dying. He read them first in English, then in Latin; the magnificent

Go forth, O Christian soul, out of this world to God the Father who created thee, God the Son who redeemed thee, God the Holy Ghost who sanctified thee, . . .

the aspirations, the psalm *De Profundis*. Then he read the prayers to be said by the graveside, and for the first time the terror of imminent death, not his mother's death alone but the death of all life, seized him. He would have liked to run away from it, out of the house, away through the fields he had walked this evening, through dewfall, through morning, over the edge of the world, away from it. He realised that his thoughts that day had been the only true ones; nothing mattered beside God and the soul's one and decisive meeting face to face with Him. To live one's life racked with pain, loaded with humiliations, abandoned by the whole world, all this was as nothing compared with the responsibility of meeting God in death; the responsibility that he with others had taken so lightly and for which he must soon answer. The slowing down of time in which his mother had suffered, that had made every hour seem as long as an ordinary week, was now reversed, so that he saw himself being swept ever onwards into time and eternity; beyond his mother's death lay only his own. About his mouth the sculptor life drew a line that instantly hardened it, that made his face seem the face of a grown man.

He took down another book from Bridie's collection, a book of meditations on the passion of Christ, and began to read, but the prayer-book lay open before him, and now and again he glanced at it, as if to assure himself of some word or phrase that had grown entangled in his mind. The candle burned away to nothing in front of him, the room sank into darkness, the dawn stole in the window and brightened the geometrical pattern of sky; everything seemed to have dropped into that deeper sleep that comes with day, only the few birds that haunted the roof-tops of the quays chirped and whizzed by the dim pane and did not disturb it.

Then suddenly the cycle of the church's life that had haunted him since the previous morning all faded away. It was like the crash of falling masonry about his mind. The body of his mother, the pain-racked,

dying body, that had been the 'Christian soul', the
'faithful servant', that was to enter 'into His peace',
was only the body of a poor charwoman, thwarted and
exploited by other 'faithful servants', by other 'Christian
souls', and now about to be put in a box and laid
somewhere to rot. It came before him in all its tender
necessitousness. 'O God!' he said, 'she never had a
chance, she never had a chance!' and began to weep
bitterly in a complete abandonment of shame and loss.
He flung himself upon the bed while the first carts
clattered over the cobbles beside the house, and fell
asleep still crying.

He was wakened by Dona Nobis, shaking him and
holding out to him a cup of tea. His mind reverted, like
bowstring to bow, to his last thoughts. 'O Jesus Christ!'
he said, and wept again.

'Tut-tut, child,' Dona Nobis scolded impatiently,
smacking his wrists, 'don't carry on like that for goodness' sake!' And immediately he stopped.

'We must be resigned to the will of God,' she continued, putting Saint Anthony on the mantelpiece to
make way for the bread-and-butter.

He drank the warm tea and gradually his weakness
of spirit left him. His mind, making the full circle
back, was half surprised at its own gathering peace.
He looked with secret admiration at Dona Nobis, sitting affectedly at her meal, her profile to him; glancing,
when her eyes turned away, not sideways but upward.
It was as though she were feeling acute shame and
discomfort at eating before him. (As she actually was.)
She ate slowly, crushing the bread-and-butter, which
she dipped in tea, under her bare gums. She looked
deadly tired.

'You ought to go to bed now, Miss Daly,' he said suddenly.

'Och aye, child, I've my day's work to do yet,' she replied, her eyes reaching the ceiling in their flight.

'Would you—could I take some of those prayer-books to read?' he asked.

'To be sure you could.' If he had tried to find a way to her heart he could not have found a better.

'They're very consoling,' he said, for want of something better to say, and was startled by her reply.

'I often wonder whether the people that wrote them know how consoling they are.'

'Why do you say that?'

'Nothing. I only wonder.'

He realised that he could not get her to talk freely while she was eating. She was too embarrassed. Dona Nobis, a great hater of conventions, had long ago transferred her natural modesty from the subjects to which modesty applies and attached them to her food and her poverty.

As she carefully dusted into her apron the crumbs from the table and launched them into the flames, she said, 'You'd want to get the priest for your mother to-day.'

'Is she as bad as that?' he asked, starting.

'Oh, nothing to speak about. But she's weak, and in case she got into that stupor again——'

'I see,' he said heavily; 'she mightn't come out of it.'

'That's the way, child.'

He dressed and went for the priest. When he came back and told his mother he cursed himself for a fool that had not warned her first. It was as if some one had drawn a brush faintly washed with grey down over her face to the throat. He knew what she was thinking, and she knew he knew. He knew she knew that too. The strands of their minds seemed to interlink in some strange fashion, so that each looked into the other's eyes and saw his or her own thoughts imaged there, and beyond and through these again the other's thoughts. The tears that started uncontrollably in his eyes were immediately reflected in hers. She put her hand up feebly and stroked his forehead. Then he sat on the edge of the bed and kissed her many times. Mercifully, the cruel pain was easier, but she was sinking fast, and, as Bridie said, it would only be a matter of time until the stupor supervened once more. They both knew this might be the last time.

Towards evening Mary Kate came in, made his tea, and went out again. Shortly afterwards he saw by the fluttering of his mother's heart that something was happening. It was rising and falling as if trying to escape. It seemed to him that he heard it thudding within her. He rose and locked the door. Then he went to the drawer where he knew the blessed candle was kept, the old yellow candle that his father's dying hand had held; with his own trembling hand he lit it, and moulded her poor cold fingers about it. His left hand holding hers and supporting the candle, he opened the prayer-book and began to read the prayers for the dying—in Latin, as he knew she would have wished. As her breathing grew more difficult he hardened his voice; the noise she made came to him over the Latin words; he raised his voice, raised it until it seemed to him that he was gabbling and shouting. He glanced from the book to her; her eyes were fixed on him, and they had a queer surprised look. The candle-light reflected itself in them. Her hands grew colder and more lifeless under his grasp; he tightened it and raised his voice still more. *Requiem eternam dona ei, Domine*. A faint knocking came to the door. It seemed to be somewhere very far away. *Et lux perpetua luceat ei*. Close to him was the ominous death rattle. This was it, the wresting asunder of soul and body. His voice pealed out over that, and he heard shouts, calls to him from the landing. Mary Kate was speaking. His nails were buried in the dying flesh. And now all recognition had faded out of the glassy eyes that fixed him in the last utter humiliation of death. He was in the middle of a sentence when he noticed it——

Then he threw the prayer-book far away from him into a corner and, sobbing hysterically, flung himself upon the dead thing that had been a mother.

VIII

MRS. DINAN was buried with a luxury which must have delighted her own heart as she looked forward to it. It is the irony of fate that the saving which poor people such as she can make guarantees them only against posthumous indignity. To have four horses drawing her bier, that had been the only one of her dreams which Phil was able to gratify, and magnificent indeed they looked on that bright summer day, more restless somehow than two, more tragic, more darkly beautiful. But who enjoyed them? Who knew they were unique and fitting? Not she certainly. Not Phil either, for it is doubtful if anything of that day remained in his mind but the clumsy swaying and knocking of the coffin which four perspiring and angry men manœuvred down the stairs, while a little crowd above and below advised and disputed and added to the victims' rage, and Phil watched from the landing, looking as though at any moment he would break through them and sweep them all away. Mary Kate kept a tight grip on his arm.

Then she, her mother, Dinah, Dona Nobis, and Willie, her young brother, got into the first carriage. As usual, said Dona Nobis darkly, there was bad blood about the carriages, and it would certainly end in a free fight before the night was out. If people didn't want a spin for themselves they wanted it for their wives or children, and, they might mark her words, it would be still worse at the cemetery. Often and often she had seen heads cracked about less.

Babe shivered in a lady-like fashion.

'Aren't the people in this quarter a disgrace?' she asked.

'We're as bad ourselves,' replied Dona Nobis shortly. 'Can't we stop at home, tell me? When you're gone you're gone, and no more about you.'

'Well, you'd like to show a bit of respect for the dead,' said Auntie Dinah.

'Fitter to show it for the living!'

'How well you wouldn't give her the little bit of butter when I asked you,' added Mary Kate cruelly. 'Maybe you're sorry now.'

But her aunt only laughed inconsequentially.

The carriages drove off. Mary Kate's attention was devoted to her mother, whom she was observing with the rapacity of a watch-dog. As they alighted at the cemetery she pulled Dona Nobis aside and strolled along with her, helping her over the high mounds of old graves and reading for her the names and dates on the tombstones. That any one should have existed before the date of her own birth was a great cause of innocent pleasure to that good soul, and the older the grave the more pleasure it gave her.

'Is me ma going to have another baby, Bridie?' asked Mary Kate at last.

'Goodness' sake, child, have sense! What put that into your head?'

'I heard her talking—about going away. And she

looks like it, Bridie, if you watch her sideways. Have a good look at her.'

'Well, divil been in it,' said Dona Nobis, dropping suddenly to rest upon a gravestone, 'if she do I'll swing out of her! As true as God I will. Believe you me, I'll put her wool in the grass, Mary Kate. She won't fool me this time like she did the last, the vagabond.'

'Because I won't stop in the one house with her if she do, Bridie,' said Mary Kate with a catch in her voice. 'I'm telling you that. I can earn my living now as well as another time, and I won't put up with it.'

'Whisht up, anyway, girl, until you're sure,' said Dona Nobis, scraping the moss off a stone with the aid of a hat-pin and examining the inscription with her myopic eyes. 'Look at that now,' she said with excitement, 'there's one of my own family died in 1854, look. Well, well, well! To think of her lying there all that time!'

Her pleasure resembled that of a geologist whose discovery of a fossil has enabled him to antedate the creation of life by some hundred thousand years.

'I'll go over and stand by Phil,' said Mary Kate, who could see no connection between her own existence and a grave, however old. 'Don't forget what I told you.'

'My soul on it, I won't,' exclaimed Dona Nobis. Sitting on the tombstone she set about adjusting her high-perched hat that had got knocked sideways on leaving the carriage.

Mary Kate experienced the sensations of the burial through watching Phil. Though he had hardened his manner, or rather stilled himself, in obedience to the new impulse that was stirring within him, he could not avoid feeling and transmitting to the magnetised Mary Kate the brutality of the decayed and broken boards that lined the graveside with their caking of white mush that had once been living, breathing creatures like those who looked on, and the bones tossed at his feet. But what he did not succeed in transmitting was the almost overpowering emotion of certain words the priest said over it. It was the gospel story of Lazarus, and as it progressed Phil felt his heart expanding as though it would burst with passion. Millions like him have felt the same.

The priest dipped the sprinkler into the vessel of holy water. Phil almost started from his marble-like rigidity when he heard the drops patter across the polished lid that shone so bravely in the sun. But he held himself in check, tightening his lips and repeating over and over to himself, 'Cease, the Heart of Jesus is with me.' It was the end. The rope scraped through the brass handles as the coffin was slid into the grave. The sweating grave-diggers shouted passionately at one another. The first handful of clay was dropped in and lay across the breastplate legend, 'Katherine Dinan, who departed this life . . .', the men lifted their shovels, and load by load the everlasting earth dropped back, its sound growing duller and duller as it left the eyes and mouth and the hollow wood behind. Everybody dropped on his knees. Only Phil remained standing until Mary Kate drew him down beside her. Even then he could not pray. He glanced up and saw the valley of the Lee far beneath him. He had walked there with Mary Kate that day his mother . . .

He remembered with intolerable distinctness a trick she played for him when he was a child, drawing back the flesh from her brows and saying, 'Chin chin Chinaman.' And she had seemed so beautiful with the wrinkles drawn from her face that he would make her do it again and again. His breath came faster. The trembling shook him from head to foot. 'Cease, the Heart of Jesus is with me,' he repeated mechanically.

Mary Kate's presence served to relieve some of the excitement that supervened, but even she did not succeed in preventing three different residents in the Dolls' House from getting away with 'a couple of bob to give the grave-diggers a wet', while the grave-diggers still hung round, and by vigorously brushing their lips with the back of their hands tried to convey to a parched larynx a sensation of Christian patience. There remained the men on the hearse and the carriages, but Mary Kate took charge of these.

She watched the carriages roll off in a smother of dust, and enjoyed the spectacle of those faced with the short walk into the city. There was prime material for a row here, she decided. When they got back it would need no more than a word for the tenement to blow up. They were all very red, some limped, and nearly every one exaggerated his or her weariness.

Phil was standing by the grave when she returned, but he allowed himself to be detached from it without a sigh. She would not let him go back by the road, but through the fields to the river, which shone in its wide, winding circuit of the flat-bottomed valley like a humiliated serpent. They strode off downhill. On Monday he was starting work as a sort of assistant to an old carpenter on the quay. He wanted to start as soon as he could, he told her, to shake off the depression. Besides, he wished to keep on the room in the Dolls' House, and how else could he do it?

'Lord,' said Mary Kate, dismayed but pleased, 'won't it be terrible lonely for you?'

He was not afraid of loneliness, but he did want everything to be kept just as it had been during *her* lifetime; with the feeling of *her* in the room he did not see how he could be lonely. Mary Kate thought this uncanny.

'One would think you were so mad about her you'd be glad to get out of it,' she exclaimed.

He shook his head.

'From to-day on,' he said, 'I want to start a new life.'

Mary Kate felt a new life was something you started on Ash Wednesday (when you went off sweets for Lent) and gave over before the following Sunday; it was something in no way connected with keeping on a room you didn't need.

'I suppose it will, in a way, be a new life for you,' she admitted vaguely. 'Starting work and all. I'd do it myself if I could only get a good place where I'd have a couple of evenings off.'

'Oh, it has nothing to do with work,' said Phil. 'I want to live differently, that's all.'

The proof of the pudding was in the eating, she thought doubtfully, and presumed that in practice she would understand better what his intentions were. Meanwhile she wanted to confide to him her fears for her mother's future, and blundered from phrase to imaginary phrase in search of a way for telling her secret. But in the end none seemed better than the natural one, and she blurted it out, just as she had done to Dona Nobis.

Immediately she regretted it. Phil took it to heart, even now. She hastened to say that she was only guessing, but the harm was already done. He made no comment except the rather inept one, 'That's a terrible sin, Mary Kate,' as if anything worried her except the gross indignity of it, the insult to her own precocious womanhood which he did not seem to realise. And, though she did not say it to him, exasperation that traffic with the devil yielded such meagre rewards. She bound him with terrible oaths to say nothing of it to any one else, and then grew easier in her mind. Whatever happened this new Phil, or however long he lasted, you could certainly trust him.

It is right for an author to dwell for a moment on this conversation, which fixed itself in Mary Kate's mind as the beginning of Phil's 'fidgets', as she indifferently called all his manifestations of spiritual enthusiasm. Actually, as we have seen, they go further back, and might as well be dated from the first moment of fear for his mother's life, or from the night he spent alone with Bridie Daly's library of pious meditations.

But only now did Phil begin to exist for her as a character distinct from every one else in the world, and only now did she begin to take an objective interest in him. That she liked him at all she only admitted to herself on the beautiful river road under the shade of the overhanging chestnuts and beeches, when he irritated her by his wandering talk about Dona Nobis. That woman's influence on him was nothing less than extraordinary, thought Mary Kate. And she would have been less than a woman if she could have listened to praise of another for any length of time. Mary Kate was all woman and it exasperated her. Besides, he was ungrateful. It was ungrateful to say to a girl who had done so much for you that Dona Nobis had been your only consolation, to say that only for her you would not have been able to endure it and might have gone out of your mind. She was close to tears. For two nights now she had sat up with him brewing him hot tea, and her lids were heavy with sleep.

Phil praised Dona Nobis in all moods and tenses, for her strength of character, for her kindness, for her lofty determination to live on in the world (where the blazes else could she live? asked the girl of herself). It was a hard decision, and it did not grow easier with time. He wished to imitate her way of living, and for that reason he was abandoning thoughts of everything else. And at that a fierce little devil of jealousy woke in Mary Kate.

She grew more silent as they came nearer town. Phil was standing the tram, and, sitting on top waiting for it to start, she let her eyes rove over the wide shallow river, staring intently at the swans and the swans' down that floated erratically on wind and stream as though it had come alive, at the men fishing from the bridge, at the bushes that came out over the low walls of the gardens and almost touched her face—at everything, in fact, but Phil. She pulled down leaf after leaf, rolled it into a tight ball, and tossed it on to the path. She admitted to herself that she had liked him far better than she had known, and tears came into her eyes at the thought that he preferred Dona Nobis without a tooth in her head. He was hard, she decided, and complained him bitterly to her own conscience for not showing more emotion and for sitting there so cool and dry-eyed beside her.

She was convinced of his brutal insensitiveness when he said he wanted to buy a watch. At this she jumped in her seat. Wasn't it an outrageous thing, she thought bitterly, to say the day your own mother was buried you could think of buying a watch, as though the dead-money was burning a hole in your pocket? And they actually said women were interested only in gew-gaws! A score of things came to her mind, things he had done or said, which, in the light of this last outrage, were shown up as selfishness. She tried to show her disapproval by being cold and distant, and because he seemed unaware even of this she grew angry. Every gesture he made displeased her. Her mind, churning within her, was engaged in the task which in the Dolls' House is known as 'blackening your face'. Mary Kate was blackening Phil's.

It was a quarter to six when they got back to town. They had not much time to choose, but Phil was easy to please. He bought a watch for five shillings. Even this made her angry. Any old thing would do him! She walked to the door and stood there, looking out at the crowds passing from work.

But she started when he asked to see a lady's watch! She looked at him in doubt. The man brought a tray of them, tiny watches with straps. Mary Kate's heart suddenly began to flutter into panic. She wanted to say that he must not buy a watch for her, but she couldn't, because he never gave her the chance, never said 'this is for you'. He merely asked with an air of aloofness which was the nicest, and Mary Kate could only fidget helplessly and say this, that, or the other was lovely. For all the time there was the possibility that the watch was for Dona Nobis!

So by the time the shopman took her hand and tied the wrist watch on she had committed herself irrevocably; and Phil took out a bank-note and handed it across the counter; and with a watch that felt like one of the faces of Shandon steeple on her wrist Mary Kate sailed out of the shop. Phil said nothing and she said nothing. There seemed to be nothing to say. They walked down the quay together, and as they came to the bridge, in sight of the Dolls' House, her face began to crinkle up like so much stiffened paper. Phil pretended not to notice. When they reached the first landing he asked in a casual tone, 'Will I call you for mass in the morning, Mary Kate?'—and then without warning she sat on the stairs and put her fists to her eyes. What else could she do? On top of doubts such as hers, to be convicted by her own conscience of pettiness, jealousy, and unworthiness of a boy she had only just admitted to her affections—this was a cruel fate for a young woman not yet sixteen.

Fortunately, Dona Nobis, who had only been waiting for Phil to come home, stepped out on the landing and passed it off as a joke. The two children had tea with her, and she went into ecstasies over Mary Kate's watch and said, indeed, she deserved it all. Thereupon Mary Kate began to see in her something of what Phil said he saw. She was a grand little woman all right.

As Mary Kate went out, Dona Nobis, speaking with great emotion, said, 'I'm very sorry to say, child, that what you asked me is true.'

IX

PHIL faced into work with the determination of working well. His reason for desiring to be a carpenter is perhaps not so obvious to others as it was to himself. To him there was simply no alternative. Saint Joseph had been a carpenter.

That reason had not entirely satisfied the good monks. They were prepared to find him a scholarship in some religious college or a small clerical job, but Phil had made his first determined choice. Saint Joseph had been a carpenter and he would be a carpenter. Even the neighbours seemed to have recognised a change of soul in him, for, since the evening of his mother's death, it was no uncommon thing to hear him referred to as 'The Saint'.

A little lane off the quays was the site of Gregory (pronounced Groggery) Mahon's workshop. As you stood at the door Shandon's grey snout was on your left, Saint Peter and Paul's church on your right. Shandon pointed nine as he knocked. His punctuality was unnecessary, because old Mahon answered the door in his night-shirt. 'Set down upstairs and wait for me,' said the boss. Phil sat down in the workshop, a double room with high ceiling and bare walls, against which were ranged planks, cut and uncut, chests-of-drawers, wardrobes, tables, and hallstands, some of them roughly painted chocolate or green. He sat there for a long time until every article of furniture had become familiar to him. He kept glancing nervously at his watch. An hour passed, and another quarter, and his zest gradually abated. At half-past ten the new boss came down, once more rubbing the sleep from his eyes. He had changed the night-shirt for a day-shirt and pants.

'Fell asleep,' he explained, with a yawn. 'Went back into bed just to warm myself before I got up and fell fast asleep. Come on into the kitchen and set down.'

Phil followed him into the kitchen and watched him set a match to the gas-cooker.

'I see you're punctual,' said the boss, with another great yawn. 'I used to be the divil for punctuality myself at one time. But as a bachelor I got out of the habit.'

He was a small man with a brick-red face and grey tousled hair. He seemed to have no eyelashes, and his red lids fluttered impatiently like his hands, which were always in motion towards something. Phil noticed that the kitchen was almost devoid of furniture. There were no pictures, not even holy ones.

'My late jade of a wife,' continued the boss, cutting himself a hunk of bread, 'was that lazy, she usedn't to get up till twelve or one, and at nine o'clock every morning'—he waved his knife to mark the emphasis—'at nine o'clock up I'd trip from this very kitchen with a cup of tea and a round of toast for her.' He was silent for a moment and then asked gloomily, 'And I'd like to know who put the hot-water bottle in the bed for her?'

'Is she—is Mrs. Mahon—long dead, sir?' asked Phil.

'Dead? Who said she was dead?'

'Oh, I thought she was.'

'The divil deaden her but she is not dead,' commented Mr. Mahon darkly. 'She cut her hook.'

'What's that, sir?' asked Phil, startled.

'I say she cut her hook, boy. Deserted, whipped her stock, ran away, vamoosed, absconded, eloped.'

He slashed tea into a basin-like cup for Phil with a sudden frenzy of earnestness.

'Hurry now,' he said impatiently, 'hurry now, for the love of God! There's half the morning gone already and a hammer didn't see a nail yet.'

He swallowed his tea with the haste of a workman snatching a pint, and still nibbling at a lump of dry bread, led the way back to the workroom. Then he fell upon the day's work with an energy that dismayed Phil, whose desire to learn could not keep pace with old Gregory's desire to put board to board. True, once or twice he had the impression that the work was being done with more energy than grace, but he felt that only idleness made him critical.

In the afternoon the old man's zeal diminished; he allowed Phil to handle a saw, and even gave him a few tips. About four or half-past a few people came in to inspect the furniture—poor folk they were mostly— and when they appeared Gregory hurried on his ragged old coat, and with his shirt sticking out from the seat of his pants and his mane of white hair wagging wildly, he steered them round from hallstand to wardrobe, speaking glibly and never ceasing to gesticulate. It appeared that if he did not actually know the visitors he knew everybody else belonging to them.

'Wisha, poor Peter!' he would say. 'It is Peter, isn't it? No? James, of course 'tis James—Jumbo I used to call him—poor James, is he in America all these years? Is he now? Is he really? Why then, would you believe me, we were in the one class in Blackpool? We were then. And do you know who was with us? The bishop's cousin. You ask him the next time you're writing to him. Many's the good game of handball we had together.'

Then turning on Phil he would shout:

'Hi, boy! Hi, boy! Have you nothing to do to say you're idling around there?' Then a dive towards him. 'Show me! Show me! Well, go on with it, can't you? Go on with it, you gom! Saw, saw, saw, saw, don't stand there with your hands in your pockets!'

Each time he was spoken to in this fashion Phil felt he would go through the ground with shame.

'I'm sorry you're not satisfied with me, sir,' he said miserably as six struck from Shandon.

'Not satisfied?' The old man was genuinely astonished. 'Who said I wasn't satisfied?'

'I thought from what you said, sir——'

'Oooooh, never mind that,' the other crowed. 'Gracious, boy, don't mind that! That's only to make them see we're up to date. That's advertising. They like that. If it's any consolation to you I think you're a grand boy—different to the other young pups I had, answering me back! I tell you, boy, you go on like that and you'll be a success in the world. You'll be a famous man, a Rothschild. And to prove it I'll increase your wages straight away. A shilling a week.'

'Oh no, sir,' said Phil, relieved but bewildered.

'Oh yes, boy. . . . Well, sixpence, anyway. Say six-

pence. To show I can appreciate a good workman
when I see him!'

So passed a week or more, and the old man, to his
own advantage, was becoming accustomed to Phil's
punctuality as Phil was to his oddity. But it was not
long before he realised that there was another side to
the picture.

That was on the morning when Mr. Mahon, after
dawdling atrociously over the meal he called breakfast (in which Phil invariably joined him), made his
way to the shop and began the sorriest pretence of
work that Phil had ever seen. He was silent and unhappy, his white head hung upon his shoulders, and
his little grey eyes moved furtively about the workshop with a conspiratorial air that Phil could not help
thinking comic. At last he raised his head, puffed out
his chest, and sighed heavily.

'Notice any difference?' he asked. Phil, who was
mystified, had to admit that he didn't.

'That table wasn't like that.'

His assistant did not contradict him. The old man
sighed and turned to his work once more. Trembling,
he reached out his hand for the saw which was lying
on the bench beside him. He grasped it fumblingly
and it fell with a clatter.

'Look at that!' came out of him in a long and eerie
wail.

Phil picked up the saw and handed it to him. He
took it gingerly. Then he began to cut, but the saw
was biting badly and slipped. He began again, sigh-
ing and gabbling distractedly to himself, and this
time the saw cut, but to Phil's amazement it cut
steadily away from the pencilled line. Still the old

man persevered, shaking and purple with unaccustomed effort. Then he rose and lifted his grey eyes to the ceiling.

''Tis Selim,' he said, and if he had said ''Tis heart disease' or ''Tis the end of the world' he could not have been more profoundly moved. Phil was shocked. 'Let me try, sir,' he said. He took the saw and cut the plank clean enough to satisfy a better carpenter than Gregory Mahon.

'That's right, that's right,' his boss said abstractedly. He resumed his work.

But his expression and behaviour went from deep to deep of gloom. Now, when he reached for a plane that was lying on the bench, almost at his hand, he approached it warily from behind, like a timid child stealing up on an unsuspecting but presumably vicious puppy. His movements grew slower and more cautious, and at the same time, it seemed to Phil, more clumsy. For all his care in trapping a chisel that to all appearances was quite tame, it rounded on him and cut his finger. The plane crashed from his hand. The saw refused point blank to cut anything except himself. Phil, who in his awkward way had to help, time and time again, eventually found himself seeing the workshop in an unusually bleak and sinister light, and the tools and planks as a sort of fossilised menagerie restored for the moment to its old life and habits. At last the old man said gloomily, ''Tis clear he have no power over you.'

'Who, sir?' asked Phil.

'Selim.'

'Who is Selim?'

Gregory shook his head and lowered his voice,

his eyes dancing from corner to corner of the workroom.

'That's three times this month,' he said mournfully. 'He's getting bolder. . . . And do you know what?' he exclaimed, flashing up for a moment, 'as true as God, only for him I'd be in Paradise!' His voice dropped again, this time to a whisper. 'I knew it the minute I looked in the door. I told you the table was shifted, and one glance at that saw——' He looked at the apparently inoffensive saw as if it might rise from its bench and bite him.

'I thought everything was just the way we left it,' remarked Phil practically.

'No, no, no,' said Gregory, 'didn't I show it to you? Felim was here for a fortnight now. I wonder what's come over him at all.'

'Who is Felim?' asked Phil, feeling that either he or the old man was astray in his wits.

'Felim? Felim is one of the Sullivans. The Sullivans and the Mahons are related. Felim is a Sullivan.'

'And isn't Selim?'

Gregory Mahon laughed. The irony of a lifetime of suffering creaked in that laugh, but it ceased abruptly.

'Is it with a name like that?' he asked, his eyes dilated with excitement. 'Did you ever hear tell of a Selim that come out of Ireland? Did you? You did not.'

'I didn't,' Phil admitted. 'Would it be a Turkish name?'

'Ssssh!' the old carpenter hushed him, looking fearfully around.

'And is it because he's not Irish he does that to you?' Phil asked perseveringly, determined to get to the bottom of this mystery. But the question seemed to startle the old man, who immediately sprang to life and grabbed him by the arm.

'Oh, no! Oh, my, no! Oh, not at all! I never said that! Oh, no, never! I might have said—but Thedd isn't Irish, and I'm not saying a word against him, remember, not a word!'

'Ted?' asked Phil, dumbfounded.

'Not Ted,' Mahon hissed furiously. 'Thedd, Thedd, Thedd. I'm not saying a word against Felim or Selim, not a word, but I don't say but I'd be happy with Thedd by himself. Even if he isn't Irish.'

Then he dried up, and not another word could Phil get out of him about Felim, Selim, and Thedd.

He was rather glad in a way of the intrusion. It gave him an opportunity to learn his work, for half an hour or less had been sufficient to convince Gregory Mahon of the malicious genie's presence, and the rest of the day Phil had to do the work as best he could. It was the first time he had had anything fully explained by word of mouth, and he worked with genuine pride and zeal.

He was an apt pupil, even the old carpenter admitted that, and in some ways he was the better of the two. For instance, he could cut a plank clean, which was more than Mahon had ever learned to do. For him a table or chair or hallstand, or anything else, was complete when it had been made to stick together and stand with no more assistance than what he called 'a wedgeen' under one leg; and it had never occurred to him that a table which was slightly wider at one end than another was any the worse for that. Neither could he understand that the four legs ought to be (if for no other reason than an irrational feeling for proportion) of either the same length, depth, or width. All his life he had been making good strong tables that were perhaps just a bit out, and selling them at fair prices, and the poorest of the poor (who were his only customers) had never complained. Indeed, why should they? Those were good tables. They were, as Gregory said proudly, rough and ignorant tables, but they lasted longer than the kind you bought in shops and cost less.

And, until the customers began to arrive, Phil practised his trade diligently, and learned not only how to make joints, but how to make them so that later they did not need 'a little bitteen of a wedge' or 'a morsel of glue' to make fixtures of them.

Fortunately, Mahon's powers of salesmanship were only slightly affected by the presence of Selim, and in his ragged old coat, with the tail of his shirt trailing from his seat, he acted as cicerone, flourishing his arms, and tracing back the real or imaginary history of the customer's family to the days when he and the bishop's cousin were both going to the same little school in Blackpool.

'John, Michael, Willie—ah, yes, of course, Willie. And do you tell me Willie is in Dublin? Ah, do you tell me so? Willie? With five children? Fancy that now, fancy that! Remember me to him whenever you're writing; he'll remember Gregory—old Greg that used to walk to Blarney with him to the band promenades in the castle gardens. Dance? You may swear we danced! Ah, youth, youth! Many's the heart Willie broke before the apron strings tied him, many's the heart he broke! Tell him so from me, the rascal!'

And to Phil: 'Aren't you done that yet, boy? My God, are you going to spend all the evening over that little job? Put your juice into it, man, put your juice into it.'

And passing him, his face red with shouting and excitement, he would wink, briefly and knowingly, at Phil.

X

THAT winter occurred the disgraceful episode of the pussy cat.

Mary Kate's guess at her mother's condition had proved correct. Babe had been seduced again (for, like certain magical draughts, Babe's virginity spontaneously renewed itself). In time Mary Kate had another brother whom she hated far more than the first. Nor if she had wanted to would she have been allowed to like him. Auntie Dinah insisted on dropping hints, and Babe and she carried on long conversations that trailed away into laughs and suggestions when Mary Kate appeared. For a full ten days after Mary Kate went round in the sulks, even going so far as to ignore her mother's speaking to her. She flew into a rage with her aunt, and when Dinah threatened to beat her, actually squared up to fight. But that did not last. At her age it was no use trying to fight.

While she was adopting this attitude a messenger arrived with a basket that contained a Persian kitten. Mary Kate could not very well ask where the kitten came from nor why it caused her Auntie Dinah so much malicious amusement. She gathered from ironic speeches, delivered especially for the kitten's benefit, that the donor was of the male sex, that his hair was dyed, that he had a paunch and suffered from dyspepsia. She disliked the kitten too, and kicked it with great gusto.

Then one evening she was sitting on the table watching some men working on a crazy chimney-stack nearby. It was seldom that life flourished above the waste of roofs one saw from the attic window. Her mother was resting after a heavy dinner and Dinah was somewhere on the next landing. The baby was asleep. Suddenly she heard a shrill voice, with what seemed to her an affected accent, calling her mother's name. 'Mrs. McCormick? Exactly, Mrs. McCormick.' The voice was unfamiliar. It was not the voice of any of the charity visitors, for all those were known and docketed, and no one of them could possibly have reached the stairs without warning. Babe sat up and listened.

Then Auntie Dinah swept into the room, hands fluttering, knees knocking.

'Oh, Jeese, Babe, give us the brat. 'Tis a stranger. Maybe she's going to give you something—maybe she'll——— Tidy up the place there, you little fool!' (to Mary Kate). 'And you, Willie, don't you as much as ask for a penny or I'll split you open! The brat, Babe, the brat!'

She snatched up the baby and whirled out of the room again; Mary Kate heard her take the stairs three at a time. Meanwhile the strange voice grew louder and louder; never at any time but Saturday night would you hear a voice as shrill.

'A friend of my husband,' it belled, and as a sort of ornament, like those Mozart loved to tag on to his melodies, came Mrs. Doyle's voice *piano*, 'Yes'm. On the top landing'm.' Mary Kate heard a couple of doors open, and crept to the landing to look down. The whole house seemed to have waked; women stood cleaning their hands in their aprons and children clung to their skirts. And then Mary Kate saw the woman was lame; she stumped from stair to stair and made long pauses to address the growing audience above and below her. Her progress was maddeningly slow, as slow as her voice was shrill. When she raised her head to shout the child saw a broad, determined, colourless face with false teeth and pale grey eyes.

'Yes, a friend of my husband.'

'Fancy that, now,' said a woman's voice, and Mary Kate was stung by what she detected in it of irony.

'So I asked my husband about her and he told me who she was—such a sad story, don't you think? And such a good woman. So I insisted on my husband sending her a little pussy cat to keep her company. A little Persian kitten. You've probably seen it about the place—so friendly—grey Persian. Of course you have! And it's probably lonely without its mother. I'd have brought her in a basket, but she's so enormous. And she won't stay quiet when she hears the traffic. Persians are so highly strung.'

Stump. Stump. Stump. She leaned heavily on her stick.

Every one in the Dolls' House by now was somewhere or other that the visitor must pass. Even Dinah had come to the door of Mrs. Vaughan's room with the big handsome countrywoman, and they stood talking, Dinah taking in every phrase and gesture. Mary Kate knew they would have a full evening's entertainment afterwards.

'Oh my! Oh my!' the stranger sighed, looking up

at Mary Kate. 'Must I go up all those steps? But what a pretty child! And what lovely hair! Just look!' she added to Dinah, 'isn't she a picture?'

The picture promptly disappeared and would have been glad to bury itself somewhere, but that escape was now impossible.

'Is that your own baby?' asked the stranger suddenly of Auntie Dinah.

'No'm,' muttered Dinah in a fluster.

'Well, it's quite a nice baby. You've nothing to be ashamed of.' She turned to Mrs. Vaughan. 'A friend of my husband. He gave her a kitten.'

'Oh yes, ma'am,' said Mrs. Vaughan good-humouredly.

'Who was that child? Not Mrs. McCormick's?'

'Yes, that's Mary Kate.'

'Fancy!' The stranger thumped her stick off the stairs. 'And I thought she was just a child herself. Such a big daughter! And such a handsome daughter, I must say. Well, well!'

Thump. Thump. Thump. Babe was sitting up in bed, frantically reviewing herself in a hand-mirror and repairing her face, while she muttered oaths and aspirations all in one breath. Then she lay back, looking prettier and more doll-like than ever, against the pillows. The terrible steps came to the door, and Mary Kate at her mother's signal opened it.

'Well, well, so you're the pretty young woman that ran away from me just now. Do you know you're a beauty? Did nobody tell you that yet? No young idiot ask you to marry him? Will you come home with me now? I'm sure you'd love to.'

Mary Kate slunk back furtively. Her expression

showed no immediate inclination to go anywhere with the tall limping woman.

'I'm Mary Verschoyle,' the latter shouted gaily, leaning over Babe as though she might be deaf. She held out her hand. 'My husband told me about you.'

'It was so kind of you to come and see me,' simpered Babe. 'I'm sure I never expected it.'

'Not that my husband wanted me to. I'm sure he'll be furious with me. May I sit down? Those stairs! But, as I say, I've heard so much of you, and when he said you weren't well my heart went out to you, poor child.'

'No, Mrs. Verschoyle,' responded Babe correctly, taking pains with her accent as with her appearance, which was wan, rather weary, virginal, and timid. 'I haven't been well for some time.'

'And I said I simply must see you. I have been picturing you all along. Very like, I must say, very like, though I wasn't counting on that great strapping daughter of yours. The prettiest child I've set my eyes on for months. Why doesn't she speak to me? Eh, Mary Kate—isn't that her name, Mary Kate?—why don't you come here and speak to me?'

'Come here and speak to the lady, Mary Kate,' commanded Babe.

Mary Kate rose and stood unsteadily before Mrs. Verschoyle, all aflame and with eyes averted.

'How old are you, Mary Kate?'

'Sixteen,' replied Mary Kate without looking up.

'She's shy, that's what it is,' fluted Mrs. Verschoyle, with all the joy of discovery. 'Look how she blushes! My dear child, to be able to blush like you I'd give ten years of my life. Ten years from one end for a year off the other. . . . Some sweets, dear Mrs. McCormick. . . . Have a sweet, Mary Kate—oh, come, take a fistful! At your age I'd have grabbed the box. . . . Do you know, dear, I don't think I like her name. Why don't you call her Mary, plain Mary? So much more attractive! Or Marie, quite a pretty name, and so suitable for people of your persuasion. . . . And this is your son? Have a sweet, little man. Oh!'—she laughed at a pitch that could be heard from the road. 'Grrrr! How *he* grabs them, the rascal! What's his name? Willie? Personally—I may be wrong, of course—I think I should have chosen Alec. Alec or Stephen, those are my favourite names for men.'

'Oh, yes . . . lovely names,' mumbled Babe, taken aback by the storm of conversation.

'And do you think—you'll excuse my saying so?— do you think Mary Kate wears her hair right? Don't you think it would be nicer in one plait down the back? Dark hair becomes so mushy when it's loose. Excellent for blondes, of course. I hope you make her wash it regularly? Don't forget now, Mary Kate, next time I see you! What a pity I didn't know—I could have brought you some little thing—— But never mind, never mind, another time.'

'Oh, please, don't think of it,' sighed Babe, with her most languishing smile.

'Nonsense, why wouldn't I? It isn't as if I had children of my own. She must come and have tea with me. I adore children, don't you? My husband would be delighted to see her. He's so fond of children too, but we don't see many. Only now and again, when my nieces come up from the country. Such a tragedy, don't you think? About us not having children, I mean?

Well, it's a good thing Gilbert has so many things to occupy himself with. And you'd scarcely believe how interested he is in you!'

'Ah, Mr. Verschoyle is so nice,' Babe flourished languorously.

'Isn't he? Isn't he? Don't you find him charming? Such an interesting survival! He always reminds me of my father. It's his oddities that date. People don't have those oddities nowadays, I think. In my young days every one cultivated being odd. Old Cork, all the characters—so quaint! Even the big people, the Parnells and the rest of them, what fascinators they were. But we don't have Parnells any more. I'm so glad you like him. I'm sure when I tell him he'll forgive me for being so forward.'

'Oh, I'm sure he has nothing to forgive.'

'And there's pussy,' the older woman went on indefatigably, ignoring Babe's leaden-footed politeness, and doubling up in her chair. 'Pussy-wussy-wussy. Has pussy-wussy forgotten me? I do believe he has! Pish-wish-wish-wish. Ah, the love, the sweetheart! Does it know its old mother after all? Mmmmm, there's a big pow-wow pussy-wussy is making for his old mammy. Do you know, I had to beat Gilbert into sending you that kitten? Not that he grudged it or anything of the sort, but somehow he thought it wouldn't be proper. Such an idea! Not proper! He's so early Victorian! Do you know' (her voice had a pounce in it) 'he's fifty?'

'Goodness, no,' exclaimed Babe, presenting to the wide world a well-defined simulacrum of amazement. 'And so well-preserved!'

'Mmmmmm,' the other hummed complacently.

'Fifty. *And* well-preserved, as you say. Not like me, though I'm ten years younger. Rheumatics! . . . A doctor friend recommended a cure. Go off everything —gradually, of course. First eggs and milk, then down to a pint of water. Complete starvation. But it's so bloodthirsty. And I'm getting old. It isn't as if we were both in the dangerous ages. I have no rivals to fear at my age. Have a sweet. Don't you hate living in this house?'

'Well . . .' Babe made a wry grimace.

'Exactly. That's what I say to Gilbert. But after all there are ways and means. Now a little cottage in the country—if it were possible, of course—a small poultry run.'

'Well, you see, all my friends are in the city,' Babe said, a faint hardening perceptible in her voice.

'Yes, yes, of course; and there are the children to be educated.—Are you fond of books, Mary Kate?'

'Indeed, she's not a bit studious, I'm afraid. She've left off going to school, though I wanted her to go to the nuns for a year. But Willie will be a scholar.'

'Oh, so you've left school? And what are you going to do now?'

'I want to go to work,' said Mary Kate sullenly.

'Work? What sort of work?'

'I don't care.'

'Well, it's not impossible. You might easily get into a shop. Would you like to get into a shop and work behind a counter?'

'I would.'

'You would what?' snapped her mother angrily.

'Ma'am,' added Mary Kate.

She knew she was not showing her best, but the

visitation was proving too much for her. She saw the
ears cocked upon the stairs, listening to every word
and preparing a treasury of this ridiculous woman's
remarks.

'I'm sure a good many shops would be anxious to
get such an attractive girl,' pursued Mrs. Verschoyle.
'But we must make sure where we're going. Think
of the dangers for a young woman of becoming the
attraction of some wretched little tobacconist's shop
and marrying somebody out of employment and with
time to court her! Now a jeweller's or a really good
dressmaker's would be an excellent opportunity for
cultivating the best class of people and acquiring a
certain good tone. Well, come and see me, child. We'll
talk it over.'

'Old fool!' thought Mary Kate bitterly.

Still the old fool bugled on as if she were wound up
for it. Mary Kate returned to her seat by the window.
She thought maybe after all Ma Verschoyle might
have influence enough to get her a job. She loathed
the idea of going into service, and that was all she was
fit for. If she could get a decent job she'd clear out.
Ma Verschoyle was just the sort of old idiot that
would take pride in a thing like that. Mary Kate
sighed.

Life was not so easy. You had dreams and the
dreams did not come off, and then somehow something
happened and you never knew what the result would
be. The great thing was to humour them, as her
mother and Auntie Dinah did. She sighed again.
Her dreams had been all of Phil, and if he had proved
reliable all might have been well. But he had the fidgets
worse than ever. She sometimes saw him of an evening

and they strolled off somewhere together. He had got quieter in himself and was for ever wanting you to call into churches 'just to say a little prayer'.

A few of his 'fidgets' rather alarmed her. He had a special walk which he usually took alone. Beginning at Saint Peter and Paul's church, he walked to the Augustinian church on the Western Road; after a prayer there he went on to the Franciscan; up the Mardyke and around Sunday's Well (prayers); along Shandon Street as far as the Cathedral (prayers); downhill to Pope's Quay (prayers); thence along King Street as far as Mayfield (prayers); down the Lower Road and into Saint Patrick's (more prayers); over the railway bridge and along the southern quay to the Capuchin church (still more prayers). Sometimes he varied the itinerary, dropping Mayfield and taking in Blackpool, the Lough, or some other outlying church, even going as far afield as Clogheen, but he always managed to visit the same number of churches. This he called his rosary, praising it as good exercise for soul and body. One night she had gone with him, and he had worn the heels off her shoes and the silence off her patience. The great thing, he said, was not to cross your own tracks nor pass by the same road twice. She thought it all a bit crazy.

Yet now as she listened to her mother and this old fool of a Verschoyle woman the memory had the power to make her angry, not with him, but with them. It was all very well wanting a job, but to be nice to a woman like that meant being as bad as her own mother, who was, anyway, not much better than the ugly word Mary Kate knew all too well. She would rather go out washing office floors like Mrs. Dinan than be dependent on that old one to do anything for her. And this pious thought filled her with a loathing of dependence in any shape or form. Charity degraded both giver and receiver. She imagined now that she knew what Phil thought of it all. Very well, she'd show them! To blazes with Ma Verschoyle and her old job!

A fruity and ornamental coda was blowing Ma Verschoyle from the bedside to the door; that she must come and see Mrs. McCormick again when she was well, and wouldn't dear Mary Kate come and see her, and really her hair would look so much nicer, and perhaps those few grapes—she didn't know whether the dear invalid liked them, personally she abominated the things, but it seemed to be done, didn't it?—and wouldn't Willie come up to her for a basket of apples? and didn't she think a creamy wall-paper would give more light than those dreadful flowers? —she hoped she would be excused for saying it, and she was delighted, so delighted!

And then she stumped, stumped, stumped downstairs, and every one came out to see, and a hail of questions, remarks, and sighs rebounded off every landing, and Mary Kate's mother sat up in bed and displayed a bangle of tongue each time her name was mentioned. Dinah rushed in with the baby in a hysteria of delight.

'Oh, Mary my mother, did you hear that one?' she chortled in a whisper. 'Hop—hop—hop.' (She imitated with cruel realism Mrs. Verschoyle's rheumatic limp while this was still sounding down the stairs.) 'Here, Babe girl, take the baby till I do her.'

She squared up in the centre of the floor, standing

on tiptoe and looking at the top of Babe's head; a sweeping brush took the place of the visitor's stick.

'Is that your own baby or have you it on loan?' she demanded peremptorily. 'How much a week? Look up and answer me properly, girl. Married or single? Yes or no? Why do you do your hair like that? Who is the child with the three squint eyes that was looking at me over the banisters? Any relation? No relation. Oh dear, oh dear! My husband—gave the poor child a pussy-wussy-wussy—answers to the name of Gilbert—a charming woman! My husband will be so glad I made her acquaintance.'

'Oh, shut up!' cried Mary Kate in a rage. She went out on the landing and banged the door behind her. Dinah's voice rose as the stick bumped the last stair and Babe exploded into a gurgle of laughter. 'Sweet Sacred Heart, he reminds her of her father!' she yelled. Mary Kate's heel drummed an exasperated rhythm on the boards. She trailed slowly downstairs. On the second landing a group of women were gathered about Doyler's mother. They were laughing. Her cheeks growing redder, Mary Kate tried to float past them by sliding on the banister, but some one blocked the way and a laugh was raised at her.

'Mary Kate, mind you don't get run away with when you go to work in the jeweliers.'

'Have the persians kittens yet, Mary Kate?'

'Oh, Gilbert gave her a fine substantial pussy cat all right,' one woman said flatly, and they all rocked at the joke.

This was too much for Mary Kate. She blazed down the stairs and away up the quay. When she had gone half-way she changed her mind and flew back

again. She had another idea. She ran through the
North Main Street, jostling the people off the footpath
and extricating herself from an occasional knot of
locals that put out their legs to trip her. At last she
caught up with Mrs. Verschoyle and dragged her
defiantly by the sleeve. The tall woman swung round
in alarm.

'Oh, it's you, Mary Kate!' she exclaimed in astonishment, and it was only afterwards that the child
noticed how different her voice sounded.

'Yes, it is me,' Mary Kate hissed between her
pants and sobs. 'Why don't you come back with me
now and listen to what they're saying about you?
Why don't you? Me mother and all. Come back now
and listen to them!'

'Why, whatever is wrong with you, child?' Mrs.
Verschoyle asked, noting the hysteria in Mary Kate's
voice.

'Making a hare of you, yourself and your old talk!'
cried the child, her more reasonable self realising that
with every word she was putting another nail in the
coffin of her fine job, but taking out in full on her ad-
versary all the humiliation of all the charity-mongers
she had ever known or heard of. 'Me Auntie Dinah
taking you off, and the neighbours taking you off, with
your old mangy cat and your fool of a husband!'

'My dear child'—Mrs. Verschoyle's face grew
purple, but she tried to laugh—'don't make a scene.
Remember there are people listening.'

'I don't care who's listening,' said Mary Kate, a
racial concept of the virago emerging from her dainty
face like a storm from the depths of a placid mountain lake. 'I'll let the whole world know. Your old

waterbag of a husband! And you talking like that to me ma about him. We all know the sort of a pussy cat he gave her, so we do.'

'Be quiet, you—you little shrew!' gasped Mrs. Verschoyle.

'I will not be quiet,' hissed Mary Kate. But her voice grew into an ominous calm as she added, 'And if you don't keep him away from my ma, do you know what I'll do? I'll scratch his bloody eyes out.'

'You don't know what you're saying,' replied Mrs. Verschoyle calmly. Mary Kate had the horrible feeling that something like pity had crept into the bold brass that was now playing so softly. So she threw her last dart and then ducked as from a blow.

'That baby you were admiring on the landing with me Auntie Dinah—do you know who that was? That was your husband's bastard?'

And as the ugly word passed her lips she was overwhelmed by a wave of shame that flooded her heart to the brim and started tears in her eyes; helpless tears that laid her all open to her enemy. But the enemy completed her downfall by merely clucking dryly with her tongue, and drawing her in tow as if she were a tender beside an Atlantic liner, whispering remonstrances and pitying chuckles.

'Now, Mary Kate, you must never say anything like that again. Never again, do you understand? It's not what you say about any one else I mind—it's what you say about your mother. Whatever she is and whatever she does—and I'm not defending her—she is your mother, and you are the first who should stand up for her. If you say things like that, what will other people say? . . . But all the same I like you for it, Mary

Kate, I do really. . . . Now, now, now, you mustn't cry! I'd like to bring you away with me out of that horrid house, but you see—you understand—even my house isn't the sort of place a young girl . . . Oh, I'm not quite such a fool as you imagine, Mary Kate. . . . And do you think you ought to wear blue? Somehow something lighter—grey or green, grass green—no, duller than that. But I don't suppose you have your choice. We'll see, we'll see. And remember you're coming to see me. When shall we say? Next week? Friday? Yes, Friday will do. I'd like to show you my garden. And remember, Mary Kate, my dear child, never, never under any circumstances, no matter what the provocation may be, *never* lose your temper like that again. You look positively hideous.'

It would be unreasonable to expect that Mary Kate should have caught more than a quarter of the shrill babillage with which Ma Verschoyle entertained her until they reached the tram stop on the Grand Parade, but she would have been less intelligent than she was if something of it had not sunk in. As it did. And gave her a terribly restless night and a lesson in human sympathy such as she had not had since the far-away evening of Mr. Vaughan's blow-out. Twenty times at least she assured herself that she would never go near Ma Verschoyle again, and nineteen times found it necessary to reassert herself on the point. And that she should have concluded on a negative must be laid to the account of Sleep, who called an unexpected closure, thus saving her from the necessity of reassuring herself once more.

XI

PHIL, whose piety had been more than half responsible for Mary Kate's outburst (he having by this time become the keeper of her conscience), disapproved strongly of it.

He explained to her that we must be continuously on guard against our natures, above all against our passions, for it was to Mary Kate's passions that he put down her rudeness to Mrs. Verschoyle. Mary Kate did not see what passions—whatever they might be—had to do with it. She had merely lost her patience. But Phil replied that patience was just the thing we must never lose. She listened to him open-mouthed. What would life be like if you didn't lose your patience? she asked herself, and knitted her brows in the effort at imagining a contest of patience in which neither party would weary. This was all a little above her head, and wherever Phil had the idea from she knew it could not have been from his model, Dona Nobis.

Strolling into his room, sitting on his table, endeavouring to discuss the world with him, Mary Kate, who had outgrown her years both mentally and physically, was already a model of eternal woman wondering at eternal boy. She smiled when she saw the mirror with its face to the wall, turned so that Phil should not be distracted by the image of his own features when he wished to concentrate on something else. At fifty Phil's behaviour would provide her with just as much amusement, for no man ever outgrows abstract interests and no woman ever grows into them. That he should insist upon making his rosary twice a week, on Tuesdays or Fridays, whether the weather was wet or fine, and visit each time never less nor more than nine churches, was diverting enough. But that he should also indulge in a whole ritual governed by the same numerical principles was astonishing, was, in fact, if one considered it long enough, frightening. The nearest approach they had come to a row was about this curious methodical piety of his.

One morning when he had called her she had drowsed on in bed, and that evening when they met she had found him not only cold but openly disapproving. He refused to call her any longer. She flew into a panic. Somehow this early mass had become a portion of her life, and Phil's calling her was her closest link with him. The bond between them was as fine as that.

'But, Phil,' she protested, 'it's only one morning out of how often?'

'It's that morning that counts,' he replied resolutely. 'That was the morning getting-up needed the greatest effort, and that was the morning your will power gave way. How do you expect ever to do anything if a thing like that can beat you?'

'But it didn't beat me,' she exclaimed in exasperation. 'I was sleepy. I can't help being sleepy, can I?'

He shrugged his shoulders in the curiously unemotional way he had developed since his 'fidgets' began.

'Well, from this on I leave it to yourself. For me to

call you after what you've done would only be weakening your will power more.'

'I think you're maggoty mean,' she flared up.

He shrugged his shoulders again and did not reply.

'Will you or won't you?' she demanded peremptorily.

'Won't I what?'

'Won't you call me in the morning?'

'No.'

'Phil!'

His good-looking face became troubled and obstinate. He thought for a long time before answering.

'All right then, I will; but on one condition.'

'What's that?'

'Every night before you go to bed you must pin a bit of paper to the door with a message asking me to call you and mentioning the time. "Call me at a quarter to eight"—something like that. Whenever that's up I'll call you. Whenever it isn't I'll let you sleep on.'

'Wouldn't you like me to sign my name to it?' she asked with heavy sarcasm.

'Yes,' he answered; 'you must sign your name to it too.'

'Well, of all the idiots!' she exclaimed in a rage, and suddenly recollected her last row with him and how much in the wrong she had been.

'Why do you want me to do that?' she asked gently, too gently, it is to be feared, for it steadied Phil in his obstinacy.

'I want to put it on you to ask.'

'But if I ask you now?'

He shook his head.

'Now isn't the morning. I want you to do it the last
thing before you go to bed, to use your will power that
far, once every day. I'm not even asking you to write
a new note every time. The same one will do, and
when you pin that up at night, even though it doesn't
take you more than three seconds, it will be a use of
your will power.'

'It wouldn't do to leave it up all day?' she asked
hopefully.

'I didn't think of that. I'll take it down and pin it to
the window-sill on the landing.'

'Oh, all right, all right,' she sighed.

The dark cloud passed over, but it left an uncomfortable feeling in her mind. She saw that Phil was
planning his life carefully, and fiercely but silently re-
sented it because she saw herself ruled out. He told
her gravely that after a certain amount of natural
irritation Gregory Mahon had now got quite used to
his knocking as nine o'clock struck from Shandon,
not a minute more or less. That was when Shandon
was right, which it wasn't always. He checked his
watch with the post office clock before going in for
the night. She realised now that he had been in no way
frivolous in buying a watch on the day of his mother's
funeral. That was the beginning of his 'new life'. His
watch had become a sort of secondary divinity whose
inexorable laws regulated his whole existence. At half-
past seven the alarm went off, and it was portion of
his duty to see that it never needed more than a half
a twirl of the key at night; he had shot across the room
to the mantelpiece and stopped it before it had buzzed
for more than three seconds. That had taken some
doing, but by thinking for the first few weeks that he

was in a house on fire he gradually accustomed himself to it. And this idea of the house on fire remained with him. His body was a house on fire; no sooner had he quenched one outbreak of sense than another appeared somewhere else. He was endeavouring to develop his will power so far that he would wake immediately before the alarm went off, and already he had succeeded, once for three mornings in succession, once for five.

He allowed himself five minutes for his morning prayer, ten for dressing; then he called Mary Kate and pinned the smudgy slip of paper scrawled with PLEASE CALL AT 7.45 AS USUAL MARY KATE McCORMICK to the window-sill. This he called his 'job docket' to put his piety on a business footing. At eight minutes to eight he set out for mass. There were two hundred and fifty-six steps between the Dolls' House and the church—he had counted them three times and struck an average—and at the pace he went he was kneeling in his usual place five minutes before mass began. He was back in his room at twenty-five minutes to nine or thereabout, made himself a cup of tea, and set out for work at three minutes to nine. He developed the habit of saving, first sixpence, then a shilling of his wages for distribution in pennies to the poor. His method of doing this was another torment to Mary Kate. He called the beggars his 'pensioners'. There was a certain day for paying each one, and while he did not like to defer payment when the beggar man or woman failed to put in an appearance, he detested having to anticipate it even by so much as a day. One had the impression that somewhere or other he had a neatly ruled account book in which payment of each penny was duly recorded. He concentrated upon saying a certain number of aspirations in the day, a number which at the end of the week totalled up to a good round sum that made major calculations easy. He instituted certain checks, and occasionally worked out how many he said in a month or might be expected to say in a year or even in a reasonable lifetime. This last figure was positively staggering, and he wrote it in great figures across a whole page of the fat exercise book in which he entered up his failings, doubts, and ideals. On Tuesdays and Fridays, preparatory to his 'rosary' of the city churches, he took no milk or sugar in his tea. He was a regular communicant each Sunday and on the first Friday of each month. He was also considering making what the faithful call 'the efficacious nine Tuesdays', which would fairly fit in with his Tuesday-Friday cult. All these things he carried out with the knowledge and approval of Dona Nobis, whose reverence for him increased as her sense of his personal dignity faded. Never had her awe of him been greater than when she dared to call him 'a little idiot'. She got a guilty yet hallowed thrill from such freedom with those she considered her superiors in the eyes of the Lord. He knew that, and knew she spoke of him in that way as she spoke of Saint Teresa as 'old Tessie'.

In one thing only was she his superior—she could sing hymns. Above all, she could sing the soothing Latin hymns he loved: *Tantum ergo*, *O Salutaris*, *Ave Maris Stella*, and the litany of Our Lady of Loreto. And Phil could not sing. The only occasion on which he had attempted to sing the litany had kept Dona Nobis chaffing for weeks, for he had no

sense either of pitch or time, and his long dismal wail
had reminded her of the night that the Fairy Woman
was keening old Mahoney on the quays. She immediately put her fingers in her ears. After that Phil
only listened; but he was a good listener, and would sit
for an hour enchanted by the sound of the Latin words.

> *Tantum ergo sacramentum*
> *Veneremur cernui,*
> *Et antiquum documentum*
> *Novo cedat ritui. . . .*

She had also the gift (which Phil did not exactly
envy her) of seeing things. One evening he arrived
with a present for her. It was a present purchased after
long self-communing. It was, in fact, a love story
entitled *Kisses for Four*, and Phil did not quite know
whether it was (from him) a proper gift. Still she liked
love stories, so there would be no harm in giving her one.

As he pushed the door in he received a shower of
cold water in his face. Dona Nobis was standing inside
with a holy water font and sprinkler. 'Turn round,' she
commanded without further explanation. He did so
and received a fresh shower on the back of his neck.
'Set down now,' she said, and he sat beside the door
and watched her. She strode round the room, and
each step was accompanied by a sprinkling in one
direction or another. Three or four times he heard her
say with gusto, 'Take that, you little bastard you!' It
was made more eerie by the relative darkness of the
room. He heard her go on her knees and give three
great casts under the bed. Then with a face that glowed
triumphant in the firelight she put back the font in its
accustomed place over the mantelpiece and leaned
back looking at him.

'Saint Teresa tells us,' she said dryly after a pause, 'that 'tis no use unless you can hit him a wallop.'

No more was said about it. Dona Nobis had a short way with demons.

Mary Kate found it difficult to extract from Phil any real entertainment about his new employment. She knew that Gregory Mahon was a bit daft, and knew and recounted to a silent and disapproving Phil the reason for Mrs. Angela Patricia Mahon's disappearance.

Which was that one morning after they had been married for two years a young woman, much younger, it must be admitted, and much more attractive than Mrs. Mahon, knocked at the door. Mrs. Mahon answered, and no sooner had she put out her head than a baby was unceremoniously thrust into her arms with the remark, 'I beg your pardon, ma'am, but would you mind giving Mr. Mahon back his baby?' Whereupon the young woman disappeared, never to be seen again. Mrs. Mahon, it was alleged, put the baby in the bed with a note pinned on to it saying that she had gone back to her mother, and hoped she would not be followed, as she would not anyway come back to the sort of man who would do a thing like this. Against the 'this' was drawn a hand in a stiff shirt cuff, and the finger would seem to have pointed to the attached baby.

If Phil disapproved it may well be because he recognised the probability of this having happened. His principal obstacle in the attempt at becoming a saint was old Greg, and his peace of mind was frequently troubled by certain contrary notions of Greg's that came under the sign of the mystic Thedd.

·He first made Thedd's acquaintance under peculiar circumstances. He was wakened one night by shouting and laughter from the quay outside. He heard a splash and at first thought it might have been a drunken man fallen into the river. But the renewed laughter told a different story. He looked out through the window. There was a light rain falling. He could see nothing at first, but after a little while he detected two dark figures by the quay wall. They laughed and screamed. Then another voice joined in, a man's, and Phil was certain it came from the river. The voice was familiar. He hastily pulled on some clothes and crept downstairs in his stockinged feet. At the foot of the stairs he donned his boots and went out on to the quay. As he did so the two figures ran away laughing in different directions. 'Nix! nix!' screamed one. Phil looked about him. Then he leaned over the quay wall and heard a splashing in the river. It made off towards the opposite bank. 'Come back, come back,' he called in a low voice. 'Whoever you are, come back.' His voice sounded very loud in the silence, and it was answered immediately by two screams of laughter that came eerily from either side—obscene, hysterical laughter that made his blood run cold. The splashing continued. Then it ceased abruptly. He screwed up his eyes trying to pierce blackness. The rain fell monotonously, drenching him.

Then a white figure could be seen dimly, climbing an iron ladder against the opposite wall, and again the laughter came like call and answer from either side. Quite plainly he heard the pad pad of naked feet on the other bank, and the voices screamed and hooted. Then everything was still once more, and he crept back to bed, drenched and puzzled and frightened.

Next morning the old man had a cold in his head. But it was not this so much as the way he talked that convinced Phil. This was a different demon to either Felim or Selim, both of which he knew well. This was clearly Thedd.

Thedd, in Gregory's theology, was the spirit of creation. With his coming arrived the spring, flowers, girls, passions, rhapsodies, long letters and poems; and spring in this sense confined itself to no season of the year. From early morning Phil's faith had to stand firm against an onslaught of philosophy and senile erotism. A double misfortune occurred in so far as Mary Kate, out of feminine curiosity, called at the workshop that morning for the first time. Thedd blew Phil and Mary Kate together in old Greg's mind; a white flame of passion must go up from the Marsh, and every sort of amorous allusion was used to incite Phil towards her—without immediate effect. But he was forced to explain his position.

'You see,' he said, almost sweating in the effort to make himself understood by this queer old man to whom he was otherwise quite devoted, 'it doesn't seem to matter what happens in this life. It's only what happens afterwards that matters. Compared with standing before God on the last day, everything we see round us is only smoke and ashes.'

'Nonsense!' shouted Gregory. 'Do you think the sunlight is nothing?'

'Not very much,' said Phil hopelessly.

'Nothing? The sunlight nothing? And the moon with the tides going crazy after it, that's nothing?

Flowers, birds, bees, worms, ships, trees, streams, rivers, oceans, fishes, mountains, fields—they're all nothing?'

'Compared,' said Phil desperately, finding it necessary to raise his voice to stem the torrent of inspiration, 'compared with having to die and——'

'Nonsense!' the old man hooted shrilly. 'Nonsense with your smoke and ashes! That radiant, that beautiful, that divine, enchanting creature that stood there —yes, there, just where that heap of shavings is— that sunbeam, you call her nothing? Where did you leave your muscle and sinew? Where did you leave it, I ask you? Or are you a man at all? Are you? When you were looking at her, didn't you want to throw yourself on top of her and squeeze her like a ripe plum? Didn't you feel your insides were going to pieces and a rush of fire coming up in their place? Didn't you? Didn't you, you inhuman monster?'

'I did not,' said Phil disgustedly.

'Inhuman monster,' Gregory said again, flinging himself on his work, which he seemed to sail through without effort, singing and shouting and stopping at intervals to pour out the accumulation of his frenzy. He cheerfully admitted to a sort of superior madness, and treated with exaggerated respect all the peculiar notions that came to him under its influence.

'Woman,' he shouted, rising in a furious perspiration and scowling at Phil, 'woman is a weir, and I'm a salmon.' And he went on with his work. After a while he shot up, still more excited, with, 'God is the jest of gestation. . . . What did I say about women?' And without waiting for an answer, growling mournfully like a beast in pain, he rushed upstairs. Phil heard him still grumbling as he clambered up and fumbled about upstairs for pen and ink. Twenty minutes later he reappeared like a man eased of his load. He carried a sheet from an exercise book on which the ink was still wet. He read his composition to Phil, and then handed him the manuscript which transcribed accurately enough the crescendos and diminuendos of his voice, and by isolating words, or putting them in capitals that trailed right across the page, succeeded in conveying something of the excitement they caused him. Nothing, alas, of his meaning, if he had any.

Again he was prepared to enter into fresh discussions about the majestic truths of philosophy, and again Phil maintained doggedly that nothing mattered for him beside the terrifying moment of the judgment seat. And again the flood of inspiration rose through the hammering of nails and squeaking of saws, and this time Mary Kate became confused in the old philosopher's mind with Killarney's lakes and fells, celebrated in song, and with the immediate necessity for an amusement park, with swing-boats, roundabouts, open-air dances, and public conveniences, to be erected on a waste spot near the Lough, and he raced off sweating and growling to write letters to the Government about it. This lasted the whole day.

Upstairs he rooted out of a heap of rags a tattered uniform, all green and white with what had been white breeches and a cocked hat with a feather, the uniform of the Irish National Foresters. And strutting round in this, with endlessly new sheets of copy-book inscribed with *vers libres*, modernist designs, economic and sociological proposals and letters to his great enemy, Bernard Shaw, the cabinet-maker looked like some figure out of a dream. He made himself a wooden sword of some laths, and went round with this swung from his belt or carried 'naked' (as he said) in his hand. His face and manner too seemed to change; they ceased to be his own, and in some way became abstract and impersonal.

He wrote dozens of letters to whatever public figures, such as Bernard Shaw, happened to strike his fancy. And these letters were put into envelopes but never stamped, and while he posted certain business letters quite sensibly, he carried these others about with him and posted them in the oddest places, such as the Bishop's palace or the home of some stockbroker.

Phil was sincerely troubled when he was entrusted with one to give to Mary Kate. For Phil, though he never remonstrated, was himself at an age to be troubled by the energy with which the old man pursued what he called 'the religion of everlasting beauty' that ranged from passionate avowals of idealistic affection to commonplace and sordid liaisons with the sluts of the quarter. He had reached the stage when obscenity imposes itself willy-nilly upon every boy; but quite unaware of this, and imagining himself unique, he repented the errors of his Creator with a mortal bitterness. Hell, during those black nights, was a living reality.

And Phil had to admit that as Mary Kate grew older she displayed a distressing lukewarmness about the fierce modesty with which he surrounded himself. She even enjoyed the letter which he brought her from Gregory. Which led them into a peculiar discussion, during which Mary Kate made the most dramatic

advance of her life, by announcing that she thought a
lot of talk was made about nothing, and, personally,
if Phil, for instance, wanted to kiss her she wouldn't
mind.

Then she looked away and tried to pretend that
she did not know how furiously she was blushing, and
Phil's eyes sank to the floor and he blushed too. There
was a dreadful moment of suspense.

'No,' he said at last; 'if I kissed you it would mean
I was going to marry you.'

'No, it wouldn't,' she retorted promptly. 'You could
kiss a girl without marrying her.'

'*I* couldn't,' he said between his teeth. 'I'd never
kiss a woman I hadn't made up my mind to marry.'

'Why?' she asked.

'Because it wouldn't be fair to marry some one else
after.'

She determined not to let him see how this thrust
had gone home.

'But suppose the girl wouldn't mind?'

'I'm not thinking about her. I'm thinking of the
woman I'd marry.'

'But she might have been kissed before that.'

'Not if she was my wife,' said Phil flatly without
looking up, his face grown redder than ever. 'I'll never
marry a woman that isn't like my own mother, and I'd
expect it of her that she'd be as I'd be.'

'Oh, but that's silly,' said Mary Kate, a little wave
of perturbation and jealousy mixed rising within her.
'You wouldn't expect any girl to be like your mother.'

'*I* would,' he maintained obstinately.

'But if she was like your mother no one would want
to marry her,' she exclaimed with exasperation.

'Why not?'

'Because no one marries mothers,' she replied hotly. 'You marry girls, not mothers.'

'Well, they become mothers, don't they?' he demanded.

'They do,' she admitted reluctantly, 'they do.' Adding as an afterthought, 'Not to their husbands, though.' Which, even if accidental, was a considerable piece of psychology.

But this conversation left them both disturbed. Phil was disturbed because her words when he repeated them later to himself made him hot all over and made his skin so sensitive that the pillow against his cheek was momentarily transformed into the cool fresh cheek of Mary Kate, and when he laid one hand lightly on another and stroked it, it was as if he were stroking some one else's hand, and the fingers that were his own seemed cool and twig-like, reminding him of Mary Kate's long translucent fingers resting on the edge of his table. He shivered with longing, and twice that night he had to get up and kneel in prayer to bring his vagrom imaginations under control.

For Mary Kate it was even worse. She had already gone through most of what Phil was going through only without his sense of guilt. And now she had to go to bed, her ears still hot with his cruel snub, and with the knowledge that unless she stayed unkissed for as long as Phil's fidgets continued (an utter impossibility, she recognised) she would forfeit her chance of being his wife; and even if she were to practise her will power to that extent (it seemed still more impossible when you thought it out in terms of will power) there was always the still greater chance of the respectable woman of forty-five or so who would somehow remind him of his mother. Like Dona Nobis, for instance! Mary Kate had no grudge against Dona Nobis, but the respectable woman of forty-five she pictured as a pious woman with one tooth.

It was a great curse, she thought, tossing restlessly in her bed, to fall in love for the first time with a boy whose tastes in women ran to motherhood, and who attached to kissing an importance out of all proportion to the event. Well, it was his own fault, she decided bitterly, finding the bed too hot for her; he couldn't say but that she had given him his chance, and when he had married his old woman and grown tired of her she would tell him so.

She pictured herself stepping into a motor-car beside a handsome young man in grey tweeds, when Phil walked up worn and old, a long streak of grey through his hair. And she would say (very sprightly of course and with no sign of grief), 'Well, Phil, I suppose you sometimes think of the night I offered to let you kiss me?' And since she suddenly found herself sobbing as she said this, and tears were a great relief, she allowed her imagination to build whole castles of such lachrymose stuff. She would be found dead, and Phil would lament over her and remember that he had not taken the chance to kiss her in life, and kiss her now that she was dead.

She sobbed at great length, and found herself considerably more cheerful.

She got up, and as she walked across the squeaking floor, her little feet shining ghostlily at her from under the sweep of her nightdress, the toes caught up, and warming one another in an instinctive embrace, she decided that Phil might go to blue blazes, and for her part she was not going to worry her head about him any more. The point was that she was getting too old to be going on like this (the night was cold) and she wanted a boy. If she couldn't have Phil, well, she couldn't, and any other boy would do just as well (it was queer how you could make up your mind like this at night)—and every one admitted she was a beauty, and boys already looked back at her when they met her in the street (Phil was a little fool).

So she returned to bed, and surrendered herself to imaginary arms and lips that with disappointing celerity launched her into oblivion.

XII

MARY VERSCHOYLE was as good as her word and got Mary Kate a beginner's job in a small but respectable drapery store. 'For,' as she said, 'of course, as a socialist and a free thinker and so on, she didn't believe in respectability, but still one couldn't be too careful, could one?' a sentiment with which Mary Kate, very much at sea, agreed.

She found Mrs. Verschoyle a queer, lonely, cantankerous, good-natured woman with a passion for interfering in other people's business, and being Mary Kate did not dislike her for it. She explained to Phil that, as a Protestant, Mrs. Verschoyle did not believe in hell (hereupon she assumed a horrified expression), had her doubts about heaven, and thought that God, if He existed at all, had a lot to answer for. Spiritualism was another of her fads; when she could go to London she attended séances, and at home experimented with automatic writing and table tapping. Mary Kate was secretly amused by these vagaries, which she looked upon as gross superstition, much as Mrs. Verschoyle was amused by Mary Kate's firmly rooted belief in the vicarious healing power of Catholic priests.

But Phil was not amused, and he stubbornly maintained that if Mary Kate was not to lose her soul she must give up altogether her visits to the Verschoyles. At this she laughed, not altogether displeased at her own daring. But she had no intention of giving up Ma Verschoyle.

Her meeting with Gilbert was something of a trial but less than she had imagined it. The reason was that she was exceedingly preoccupied. To every girl on the dim border of womanhood comes the hour when she says to herself, 'I will be kissed, I must be kissed,' and deliberately sets out to prepare the stage for it. This hour had arrived for Mary Kate, and that was why she could not be bothered by Gilbert Verschoyle. In her own blood she had written this resolution, and the scrap of paper recording it faced her whenever she opened her prayer-book.

She had gone there to tea one Wednesday evening, and, as tea was being got ready, listened to a great rigmarole from her friend. She was giving Mary Kate one of her usual terrific jaws on the subject of behaviour, and, as usual, the latter was listening with one ear open for the occasional scraps of information that she found useful. In theory at least Ma Verschoyle was against the middle classes. But at heart she was middle class herself, for all her doubts and theories had formed late in life, and beneath all these she was a great respecter of forms.

'A perfect lady,' she told Mary Kate, 'is a cross between a pomeranian and a she-ass. You'll learn as you grow older that the best of them is inferior to a good charwoman. A charwoman can be entertaining. And they try to erect barriers between themselves and somebody a class lower, and the barriers are just as stupid as themselves. If they were farmers they wouldn't know how to keep a sheep on one side of a gap. Now a really intelligent creature raises a barrier that no one except another intelligent creature can pass. A dozen people get into her life from any or every class—and those are the dozen people she really wants to meet. But those little middle-class-minded lower classes with their class distinctions! It doesn't matter what you think; it matters whether or not you talk of eating your soup—such an idiotic expression!—and whether you shake hands with a man when you're introduced. As though it didn't depend on the man whether you wanted to shake hands with him at all!'

'And don't you?' asked Mary Kate retrospectively.

'Don't you what, child?'

'Shake hands with a man when you're introduced?'

Ma Verschoyle suddenly remembered that a respect for forms was what she had really been trying to teach Mary Kate, and immediately began to explain. Mary Kate decided that when next a fellow was introduced to her she would not shake hands—whether or not she wanted to. There was something of the snob in Mary Kate. And just then Gilbert came in.

Mary Kate grew pale. She started to rise, and was very decidedly pushed back in her chair by Mary Verschoyle, who introduced her husband with grave formality.

Mary Kate went on with her tea, and she heard Mrs. Verschoyle continue over her head.

'My husband was such a friend of your mother's, Mary Kate. You remember that kitten he gave her? You have it still? You don't see as much of Mrs. McCormick now, Gilbert. What a pity! And I'm sure she leads such a lonely life.'

Mr. Verschoyle made a grab at the bread plate. Seeing his white hairy wrist so near her, Mary Kate controlled herself sufficiently to look up. She realised that he was the original of Auntie Dinah's portrait of a lover. He must have been a handsome young man, she decided; there were fine lines in his face, but his chin had dropped and a sulky, insolent smile hovered about it and about his mouth; a smile that betrayed his abject fear of his terrible wife.

Mary Verschoyle consistently preached abnegation, preached and practised it. It was in consequence of her theory that husbands can do no wrong that she had visited Mary Kate's mother, and the result was the breaking off of his relations with Babe. Now Mary Kate saw, for the first time, that far from being a fool, Ma Verschoyle was an unusually intelligent woman, and that it was her intelligence that her husband was afraid of. She had devised a means of controlling him which he could not understand, and no other method would have been effective. She never flew into a rage with him; what was more, she never fell back upon the most natural weapon of an intelligent creature— irony. She controlled him from an immense distance as it were, and in her high observation post she pressed the buttons and pulled the levers that regulated his movements. And if Mary Kate had known more of life, she would have realised how much Ma Verschoyle's impregnability depended upon what she called the 'tragedy' of her childlessness.

But she was upset by the meeting.

She had arranged to meet Doyler that evening. The appointment had been made in a fit of pique with Phil, but when she recollected that Doyler

showed all the signs of 'going to Dublin', and made up
her insipid face to look like nothing on earth, and
glanced once more at Gilbert Verschoyle, she became
timid and depressed. . . .

When she and Doyler emerged from a lane, and
Mary Kate heard her companion saluted familiarly
by strange young men, she grew still more alarmed.
Her resolution to be kissed, written with a new steel
pen in blood drawn from her first finger, had ceased
to count. Phil's long, dark, disapproving face came
before her in a vivid, startling way, and she realised
if she were to keep her resolution she would be elimi-
nated for ever from his list of possible spouses. And
she wanted Phil and no one else.

She found herself standing in front of two young
men whom Doyler, with giggles and crude jokes, was
introducing. Mary Kate remembered just in time
that you did not shake hands, and bowed jerkily,
ignoring an outstretched palm. She heard herself
speaking in an alarmingly affected accent, an accent
which she knew was copied directly from Ma Verschoyle, but which she was quite incapable of throwing
off. This increased her uneasiness, because it made it
clear to her that, whether you liked it or not, the game
of man and woman was played according to a set of
rules that you had to obey even at the risk of appearing ridiculous. She knew without asking herself that
it represented nothing of the young men, who seemed
quite decent fellows, and nothing of Doyler, who, said
Mary Kate to herself in a burst of bad temper, was a
brazen bitch. She answered everything too pat, she
who the whole world knew hadn't a word to throw to
a dog.

And with despair she found herself being paired off with a nice young man in a grey suit and a soft hat, and saw herself striding, hard at Doyler's heels, beyond Victoria Cross in the direction of Bishopstown. The young man was real nice, a perfect gentleman in his way; and Mary Kate, whose mouth was as dry as the Sahara, would have given worlds to be able to take him into her confidence; to drop once for all this God-forsaken accent she was acquiring against her will, and tell him that it was her first time going with a fella' and she was frightened out of her wits, and she hoped he wouldn't think she was the same sort as that little pimp, Doyler, who hadn't a clean shift to her back and spent her whole week's wages on grandeur. But somehow the words did not come, and Mary Kate's wit, fluttering wildly around at a great distance from Mary Kate's excited body, knew that the said Mary Kate was behaving like a little fool, saying 'ye-e-es' and 'no-o-o-o', and, most deplorable of all, 'pa-a-a-wdon', a word that was never used by anybody outside the Verschoyles.

They went up a lane that Mary Kate learned afterwards to call 'Cait Shea's Boreen', shady and secluded, and darkening now with the approach of night. The young man put his arm about Mary Kate's waist, and she made a quite instinctive casting up of eyes to heaven and murmured to herself 'Merciful Hour!' Then the first pair, who had been carrying on all sorts of fantastic wrigglings before her astonished eyes, suddenly slid into a ditch. 'Merciful Hour!' thought Mary Kate again. It was only to be expected that the nice young man should thereupon steer *her* into the ditch, and draw his arm tighter about her waist. When he nuzzled himself into her neck it was so uncomfortable that Mary Kate made some quite perfunctory twistings of her head, and at last allowed her mouth to be caught on an upward curve and her head to be forced back on to her shoulder. As his lips went home on hers she shivered. 'Onions!' she thought despairingly. It was her luck. And to have lost Phil for this!

'I think we ought to be going home now,' she said, firmly detaching herself.

'Oh, not now, surely!' exclaimed the young man in astonishment. Mary Kate felt that perhaps she was displaying unusual ignorance.

'If you think it wouldn't be right, sir,' she replied, and meekly surrendered herself afresh to his outstretched arms. She found that the taste of onions did not improve on acquaintance, and with a mind that was very far away, though somewhat calmer, she watched this Mary Kate who was leaning against a young man's shoulder in a dark lane, under a sky daintily bespangled with moist silver stars, and decided that it was mostly a mug's game. So much for the resolutions you solemnly wrote in your own blood! She liked Phil better than ever, now that he was irretrievably lost to her. She liked his churches and his statues and his dim lights, she liked his gravity and his starry coldness.

It was only natural that she should be silent. And it was also only natural that the young man, already dazed by her lady-like behaviour and accent (which wilted under no caress, and to his passionate 'Do you love me?' returned a nonchalant 'Pa-a-awdon?')—it was only natural, I repeat, that he should have mistaken all this abstractness for a perfection of soul consonant with her beauty.

By this time the wheel on which mortal beauty swings had brought her face to face with the sun. Her features had gradually lost those links with race which sharpen the faces of children. In ten years' time these would begin to reappear, but faintly modified. In old age she would resemble herself in childhood as she would resemble her mother, for the sun brings out that which is our own; winter gives us back to our ancestry, as it were, a preparation for the tomb.

Her face had a rare quality, which can only be described by saying that it seemed to have been modelled upon a much larger scale and then reduced, so that the modelling seemed inhumanly delicate, a marvel of sensitiveness. It was small wonder that the impatient young man should cover it with kisses, kisses which Mary Kate's hand would quietly but firmly wipe off, with no consciousness of injustice to him. In the few moments' respite which he gave her from those silly questions about whether or not she loved him she decided to call a complete halt to this sticky and malodorous amusement.

She said farewell to the young man at the tram stop, a ceremony that was very necessary, as it didn't do, said Doyler, to let a young man know you were staying in a place like the Dolls' House. They made an appointment for next evening which Mary Kate resolved not to keep.

But when the time came for her to show an interest in something else her self-control failed, and it was only when she hurried off with Doyler, half an hour late for the appointment, that she felt really happy.

She was so happy that she set out to be nice to Mr. Robert Moran (whom she spoke of to Doyler as 'Mr. Onions'), laughed at his jokes, and thus completed her conquest of him.

But her chronicler, as a disciple of the realist school, feels bound to add that to her Mr. Moran was never more than a toy. He feels reluctant to probe this trait in Mary Kate's character, a trait which undoubtedly temporarily broke the heart of Mr. Robert Moran, as it was later to break other hearts than his. He is aware that a more faithful pen might bluntly describe Mary Kate as selfish. But his plane of reference is different, and to use such a word as selfish would be to introduce an anomaly into his narrative. If the poet in Mary Kate had left behind a printed record of her dreams his task would be an easier one, for artists need no defence however numerous their cold attachments. All that they take from life they give back a hundred-fold in colour and melody and rhythm.

Mary Kate was a poet though she did not write, a musician though she neither played nor sang, a painter though her pictures were herself. Emphatically she was not selfish.

As Mr. Moran and others knew, it was a privilege to have one's heart broken by her.

XIII

AFTER Mary Kate had celebrated her sixteenth birthday her father, her almost mythical father in Dublin, made an undramatic reappearance with a letter and a ten-shilling note. After this he wrote now and again, occasionally enclosing a postal order that threw an immediate if transitory glow about the peculiar economics of the attic. For it was one of the family's good or bad points that money melted in its hands, and on nothing so emphatically as eatables. An uncovered and greasy table set with an astonishing array of foodstuffs was the usual sign of a letter from 'father'. Mary Kate, coming home from work, would sometimes be met by Willie striding along the lane with a borrowed frying-pan or saucepan in his hand.

'What is it, Willie? Where did ye rise the meat?'

'A letter from me oul' fella'.'

'And what have she?' She was Auntie Dinah.

'Ah, grand tings. You'd never guess.'

'Give it up, Willie.'

'A side of mutton and a cake with lovely icing she bought in town.'

'Yerra, go on!'

'And look—a bottle of sauce! And she have—do you know what she have? A bottle of corjal!'

'Style in our house!' said Mary Kate contemplatively.

'Ah, boy!' said Willie blithely, and as he reached the foot of the stairs set up an ear-splitting whistle that was designed to inform all whom it might concern what style there really was.

Mary Kate joined in these repasts with a healthy gusto that differed from that of the others only in a feeling of gratitude to the giver. She preserved a certain sentimental attachment to the father she had never seen, and when the meal was over her greasy fingers would stain the casual notes he scribbled. She had always cherished the feeling that a father would inevitably understand her so much better than her mother did. Her almost forgotten passion for Mr. Vaughan, that had risen directly from the comfortable warmth and odour of his person, had been sublimated into a desire for understanding from some equable, dispassionate, pipe-smoking man who would at the same time respect her comfort by not squeezing her and caressing her neck under the blouse.

'What do he say now?' asked her mother, who in the excitement occasioned by spending the postal order had not bothered herself with the note.

'He wants to know when you're going to come up to him,' Mary Kate explained.

She saw with something like jealousy that her father still invited his erring wife to come and live with him—in ignorance, no doubt, of how much she had really erred. And Mary Kate disliked her mother for the coolness with which she received these proposals. It wasn't even as if she was being asked to live in poverty, as Mary Kate, in her irritation, noted. He had a house of his own just off the South Circular Road. Three fine bedrooms, a sitting room, a kitchen, conveniences, and a bit of garden (with gas thrown in). Could she ask for more? She could.

'Is it me go up there to him?' she asked loftily. 'Himself and his three bedrooms and his kitchen. I know what he wants. 'Tis a housekeeper he wants, and he thinks he'll get one cheap in me, but believe me, I won't work my fingers to the bone for the best thing that ever got inside a pair of breeches. Cock him up with his kitchen!'

'Don't go, don't go, Babe; there's a good girl,' babbled Dinah, swinging a sardine exultantly by the tail. 'Sure, all men are just the same. Wanting you to get meals for them at all hours of the day, and if anything goes wrong 'tis your fault. As if we didn't know them!'

'How glad you were to get the money from him all the same,' grumbled Mary Kate.

'Well, and isn't it his duty to support his wife?' barked Dinah. 'Couldn't your ma take him into court in the morning and make him provide for her?'

'To be sure I could,' said Babe. 'And you mark my words, but he'd pay up then.'

'I'm not so sure of that,' said Mary Kate brazenly.

'Ma, me da wants you,' chanted Willie. He had adopted this as a war cry, and thought it very funny. Mary Kate didn't.

The foregoing conversation will probably explain her state of mind when eight or nine months later her father suggested her going up. There it was, in his own writing, and it couldn't be hidden from her. Wouldn't Mary Kate come up and keep house for him, seeing that she was seventeen and already at work?

To a child normally brought up there would have

been nothing attractive about such a proposal. Leaving a job where you had a certain amount of liberty, and where you were among friends, to go and live among total strangers and keep house for a man you had never seen and for whom nobody had a good word to say! Not even her mother, who, one might think, would have been glad to get rid of her. To be sure, her mother put up no very strenuous opposition either, but that was for financial reasons. Mary Kate's going to Dublin would more or less assure those very useful additions to the family income which were now in danger of being cut off. So she contented herself with sundry shrugs of her girlish shoulders and remarks such as if Mary Kate liked it—but if she were in her shoes—and, anyway, they'd see how long she stuck it.

Of her father, of the man himself, she could learn nothing. No one seemed to have known him: least of all her mother. 'Oh, he's all right. He's a nice sort of fella',' that was as much as she could find to say of him. Babe had a short memory for bedmates.

The strongest and most embarrassing opposition came from Mary Verschoyle. Indeed, Mary Kate left the house with the feeling that she had mortally offended that good soul. 'To throw away her prospects in such a fashion, and go where she would meet no women that she knew and could trust. She didn't want to frighten Mary Kate off her own father, but really, had she thought about it? One never knew what sort of man he might be——' and so on, and so on. And all the opposition only served to increase Mary Kate's determination to go. She revelled in opposition. She had broken with Mary Verschoyle—well and good, she would break with every one else if necessary to make her sacrifice the greater. She was fully prepared to deserve a father now she had him.

It was Phil, who put up no opposition at all and even went out of his way to encourage her, who made leave-taking hardest. She was distressed. She would have wished him a thousand times over to forbid her going, and somewhere at the back of her mind cherished the idea that if he did she would obey. But Phil did nothing of the sort, and his encouragement only exasperated her. Phil received her protests in his usual stolid fashion.

'Well, what do you want?'

'I think if you were going away I'd tell you I was sorry, anyway.'

'That wasn't what you asked me.'

'What did I ask you, then?'

'You asked me whether you ought to go up to your father.'

'Oh, all right, then, I'll go—I'll go. Anything to satisfy you. I suppose you'll be pleased when I'm gone.'

'Of course. I'll be pleased that you're doing the right thing.'

'You'll be pleased to get rid of me,' said Mary Kate, with a sniff.

'I never said I would.'

'Oh, I know what you think all right,'—Mary Kate was growing sniffier and angrier.

'Well, if you know what I think why do you ask my opinion?'

'You're a—a—cold-hearted creature, that's what you are,' said Mary Kate.

It wasn't as if she knew quite well that Phil was cold-hearted; she realised that of the two he was prob-

ably the more easily distressed. But never, except by
one of those happy accidents by which you suddenly
discovered what his feelings were, would he have said
the few simple words required of him. Ask him, for
instance, as any girl might ask any boy, whether he
thought you were good-looking, and he would keep
you for half an hour explaining what he meant by the
word 'good', and pointing out that to him an old
woman sitting over the fire saying the rosary might be
more beautiful than any of the girls he met walking
Patrick Street. And to close the argument he would
smile and shrug his shoulders helplessly and remark,
'Well, you asked me whether I thought you were
good-looking.'

'I suppose you won't even write to me?' she asked.

'Oh, I'll write to you,' he said, growing a little
redder. She knew this was a bad sign.

'How often? Every week?'

'Every fortnight.'

'Week,' she repeated peremptorily, stamping her
foot. But he shook his head and smiled with the same
charming, unshakable gravity.

'I'll tell you, Mary Kate,' he explained. 'I knew
you'd ask me that, how often I'd write, and I made a
vow that whatever you said I'd go half-way. If you
had said every day I'd have written every two days,
and because you said every week it's got to be every
fortnight. You see, I made a vow.'

She stared at him blankly, impressed again by the
insane methodicalness with which he ruled his life.

'I believe,' she said seriously, 'if I was dying it
wouldn't make any difference to you.'

'If you were dying' (even as he spoke he was

weighing up the question), 'if you were dying it would be different.'

'That's a relief, anyway.' She laughed nervously, a little put out by his tone.

'I'll write to you every second Tuesday,' he went on, smiling. 'You can write to me every second Friday.'

'If I write to you at all.'

'It won't make any difference to me. Until I see you again I'll write.'

And she had to try and find a grain of comfort in the knowledge that if the skies fell he would.

As the time came for her to leave she grew into a pleasant despondency. All her old haunts became especially dear to her, and she spent long hours wandering up laneways and boreens she had not visited for years. Phil came with her once or twice, but as she insisted on stopping to say a few words to any of her old acquaintances that they met, as well as introducing him to them, and as most of these were girls, he very soon tired of it. She could not understand his great hatred of 'girls', particularly such as were young and pretty and vivacious, but so great was his detestation of them that at last if she stopped to speak to one he refused to wait for her, and continued on his way 'at exactly the same pace as before'—so he informed Mary Kate, who suspected that he had trained himself to judge his pace as he judged his time. And even the fact that she was running after him, even that she was whistling and calling to him to go easy, did not make him abate a fraction of his speed or cause him once to look round. He was a real daft youth, thought Mary Kate.

XIV

MARY KATE'S first impression of Dublin was that it wasn't sufficiently like Cork.

This was in itself a bitter disappointment and enough to plunge her into a passion of melancholy (quite real this time) that lasted for three days, during which she wrote to Phil a long letter of regrets and hopes, begging to be remembered to a list of people that looked even to his reverent eyes like a litany, requiring the interlinear insertion of *ora pro nobis*. Besides, as he didn't know more than a third of the people mentioned, he judged it to be what in all truth it was—a song of home-sickness.

Then began for Nicholas McCormick and Phil a miniature bombardment of associations which showed that little by little Mary Kate, in her own queer way, was growing acclimatised. Phil, to be sure, understood, but it may be imagined that her father looked upon it as a mild form of insanity. It is difficult to take seriously a daily discovery of some likeness which does not in the least enter into your calculations, as to be told that the postman is the dead spit of some one that collects the pennies at the side door of Saint Peter and Paul's, or that a man has just passed by wearing a suit like the suit Mr. Vaughan wears of a Sunday, or that the road into Miltown reminds your young daughter of another road from Barrack Street to Pouladuff. And he might be excused for imagining that Mary Kate really had a slate loose when she reported triumphantly that, in a hardware shop in George's Street, she had seen a basin and ewer 'the very same as the ones we have at home'. He could not have guessed how this process of identification was fashioning Mary Kate's attitude to a strange city, whose strangeness was a menace to her peace of mind.

When this process had gone sufficiently far she was able to enter into the spirit of her housekeeping, to look about her for the first time, to savour the joy of three bedrooms, a kitchen, and conveniences, and to examine the father who had been so lately presented to her. She found them all good, first by long chalks the conveniences, which did not in the least remind her of the *Honi soit qui mal y pense* arrangements of the Dolls' House, second, her father, and last, the joy of complete privacy even in her own bedroom. When her father was out she sometimes sat upon the stairs help-lessly and sang with the sheer joy of space, even as the angels must have sung when sun, moon, and stars were tossed from God's hands and the walls of space fled from them, above and beneath.

But it must be confessed that only filial piety in-duced her to set this great gift last. Her father, though second upon her list, gave her nothing like the complete satisfaction that this would imply. The truth was that she did not know what to make of him.

In response to her first hinted strictures on him, Phil very sensibly replied that you couldn't pick up a father at the age of seventeen as though you had been

living with him all your life, which rebuke silenced
Mary Kate for some weeks. Silenced her without con-
vincing her. It wasn't that she disliked her father—on
the contrary she liked him very much—but she had
the feeling that if he hadn't been her father she might
not have liked him at all. To begin with, his conversation was too much like that of the young men she
knew already and not sufficiently like that she had
imagined for the man (equable, dispassionate, pipe-
smoking) whom she had chosen to idealise. Also,
he drank, and since her disillusionment with Mr.
Vaughan, Mary Kate disliked drink, though it is true
that her father never drank himself into such a beastly
state. Also, where she had thought of a lonely man
longing for the company of his young and vivacious
daughter, she found him with a host of acquaintances,
some of them women as young and vivacious as herself.

Against this she set his very tangible virtues, which
were that he was affectionate and that he did not row.
This was a great thing. He did not row, and she might
smash a cup or spend an unnecessary sixpence without bringing the house down about her head. She had
even approached him with the suggestion that they
might have Phil up for a couple of days, and secured
his ready consent. So Mary Kate wrote to Phil and
asked him to fix a date for coming—not too late, so
that she could look forward to it, and not too soon, so
that she might see herself all the sights she wished to
show him. An invitation which Phil read as another if
more cheerful song.

To this job of seeing the city in all its myriad aspects
she set herself with great enthusiasm. Guinness's

barges, with their red funnels that you could lower as you went under a bridge, almost reconciled her to the menace of drink. She followed them down the river, and the quays that were so like the quays of Cork, with their ships and foreign sailors that were so like the ships and foreign sailors at home, were at the same time a heart-break and a delight. Only the accents of the people left her a little lonely, they were so nonchalant and monotonous, and Mary Kate longed for the sinuous, excitable, whirling timbre of the southern voices.

She began to realise that it would be almost impossible for her to keep up with her daily mass, for, as she explained to Phil, it was the thing for her father to have parties that kept her up till all hours. She gathered from Phil's reply that for the first time he had begun to think seriously about his wisdom in advising her to come up. She even got to like the parties so much that the disappearance of her daily mass did not trouble her terribly. She liked one or two of the girls that came to the house, and gradually grew accustomed to their outlook on things in general.

It seemed to be nothing unusual in their experience for a married woman to live with a fella' at the same time, while it was an accepted thing that a fella' might lawfully amuse himself with a woman other than his own wife. For Mary Kate to acclimatise herself to these propositions involved a process not unlike that which she had gone through on her arrival with regard to her surroundings. It required that she should meet easily recognisable types, and provided Mary Kate met those she was not horrified. It was they who trained her to smoke, and for a week or more had great fun tempting her to join them in their drinks. But first she got into card-playing, and it was only when she was passionately interested in a game that she became a more natural, free-and-easy Mary Kate. They were pleased and surprised by her conversation, which, as they said, was 'something rich', and with a little heap of coppers before her, her narrowed eyes a little red and running from cigarette smoke, a very frank sally on her lips, she was clearly the sort of girl who would improve under the influence of liquor. When she was teased she would get wild and shout. One night she took a sip of her father's whiskey and water, and afterwards, in moments of excitement, she would call on him or on some other man for a mouthful. 'His house was Liberty Hall', her father declared, and he would have been shocked at his daughter if she had not been ready to sit upon some young man's knee or take a kiss without squealing. Having already learned all that was to be known about 'coorting', and grown as accustomed to it as to her prayers, it would have been hypocritical of Mary Kate to pretend she disliked it.

She sometimes woke in the morning with a queer head and the feeling that there was something unreal about it all. The party that had been the evening before had vanished, and those who made it up seemed like so many evocations, gone Heaven knew where. The house was strange, the bed beneath her was strange. Nothing was stranger than her strange father, and again, if she had gone down and laid the table for breakfast and found that he did not rise, and gone to look for him and discovered him nowhere, she would not have been surprised. She realised with stupefaction that to this very day she knew absolutely nothing about him, did not know where he worked, if he worked at all, and knew as little about the men and women that came in nightly and moved about as though the house were their own. And the stranger it became, this strange life, the more she liked it, for always about it there was the sense of mystery and impermanence.

Laying the table for her father's breakfast, she wondered whether the kaleidoscope pattern she had seen last night would recur that evening, for it was almost as a pattern that she saw it. And over the gas stove while she made toast for her father's breakfast she sang:

> I dreamt that I dwelt in marble halls
> With vassals and serfs by my side,

or

> I feel like one who treads alone
>   Some banquet hall deserted,
> Whose lights are fled, whose garlands dead,
>   And all but she departed.

The gas oven with its bower of rosy flame always made her sing.

Sometimes, when breakfast was done and she had cleared away, and he had gone to work (often with three or four of his guests who had stayed on and slept anyhow and anywhere), Mary Kate would have given worlds to have been able to walk out into the bright native air of home, under the familiar houses, and spoken for hours to the familiar people—Scrap, who plied his trade next door, and Kitchener the cobbler, and Gregory Mahon. For it seemed as if none of those guests of overnight lasted into the day, at least, any later than breakfast time.

Something of the uneasy, nervous pleasure she derived from these evening parties transpired in her letters to Phil. She knew how it would shock him, and for this reason laid on the colours thick. Oh, great fun they were having!

Great fun, indeed! She was getting to like her father better, so she explained to harrow Phil's uneasy conscience, which was already stricken enough. Though he did take a drop, still there was a difference between that (especially when taken for company's sake) and making a beast of yourself. Besides, he was very fond of her, and came into her room every night to have a chat before he said good-night. It was a queer thing he wasn't married properly. Somehow he was so very game and like several young men she knew that you couldn't imagine him without a wife of his own, and indeed he was more like an unmarried man than a father of some seventeen years' standing. Which, of course, made it more difficult for her to get on a proper footing with him. He wasn't the sort of man she had expected to find, and you found it a bit hard to talk to him as you would to a father. Also, she knew from a few words she heard dropped that if her mother wasn't there, he wasn't without having a girl himself. It was different, of course, with a man, who could do that sort of thing when a woman couldn't. She didn't like that sort of thing herself, but when you knew him you understood it better. Besides, he was rather good-looking; a bit plump and going grey, but tall and attractive.

In these artless letters of hers, Mary Kate revealed

to Phil that she was being impressed, far more than she herself knew, by the peculiar standards of life in her father's house.

Sometimes now when he had taken his breakfast and gone out to his mysterious tasks she would undress and creep back to bed. When she could sleep she slept, but there were days when she lay broad awake for an hour or more, thinking how much nicer a life this was than the life she had been used to, and wondering what the chances were of its continuance. She had the uneasy suspicion that some day her mother would die and her father would marry again, and that his affection would not survive the wedding ceremony. She supposed that then she would have to go back, unless before that she captured some Johnny who would be able to look after her as well as her father. Not that she could really face with equanimity the prospect of married life with any of the five or six Johnnies of her father's acquaintance who seemed even remotely marriageable. She turned them over in her mind. They all had faults, glaring faults, from their accents which she disliked to their dolly and effeminate attention to appearance. Besides this, they seemed to be deficient in general interest. There were certain things you could talk about for quite a while, and his inability to hear them mentioned, much less talk about them, was a great drawback in Phil; but after all, argued Mary Kate, there must be at least one or two other things you could talk to a girl about and not send her to sleep. Only these Johnnies didn't seem to know about them. Which was rather astonishing when you came to think of it, for Dublin, they said, was so many times the size of Cork, and one would expect that subjects of general interest would accordingly be more numerous.

Still, she did not feel that her old life would be anything like easy to pick up again. And now it was not so much the mere fact that her mother had two fatherless children and a bad reputation that troubled Mary Kate, it was the untidiness and uncertainty of it all; the Dolls' House, which to her sorrow she had to admit a stinking place; Auntie Di, who was good sport but a terrible cross with her laziness and extravagance; her mother, still as young and pretty as she was seventeen years ago, but who through some misfortune of temperament seemed incapable of plucking the fruits of evil one heard so much about, and sat helplessly over the ashes reading rotten stories.

Even Phil. Whatever was to be said against the Johnnies, 'the Dublin Jackeens' as in the privacy of her own thoughts she called them, they seemed to be able to make it out fine, and as between Phil and his awful little job, and his mad boss, and his one room on this hand, and on the other a nice sort of Johnnie that hadn't a bit of brains but had a house with four rooms, a kitchen, and conveniences, and with whom you wouldn't have to go begging your dinner, it was a nice fix for a young woman of seventeen to be in. At that hour of the morning, and in this position of enviable sloth, Mary Kate could discuss it with herself quite reasonably, but up and about, wandering along to quays as far as the boat-houses at Ringsend, it faded from her mind, and she thought eagerly of Phil and Scrap and Gregory, and wished she was at home, and wished the night would come soon, and wondered who the Johnnies would be if they turned up.

She liked her father more and more. He came into her room regularly to kiss her good-night, sat on the edge of her bed and talked to her, then covered her up and quenched the light. She got into leaving one shoulder uncovered so as to give him something to do.

She told him about Phil, and he listened eagerly. He was lonely, she felt, and enjoyed talking to her. He did not discuss his work or his friends, but always herself.

Sometimes they spoke of her mother, and he grew gloomier. Against her, she felt, he guarded some great bitterness.

XV

POOR Phil! Poor, steady, hard-working, schedule-governed, self-centred, saintly Phil!

It would be necessary to say all this and a great deal more if one were to convey any idea of Phil's state of mind about Mary Kate, who had now been away for more than a month. What we have learned about her from her letters is only one side of the picture; there was also the other side that was Phil's. By this time he had received six letters revealing to his extremely straightforward mind a process of moral dissolution as relentless as it was swift. He carried those letters about with him, and now and again, when he knew quite well his thoughts should have been elsewhere, he opened them and read through from beginning to end. By the time he had finished reading the first letter he would be almost reassured —well for him if he could have stopped there. But from his reading of spiritual books he had developed an eye for moral drama of the simplest kind, and inevitably he would read on, and before he had reached the last of the series he would be seized by a whirlwind panic which swept his imaginations forward to all sorts of obscure and gloomy endings. It is true that he had no great passion for soul-saving. A natural delicacy told him that any form of moral superiority is quite indistinguishable from vanity, and on no occasion had he ever protested against anything done by anybody else. He listened to terrifying blasphemies without turning a hair or administering a rebuke. He allowed himself to be sneered at without showing any desire to defend himself. He was humble.

But humility did not enter into his feeling for Mary Kate. One cause of this was that he identified himself with her. Another may have been that he had no idea of where she really began. He presumed from the fact that she wrote down things she had never spoken that she had but recently made their acquaintance. Which, as we have seen, was an error.

But he was surprised and slightly hurt when she made clear the subject of her meditations as previously set down. It was a blow to find that Mary Kate worshipped material success: but that she should only now have begun to worship it, only now taken to criticising his place in life, made it worse.

One morning he came to work and knocked twice without receiving an answer. This had happened before, and Phil knew there was nothing for it but to wait. So he waited, whistling moodily, his peace of mind suddenly deserting him. Another man would have made nothing of it, but finding the door closed before him had broken his courage, why he did not know. It wasn't Mary Kate's last letter, for that, when you came to think of it, counted for nothing, yet it seemed silly to suppose that a locked door was any more important. It did not occur to him that he was lonely for Mary Kate, that without her early mass had become something of a drag upon him. That he missed her he admitted, but the extent of his longing was hidden from him, even when the old church with its yellow candles and whispered Latin gave him the sensation of being alone in an empty house. The mere suggestion that he was depressed by her absence he found irritating, and in Dona Nobis's redoubled attentions he read this conventional pity. Much as he liked getting letters, however shocking, from the girl, he felt that he had given Dona Nobis no reason for inquiring about her every time they met.

Eleven had been some time gathered to the dwindling forenoon when Gregory appeared, minus his hat. He had red rings about his eyes. No sooner did he see Phil than he put on a great show of haste and worry.

'Oh my! oh my!' he exclaimed, mopping his brow with a handkerchief. 'Such delays, such delays! How some people ever get their work done! A cousin of mine' (it seemed as though he were ramming the cousin in the lock and shaking him vigorously), 'a cousin of mine on the south side, I was staying the night with him; such old talk you never heard about Parnellites and the divil knows what else—all ancient history. How that man ever gets his day's work done.' (He was in the hall now, refusing to be abashed by the stillness that reinforced the falsehood with its brazen throat.) 'And such dawdling about with breakfast!'

Phil knew darkly the brand of cousin old Gregory spent the night with, and a sudden feeling of nausea overtook him as he climbed the stairs. No sort of good life could make up for a job like this. Mary Kate's scorn was justified. And so bitterly did this new feeling oppress him that he found himself compelled to seek conversation as a necessity, while in a spirit of pure

contradiction Gregory was less talkative than usual.
Perhaps, thought Phil, in automatic pious hope, his
conscience was at him.

But it is more than likely that what Gregory suffered from was not conscience, but fidgets. He bustled
round, making odd remarks about cousins and their
peculiarities, the great folly of thinking historically,
and the astonishing laziness, unpunctuality, and untidiness (not to say dirt) of the Irish people in general.

"Tis an amazing thing!' he proclaimed, giving a
backward nail a thump. ''Tis. A terrible thing! We're
held by all competent observers to be the cleverest,
quickest, most ingenious race in the whole world, and
we can't be in time for anything. Will we be in time
for our own funerals, do you think? Will we? 'Twould
astound me if we were. And what sort of cleverness
is that, being always late? Sure, isn't that proof posi-
tive we're not clever? Phil, my boy, I prize a punctual
man above gold and jewels.'

'You seem to be in good form to-day, for all that,'
said Phil.

'Oh, not complaining, not complaining,' said
Gregory vaguely, feeling that he might be compro-
mising himself. ''Tis the way I wasn't feeling myself
at all after you left last night, so I went over to the
cousin's for a bit of company.'

'Did you ever feel,' asked Phil, 'that you'd be better
not to be alive at all?'

'I did,' said Gregory. 'Someway like that I was feeling yesterday.'

'Feeling if you didn't get a breath of fresh air you'd
choke?'

'Suffocate,' added Gregory succinctly, lighting a

pipe, which was a rare luxury usually only indulged in after a visit to his 'cousin's'.

'And that the heart was after dropping out of you?' continued Phil, closing a record break in speech.

'I did, begod, I did,' assented Gregory, going blue over the effort to make his pipe draw.

'Well, that's the way I'm feeling now,' said Phil recklessly.

'Want a change?' asked the carpenter.

'I do.'

'Well, and do you know what's wrong with you?' asked Gregory, letting the pipe go out as he pointed it accusingly at Phil's chest.

'What?' asked Phil.

'You're in love,' said Gregory.

Phil laughed dryly.

'Mad in love,' said Gregory, not realising the extent of his own give-away, but Phil only shook his head and smiled wanly.

''Tis not, then,' he answered, feeling that Gregory would get a great shock if he knew how much mere disillusionment with his work there was in it.

''Tis,' retorted Gregory, with a sudden roar. 'Amn't I old enough to be your father, and don't I know the symptoms well?

'I don't care whether you are or not,' replied Phil. 'You're wrong all the same.'

'And what's more, you're lonesome after that girl.'

'What girl?' asked Phil, for the first time being dishonest, and betraying himself by a blush that flowed helplessly over his dark face.

'That little girl that went to Dublin. What's her name?'

'I am not,' said Phil flatly; 'no more than she is after me.'

'Don't tell me,' replied the carpenter contemptuously. 'A woman is like a bit of red flannel. Maybe you won't notice it when you leave it off, maybe you won't—but believe you me, you're apt to get a horrible bad cold after it. My soul you are.'

Phil smiled wan superiority.

'What took her to Dublin on you, anyway?' asked Gregory.

'She went up to her father.'

'To who?'

'To her father.'

'Is it to McCormick?'

''Tis.'

Gregory nodded gravely and flew at a plank with a saw. Above the screech of the saw and his own panting he flung back a question. How she was getting on. To which Phil yelled in reply that she was getting on grand. At which Gregory nodded again and spat significantly. Phil caught something that sounded like 'and she such a nice girl too'. His curiosity was roused. It had not occurred to him that Greg might have known Mary Kate's father in the days when he had lived in Cork. Even now he wasn't sure but that Greg was just inventing an imaginary McCormick to satisfy his curiosity—that would have been like old Greg— but it was a risk he had to take. Accordingly, he watched for another opportunity to interrupt the morning's work.

'Did you know Mr. McCormick, Mr. Mahon?' he asked as Gregory finished with his plank.

'I did,' the other replied darkly. 'Believe me, I did.'

'Do you think she ought to have gone up at all?'

The question seemed to stupefy the carpenter momentarily. He looked about him, speechless; Phil knew he was searching for a happy illustration, but continued, to cover up his hesitation, 'Because I told her to go, and I'm thinking now maybe I shouldn't have.'

Gregory's eyes lit up. It was like the lights springing up on the stage as the overture ends. He pounced upon the plank he had just cut, and settled half of it into the vice.

'See that?' he demanded exultantly.

He gave the handle of the vice a twirl.

'See that?' he shouted in a voice of uncontrollable emotion; 'well, that's it. Squeeze, see? Youth, beauty, innocence, all out like that.' He chuckled with sheer delight at the vividness of his own imagery, and then fumbled blindly in the nailbox for a suitable nail.

'I ought never have told her go,' groaned Phil, miserably conscious of his own share in sending Mary Kate away. 'But how could I tell her father would be the sort to encourage his own daughter in that way?'

'That's good all right,' the carpenter shouted in response. 'His own daughter as you say. What did she tell you about him?'

'Nothing but what I told you,' replied Phil. 'Why?'

Gregory gave a demented chuckle, and with a terrific smash nailed the plank to the bench, driving the nail head half-way into the timber.

'Because she's no more his daughter than she's mine, let me impress on you,' he bawled joyously, his voice seeming to emerge from the hammer stroke like

Jehovah's from the thunder-clap. Between the probable effect of the latter on Phil and the certain effect of the former there was little to choose, but Gregory, conscious only of having completely dispelled an illusion, took up his plane.

'Do you mean,' asked Phil, putting his hand firmly on the edge of the plank to assure a cessation of toil, 'do you mean he's not her father?'

'Of course he's not,' stuttered Gregory. 'Did she tell you he was?'

Things began to whirl with extraordinary rapidity in Phil's head, so that it was some time before he spoke again. Consequences were not his strong point, and human relations here seemed to have got into a terrible tangle. Only one thing emerged, that whatever hope there was for Mary Kate before, there was none now. One question suggested itself to him, and he asked it dryly, incapable of fully understanding its meaning.

'Does he know that?'

'Well, to be sure he do,' said Gregory. 'Who'd know better?'

'But Mary Kate's mother——' Phil protested weakly.

'Is it Babe Matthews?' asked Gregory contemptuously. 'Well, maybe she thought she'd delude him, but was there ever a man in his senses yet taken in by what Babe Matthews said? Sure, you couldn't believe your own four bones on that one's evidence.'

Phil sat down, too dazed to speak.

'What ails you?' asked the carpenter.

''Tis a shocking way for a young girl to be,' he replied; 'imagining a man is her father and he nothing at all to her.'

'Never fear,' Gregory assured him; 'she know well enough.'

'She do not know, then,' retorted Phil, who in moments of depression had a tendency to drop back into dialect.

'Maybe she don't after all,' surmised Gregory wisely, fingering his chin.

''Tis an awful state to be in.'

''Tis, bad.'

'What would I do at all, Mr. Mahon?'

'You might write,' said Gregory unhopefully.

'I might do that.'

'And on the other hand it might be as bad a thing as you could do.'

'It might be,' agreed Phil, having pondered the suggestion awhile.

'Or you might get the priest to write.'

'And that might be a bad thing too,' said Phil to anticipate the native process of elimination.

'It might indeed. Or you might go to Dublin and bring her back yourself.'

This was the first thing that had occurred to Phil, but, heard upon the carpenter's lips, it sounded more practicable, as though it could solve all his difficulties of courage and conscience at one stroke.

'I might do that,' he said, rising and untying his apron.

'Where will you get the money to go?'

'I have a couple of shillings saved,' said Phil.

'Will it bring you there?'

'It might bring me there all right.'

'I'll give you whatever I have,' said Gregory. 'I like a boy with a bit of the divil in him.' He dipped his hand in his trousers pocket and counted out four shillings and eightpence on the bench. 'I'll give you the shillings and keep the eightpence for the gas,' he said. His hand shook badly as he collected the coppers afresh. Phil knew he had had over two pounds the day before. That was the way family gatherings worked out. He put on his coat.

'I might have to walk back, but I'll do my best,' he said.

'Eh, you'll always get a lift,' said Gregory. 'If you were stuck anywhere you might write to me and I'd see could I sell an old table or something.'

'I might do that,' admitted Phil, putting on his cap. 'Good-bye now, Mr. Mahon,' he said.

'Take nice care of yourself,' said Gregory.

'I'm getting as big an idiot as himself,' thought Phil the moment he put his foot outside the shop. This escapade would mean that his savings would be gone for ever. But worse, he who was in all things anxious to submit himself to authority was now flung on his own two legs to fend for himself, and it daunted him. But there was what Gregory called a 'black strake' in him that made him indifferent to opinion, even his own, which may mean only that his logic was but another form of emotional energy. So leaving his 'conjuring box' (as the common saving box is called) a wreck, and pinning to his door a notice, 'Away in Dublin, Back in a Few Days, Philip Dinan', he cast his last look on Shandon and rushed off to catch the midday train to Dublin. Dona Nobis was out or he would have said good-bye to her.

In the train his panic started afresh, but by saying a great many aspirations he managed to divert his attention from his flight as well as from the changing beauty of the landscape, of which he saw nothing. However, at Thurles a young priest got into the carriage, and Phil, taking this as a good omen, was consoled, and shyly drew him into conversation. The young priest discussed the All Ireland Final for which Tipperary was again a good favourite, and Phil was surprised at the questions put him about Cork's team. Phil hadn't even known that Cork had a team.

Fortunately, the young priest put his silence down to shyness, and promised to look after him in Dublin.

XVI

As the train steamed into Kingsbridge and every one except Phil started to look out his or her belongings, he made one of his lightning good resolutions.

The young priest shepherded him on to a car going citywards, and as they passed a church half-way in was astonished to see his charge leap up suddenly. With thorough-going saintly rudeness Phil touched his hand, said a hasty good-bye, and made off down the car.

'Come back!' shouted the priest; 'we're not there at all yet.'

'I know that,' said Phil without looking back, 'but we passed a friend of mine just now.'

The Friend was the Occupant of the nearest tabernacle, for Phil had decided that he would visit every church on the way from the station to Mary Kate's dwelling on the South Circular Road, that he would say a decade of the rosary in each of the churches, and that somehow or other he would make it five (or if necessary ten) so that he would make his rosary complete. And the ten commandments, or Mary Kate's virtue, or the freedom of Ireland were for the moment of far less importance than the necessity for doing this properly.

Phil had no knowledge of the proposition he was undertaking, and very likely if he had would have

paid no attention to it. For he was quite satisfied that
God spoke to him distinctly in these flashes of inspiration, and that to deny them would be to deny
something even more important than revealed religion. If his mind had run to freakishness, and if the
momentary inspiration had bade him turn twelve successive cartwheels on the road (as it might have done),
Phil would immediately have attempted to obey,
though the mere fact that hundreds of people were
looking upon him as a lunatic would have been gall to
his hyper-sensitive soul. So if we say that Phil was
rude to the priest, we need not suppose that he was not
hurt by having to be rude. But his duty was to his
voices, and his voices had not indicated that the priest
might be warned.

The result was that, having said a decade of his
rosary, he took a tram that went in the wrong direction, asked the conductor to drop him at the first
Catholic church, and was dropped at it without dis-
covering his mistake. He had visited a third chapel
before he became aware of it. Then, of course, his
rosary was irretrievably spoiled, and he had to go
back to his starting-point to try again. All of which
took time.

I doubt if even one of my readers has attempted
anything of this sort in a strange city. Consequently,
they can have no conception of the difficulties and
delay involved, as well as the irritation to a sensitive
soul of having to give tram conductors the impression
that you have gone out of your senses. Fortunately,
the conductors were all Catholics themselves and more
inclined to treat lightly a fellow-Catholic's mild bout
of religious mania.

Only Phil had not known how many different ways there were of reaching his goal, nor had he realised the size of Dublin. The result was that a process which should have been simple became exceedingly complicated, and his mind was not used to handling complications. He felt dizzy. Darkness fell without relieving him of his responsibility, and made it still more difficult to fulfil. He was no longer quite sure what it was he wanted to do. He seemed to have visited dozens of churches and said dozens of decades of the rosary. Besides, he was hungry, and this aided his tendency to give at the knees. At one time he almost fell into despair. Lights whizzed everywhere about him, far brighter than the lights of home, and trams clanged, and every voice he heard spoke with the same astounding foreign roughness. He found them all joining in a sort of haze about his head, a haze that was only temporarily dissipated during the minutes of peace and silence which he spent in the churches. By the time he had satisfied or half-satisfied his conscience he was a very bedraggled, downcast youth who for all his close on twenty years was as timid and self-conscious as a child. Sweat poured from his face, and in characteristic reaction he began to see that his whole life since his mother's death had been a parade of tiny self-assumed duties, which would have contented nobody but a complacent child with no understanding of God's majesty or his own pettiness. Hell-fire opened out before him as, very reluctantly, he walked the few hundred yards that now separated him from Mary Kate.

It was she who answered his knock. Incredulous and startled, she let out a little cry that shook the last remnant of courage from the disconsolate Phil. She let fly a volley of questions which he made no attempt to answer. Then Nicholas McCormick appeared in the hallway.

'It's Phil, father,' Mary Kate shouted gaily. 'You know—Phil from Cork. And he never even wrote to tell us.'

'Come in, come in,' said the other man. Phil was already standing in the hallway, and showed no signs of going farther. 'Don't be shy. There's only a few friends inside. Or maybe you'd rather speak to Mary Kate awhile.'

'Maybe he hadn't his tea,' suggested Mary Kate. 'I'll bet you he hadn't. What time did you leave, Phil?'

'Take him in and give him a cup of tea,' said her father.

He walked into the kitchen with them and lit the gas. Then he stood in the doorway and asked a few questions. About when the train got in, and what way did Phil come, and how was everybody in Cork, and how especially were Babe and Dinah. All polite, distant sort of questions, put in a way for which Phil was not prepared. He had come with the idea of standing at the front door and having it out in sobriety and firmness, but now he was sitting in the man's kitchen talking respectfully to him. And after McCormick left them it took him quite a while to muster enough courage to speak to Mary Kate. Meanwhile she bustled round getting tea. All nice girls look nicer in an evening atmosphere of aprons and gas stoves and tea-cups, and Mary Kate was no exception. Besides, she was excited and pleased, and the combination of emotions made her look her best. She sat down to tea with Phil and gabbled on endlessly about the differences (real or imaginary) between Cork and Dublin.

At last Phil replied humourlessly that he didn't like Dublin.

'Ah, wait till you see it to-morrow,' said Mary Kate. 'I'll take you for grand walks, Phil, all down along the river and up the canal.'

At this Phil stopped eating, pushed his tea-cup and plate away from him, and blessed himself. There followed a few moments of silence, during which Mary Kate sat stiffly, her hand with a morsel of bread in it half-raised. Phil crossed himself again and she put the bit of bread into her mouth.

'You will not,' said Phil. 'I'm going back to-night.'

She stopped chewing and her eyes opened wide.

'What are you talking about?' she asked thickly from a full mouth. 'Sure, you can't go back to-night; what ails you?'

'I'm going to start, anyway.'

She swallowed the mouthful of food with a grimace of choking.

'What brought you up so?' she asked, uncertain whether to be alarmed or angry.

'I came up to see you,' he replied.

'Only to see me?' she asked, anger fading and alarm growing.

'And to ask you to come back out of this.'

'What's wrong with you, Phil boy?' she asked wistfully. For one half-moment she had been possessed by the wild idea that Phil had found himself unable to live without her, and the possibility that this gloomy, cryptic Phil who was so unfamiliar to her was Phil in the throes of a sinful passion, though untenable for more than the half-moment, shook her into a sort of frightened tenderness.

'I want you to get out of this place,' he went on, disturbing afresh the images in the kaleidoscope of her mind, so that it was a different, uncompromising, almost belligerent Mary Kate that faced him now.

'Well, well, well, Phil,' she replied with exaggerated coolness, 'isn't that a queer thing for you to say to me? Now if it was anybody else said a thing like that to me I mightn't take it so easy.'

'Well, that's what I came to Dublin to say to you, anyway,' said Phil, and for a moment he thought of dropping it all, of warning Mary Kate and leaving it at that. When he closed his eyes he saw a dazzle of trams and cars, his ears pounded afresh with their clanging, and he felt sick.

'But, Phil,' Mary Kate protested, and the superficial pattern was slightly different from what it had been, bringing forth a more courageous Phil. 'You can't expect me to go back—not now, and I after leaving my job and everything to come up here.'

'This is no place for you,' he retorted.

'And why not, Phil?'

'Because it's no place for any young girl,' he said hastily.

'You don't know anything about it,' she said, irritated by his tone.

'I know that much.'

'And you seem to forget, Phil, that I'm quite well able to look after myself.'

'You are not.'

'And what's more, it isn't as if I was living in a

stranger's house. You must remember that I've my father to look after me.'

That drove Phil into a gloomy silence from which she failed to rouse him. For all that, his words had had their effect. All the colour had ebbed from her face. She had not the faintest conception of what was in Phil's mind to have hurried him from the south of Ireland, but so great was her sense of the unreality, the impermanence of the life she was living, that it needed only a breath to blow it all away. Already in her mind's eye she saw it being whisked away by Phil. Anybody else could have done as much. And she dreaded its being whisked away. Never had she thought it would have been so important to her. To herself she said jealously, 'I won't go, I don't care, I won't go.' After all these years she had found her father and would not be separated from him.

'Is it anything you heard?' she asked after a silence.

'It is,' replied Phil.

'Is it something about my ma?'

'No.'

'And you won't tell me what it is?'

'I can't,' he said dully.

At this she began to cry, and Phil made no effort to console her.

''Tis an awful thing,' she sobbed, 'people knowing things and I not knowing them at all, and giving up my job and coming here. There's some misfortune on me since the day I was born. Why is it some people have all the luck and have good homes and decent mothers, while others grow up like me? And you don't know how crazy I was to stay with my father, Phil. Oh, Phil, are you sure I oughtn't to stay?'

'I am sure,' replied Phil, and immediately Mary Kate went off into a worse fit of sobs that sounded to his ears like nothing but 'Hoo-hoo-hoo'. For all his distress, he decided cynically that if girls could get a look at themselves crying it would put a stop to that stupid practice. And at this moment the door of the parlour opened and Nick McCormick came in. For a second or two Phil wondered if he hadn't made a terrible mistake and thought frantically for some way out.

Mary Kate hastily dabbed at her eyes with the first thing that came handy, which was her sleeve, but even if he had not seen her do this her eyes after the operation would have been enough.

'Hullo,' exclaimed McCormick. 'Anything wrong?'

'N-n-o, father,' she sobbed in quite unnecessary folly.

''Tis the way I want Mary Kate to come back home with me,' said Phil, taking the bull by the horns, not in any spirit of heroism, but with something like suppressed hysteria—hysteria which conveyed to the two onlookers an impression of cold-blooded impertinence.

'Oh, do you?' asked McCormick, whose astonishment momentarily gave check to his anger. 'And is Mary Kate crying to go or crying to stay, would somebody tell me?'

'I think she's crying to stay,' replied Phil in a tone which invited bloodshed.

'Blast your impertinence!' shouted McCormick, losing all control of himself. 'Get out of this.'

Phil stood his ground, his dark face gone startlingly pale, his hands clenched at his sides.

'I'm not going without Mary Kate, all the same,' he said.

At this there was commotion in the parlour and two men slipped in, followed by three or four girls who hung about in the background. 'What's wrong? What's wrong?' the voices asked.

'Get out!' shouted McCormick again.

'One moment, one moment,' a young man said, pushing his way between them. 'There seems to be a misunderstanding.'

'There's no misunderstanding,' said Phil, suddenly growing excited.

'What is it you want?' the man said.

'He wants a damn good hiding,' said McCormick threateningly, 'and he's going to get it.'

'I want to take that girl out of this,' cried Phil, 'and nobody's going to stop me either. And nobody's going to give me a hiding either.' His voice grew into an unnatural, a schoolboyish shrillness.

'And why?' asked the man, who was all the time holding on to McCormick.

'Because this is no fit place for her,' replied Phil.

'Oh, you're very cocky, young fellow, aren't you?' the man asked.

'And if you want to know,' screamed Phil, 'I think you're no fit company for her.'

The young man grew white and stormy.

'I'd say her father was the best judge of that,' he said, keeping himself in.

It was then that all Phil's tact and good sense deserted him. It must be remembered that he was already demoralised before he reached the house, and he, who for years had lived in a sort of emotional vacuum, was the last person who should have been asked to face such a painful scene.

'He's no more her father than I am,' he shouted, and before he could say another word McCormick broke loose and lashed out at him. The blow caught Phil in the mouth and sent him crashing into the fireplace. The rest of that extraordinary scene was a matter of seconds. Nobody who had known Phil previously could possibly have recognised him now. He grasped at the first weapon that came to his hand—it was the poker—and struck back with it. A red spot appeared on McCormick's cheek, and when he put up his hand it came away covered with blood. The second of the young men had Phil by the arm. Phil was foaming at the mouth with rage, and if he could have broken free would certainly have been responsible for further damage.

'Easy now, easy now,' his captor said warningly, 'you've done harm enough.'

'I'll show him,' stammered Phil, half crying with rage, 'I'll show him. Let him come near me now and I'll lay him out.'

But a change had come over McCormick. His handkerchief all reddening with blood pressed to his cheek, he turned upon Mary Kate.

'I see how it is now,' he said bitterly. 'That's what your friends are like. Well, you can go to hell with him now if you want to.' And turning on his heel he went into the room.

After a few moments Mary Kate went in after him. Then she came back and returned to the room with a basin of water and a towel. They heard her inside, bathing the wound. Phil sat on a stool by the fire in a sort of dumb stupor of remorse and terror. The girls came up and looked at him curiously, but he did not raise his eyes or speak. There was blood dripping from his mouth. They discussed the affair in excited whispers with the two other men.

At last one of these shook Phil by the shoulder and said, in a good-natured whisper, 'Hi, mister, are you going to stop there all the bloody night?'

'I'm going when she comes out,' he replied, drawing his hand across his eyes, and got up. After a little while Mary Kate came out with the basin of water and threw the contents down the sink.

'Are you coming, Mary Kate?' asked Phil.

'I suppose I'm better,' she answered dully.

'But you've nowhere to go, Mary Kate,' a tall young man said hastily.

'I suppose I'll have to go home,' she replied in the same hopeless way.

'Well, 'tis too late to go anywhere now,' the young man said. 'You'll have to wait till morning.'

Mary Kate looked at Phil, who shrugged his shoulders.

'Where would you stop if we waited, Phil?' she asked.

'Never mind about me,' he answered. 'I'll be all right.'

'Leave him come home with me,' the young man said good-naturedly.

Phil put on his cap.

'Well, good-night, so, Mary Kate,' he said, and went out.

'Tell him I'll come for him in the morning,' she called after the man who was to be his host.

That night McCormick did not come into her room, nor did she leave her shoulder bare for him to cover. She lay awake and trembled when she heard his step pass up the stair.

XVII

FOR two reasons these chapters might be called Chariots and Roads for Chariots.

Next morning, Mary Kate, who had not slept, crept down the stairs and laid the table for the man she still by force of habit called father. The kettle was boiling before she noticed the stillness in the house. Then she saw the envelope standing on the mantelpiece. It contained two pound notes. She put the money back in the envelope and left it where she had found it. Then she made up a packet of meat sandwiches for herself and Phil. Besides these she brought away with her only the little bundle of clothes that had accompanied her from home—the piece of brown paper in which they had been wrapped was still lying in the drawer. She knew that this departure would be something she would always remember. Foolishly she bent and kissed the white table-cloth. The street outside was sunlit and cheerful. It brought a fresh aching in her heart.

She called for Phil, who was walking up and down outside her friend's house. He looked cheerless too, and at that moment she hated him. She hated him more than ever when he explained that they must rely on getting lifts until they were within reasonable distance of home. She was a fool, she thought, not to have taken the two pounds. It was like her to do a silly thing like that out of pride. Or had it been pride?

They took the tram to Inchicore and started on the main road for Cork. It was a fine, clear, still day with a roseate warmth in the air. Already she was feeling reconciled to the long journey home and to Phil. But they rarely spoke. She knew that Phil's thoughts were on the scene of the night before, and that he was suffering agonies of remorse and shame at the revelation of his own queer, suppressed character which it had afforded.

But the morning went by and no lorry passed that would stop for them. They continued walking, Phil, in ignorance of the weariness that was on her, trudging a yard or two ahead.

In the afternoon a lorry, driven by its owner, pulled up for Phil's signals. The young man was curious and obliging. It was only an old Ford. There was not much room, but they managed to squeeze in, Mary Kate in the middle. She took off her shoes and pressed her anguished feet together on the footboard.

'You must have walked a good bit,' said the driver.

'We're walking all the morning,' she replied, with a grimace.

The driver looked cautiously from his wheel to her feet, not without being seen by her.

''Tis a wonder ye wouldn't take the train,' he remarked, his eyes travelling upwards until they rested upon her face.

'Maybe if we'd the money we would,' she retorted.

''Tis reason enough,' he admitted. 'I suppose himself is your husband?'

'Aren't you glad he's not?' she asked.

The driver turned a heavy face upon her and gave her a long look (to his own imminent danger, the lorry swaying perilously with its load).

'He would be your brother, so, I'd be inclined to say,' he went on censoriously.

'You'd see a worse likeness,' admitted Mary Kate.

The look was repeated. Clearly the driver was not at home with Mary Kate's metaphysical niceties.

'For heaven's sake mind the ditch!' she exclaimed.

'You've no call to be frightened,' he reassured her. 'So you're not married?'

'I'm not,' she replied quietly.

'I'm going to be married myself in two months' time,' he said, his eyes fixed on the road before him.

'Are you now?'

'I am.' His eyes, growing brighter, began their roving quest of her face. 'Four hundred pounds I'm getting with her.'

'Four hundred!'

'Four hundred.' The operation was complete and he was full on again. Mary Kate felt bound to show interest.

'And what's she like?'

'What's she like? Well, I suppose she's all right.'

'Is she about your own age?'

'Oh, ay.' His tone was purposely vague. 'About that. 'Tisn't every girl you'd get that sum of money with.'

His eyes dropped again to her feet and he regarded them intently for a moment.

'Ah, I dunno,' she added after a while. 'Money isn't all that to a man.'

He started right round in his seat.

'What's that you say? Money isn't all that? Four hundred pounds?'

'Well, 'tisn't everything. Even four hundred pounds wouldn't pay you for having to live with a woman you didn't like.'

'Hoo-hoo!' He gave a short rasping laugh. 'That's good all right!'

'Wouldn't you marry a girl you were in love with if she hadn't money?' she asked in consternation.

'Be Jase, I would do nothing of the bloody kind,' he said emphatically.

'Well, well,' said Mary Kate, 'aren't you a hard man?'

'I am just that,' he replied, impressed. 'You seen through me. I'm a terrible hard man. And do you know? Would you believe me? My bloody fool of an old fellow thinks I'm a softy. As sure as God he does.'

He nodded twice to his own reflection in the driving screen, as if to say, 'Sucks to you, old man!'

'He don't know how I spends me time when I comes to Dublin, though,' he went on. 'I tell it to you for you know now the sort of man I am. I knocks down a fine time in Dublin unknownst to me old fellow, and 'tisn't out of my own pocket either.'

He nodded once more. Clearly a splendid reflection of himself was forming in the uncertain mirror of the windscreen. He was looking deep down into it. He drove on in silence. They passed a great many churches, and Phil more than once suggested that they might pull up and say a prayer, but the hard man only nodded and said 'ay' in an abstracted fashion. He looked again at Mary Kate's toes.

'Mind you,' he said warningly, 'she's a bit heavy on her feet.'

'Who?' asked Mary Kate, but his look implied such a perfect understanding that she needed no answer.

'Ah, well,' she replied philosophically, 'that's only a small thing.'

'I dunno so much about that either,' he said. 'And mind you, I wouldn't say she was so very handsome. Not as handsome as you,' he added with heavy gallantry.

Mary Kate laughed, and her laugh made the driver think he had said something witty.

'They'd better mind theirselves,' he shouted threateningly.

'Ah, you wouldn't leave her now,' she said coaxingly.

'Wouldn't I? Eh? Is that all you know? Mind you, I wouldn't be so certain of that in your place.'

After a long pause to give effect to his words he fished about in his pockets and handed her a little case.

'She didn't get that yet,' he said complacently.

Mary Kate opened it and looked inside. It was a ring.

'Oh,' she exclaimed innocently, 'isn't that lovely? Did you buy her that in Dublin?'

'She didn't get it yet, I said,' he responded emphatically.

They drove through the midlands with their little flat ungracious towns where every tiny shop seemed crushed by a heap of masonry, so that it spewed half its stock on to the broken flagstones outside; towns without one leisurely or even cheerful building; towns of water-tight beliefs. They passed through the wide darkening plains where a faint blue mist suckled the fences, and Mary Kate thought the highways were rather like the towns, for every turn brought only another dull stretch of road and another deceptive turn that seemed to promise a mystery but gave none.

When the driver stopped the car and he and Phil were standing beside it, he gave Phil a long knowing wink. Phil watched it in dismay and doubt.

'She's not your wife?' the driver asked, jerking his thumb after Mary Kate.

'She is not,' said Phil.

'And she's not your sister either?'

'She isn't.'

The driver gave a little gasp of mirth.

'I'd be careful so if I was you,' he brought out.

'What's that?'

'I'd be careful, I say. Mind you, there might be more than you after her, and maybe people would stand a better chance.'

'I'm not after her,' said Phil innocently.

The driver looked him up and down with astonishment.

'What's that you say? You're not after her?'

'I am not,' said Phil stoutly.

'Not after her?'

'No.'

The midland silence crept back but for the squeak of a bird rising from the wide plains and the rattle of a distant cart.

'Not after her? Bedamn, but that's the queerest thing I heard this long while,' said the driver slowly, but he made no further comment, unless his deeper reverie could be called by such a name.

At last they reached a cross-roads where his way home parted from the main road. He stopped the engine and Mary Kate and Phil got out.

'If I had your direction,' he said to Mary Kate, 'I might write a letter to you.'

'My direction?' she asked, puzzled.

'Ay, your direction. For to put on the letter.'

'Oh, my address,' she exclaimed. She gave him the address, and he closed his eyes for a moment and let it sink in.

'And if I was to give you my direction,' he added, 'maybe you'd send me your likeness.'

'I would, to be sure,' she answered, not quibbling over the dialect word.

'Memorise this, so,' he said, and she repeated the address until she had it, even to pronunciation, correct. After this they shook hands very solemnly. He started the engine afresh.

'How will you get home now?' he shouted just as the lorry was starting.

'Oh, we'll be all right,' she called out.

'Don't forget the likeness,' he yelled, looking back at her, his head stuck perilously through the window. By the time he got to the corner that would hide him from view he was almost hanging out of the window in an ecstasy of farewells. When he reached home two hours later he was sorry he hadn't driven them as far as Limerick Junction and seen them on to the train, and by the time he woke next morning he could have cut his throat for not having united Mary Kate and the ring and brought them home together. He blew spits through it and made a shot at the candlestick with it. He was a big-hearted fellow, but as he said himself, 'hard', or as his old fellow said, 'soft', which is the same thing only looked at from a different angle.

XVIII

THE young man's chance of getting Mary Kate inside his ring would scarcely have been disimproved if he had acted upon the inspiration that came two hours too late. As it was, the proximity of trees, streams, and fields, the stillness and the coming night, caused the gratitude which that child of the city might otherwise have felt to evaporate with startling suddenness. No sooner had the truck disappeared than she felt the first pangs of fear, loneliness, and depression.

'What are we going to do now?' she asked Phil.

'We'll have to try and get some place to sleep,' he replied.

'Couldn't we look for another lorry?'

''Twouldn't be any use now. 'Tis too late for lorries.'

'I'm in dread to sleep out,' she said, shivering.

'There's nothing to be in dread of.'

'I don't know, Phil, all the same. 'Tis uncanny. I never done the like of it before.'

'No more did I, but sure that makes no difference. A lot of people do it day in day out and they have no choice. We've nothing to complain of. Come on now and we'll look for a quiet place up this road.'

They followed the lorry's tracks for some little way, and then Phil wisely decided to leave that road and try a still less frequented one. Wisely, though it may have been mere good luck that threw the cottage in their way. It was just off the road, in the elbow of an avenue that went past it. It looked as if it had been a gate lodge, for the gate was still there, though the avenue was apparently untrodden and choked with grass and weeds. The house too looked untended; the windows were boarded, but the hasp of the door was broken, and when Phil put his hand to it he succeeded in pushing it in without difficulty. Mary Kate gave one look in, saw how dark it was, and screamed.

'Come on, come on,' said Phil. 'This is a fine place. There's straw and all here.' He struck a match. 'And look! 'Tisn't so long ago since there was somebody here, either; there was a fire in the hearth. And there's an old table. Sure, this is fine. You can lie up on that, Mary Kate. Wait till I put a bit of straw on it.'

It was true for Phil. It was not so long since the house had been occupied, and it was probably used as an occasional rendezvous by tramps or beggars who had stolen the straw that lay about. But the tramps had left something better still. As Phil struck a second match he saw on the mantelpiece the half of a candle erect in its winding sheet.

'This is a lovely house,' he said in ecstasy as he lit the candle. 'You wouldn't get as good as this anywhere.'

'Don't you think we'd be better sleep in a hay-rick somewhere?' she asked timidly. 'I often thought it must be nice like that out in the open air looking at the stars.'

'We would not be better,' replied Phil practically. 'We'd be nice fools to leave what the Lord sent us. And you'd get your death sleeping in hay-ricks.'

'I feel I'm not going to over-sleep myself in this place, anyway,' said Mary Kate prophetically, casting timid glances at the shadows that grew uneasy even in the littlest wind.

'You'll sleep grand,' said Phil. 'Wait'll you see.'

He shut the door and Mary Kate took out what remained of the packet of sandwiches. They ate them, Phil sitting on the floor, she on the table.

'Will I quench the candle now?' he asked.

'Why would you?'

'Because it isn't our candle,' he replied, and she knew by his tone that the 'fidgets' had seized him while he ate.

'It isn't anybody's candle,' she said emphatically.

'It must be somebody's candle, and, anyway, we ought to get some sleep.'

'Even so, can't you leave it lighting and talk to me a while?'

'Now, now, now, Mary Kate, we'll never get to sleep at all if we begin like that.'

He rose and blew out the candle in an excess of confidence. He was frightened of a good many things himself; of ghosts, of rats, of tramps, and of other un-named things; frightened perhaps as much as Mary Kate, but it would have appeared a betrayal of his trust to yield to fear at such a moment. She heard him kneel in the straw. He was a long time praying, and her mind wandered away into the vastness of the night, out into the central plain of Ireland, with its trees and fields and stars among which she was lost like a flea in a blanket, and back to the city where Nick McCormick was perhaps saying farewell to his guests, perhaps brewing himself a cup of tea on the gas,

growing older and lonelier and more reckless. Both
of them unimportant to her in that mood which is
perhaps the oldest of the melancholies by which our
nature is beset, the oldest, the most transient, and yet
the most overwhelming. She heard Phil say 'Good-
night', and the shock breaking in on the bubble-like
detachment of her brooding started the tears wildly
from her eyes. She heard Phil roll himself up resolutely in the straw. He could sleep, because the
trouble he had brought upon herself and Nick meant
nothing to him. She heard the sob break from her
without being able to stop it.

'What is it?' he asked, the rustle of the straw magni-
fying his alarm.

Still she cried.

'Mary Kate, what is it? Can't you tell us?'

She heard him fumble his way towards the table
and in some strange fashion felt consoled. His hand
caught hers and held it firmly.

'Mary Kate, tell me what it is.'

'I'm afraid,' she sobbed.

'Afraid?' He laughed. 'You're a funny girl, Mary
Kate. Are you really afraid?'

'I am, I am.'

'Will I light the candle?'

'Don't, Phil. Don't do that.'

'All right, then, I won't. Will you lie down beside
me?'

It was hardly the same Phil she heard speaking.
Surely the Phil she knew would never suggest anything of the sort. There were things in him one did not
dream of. She put out her other hand and meekly
covered his.

'I will, Phil.'

She climbed down from the table and went with him over to the corner where he had lain. He sat down beside her, his hand still holding hers.

'Are you all right now?'

'I'm grand, Phil.'

But she still continued to sob. He put his right arm about her in a queer, awkward way, and then, as if it were the most natural thing in the world, brushed her hair back with his free hand.

'You're not afraid now?'

'No, I'm not afraid now, Phil. I think I'll lie down.'

He would have disengaged his arm afresh but she held on to it, so he lay back beside her, pitying, and at the same time frightened.

'Will you try and go asleep?' he asked in a whisper.

'I can't sleep,' she brought out in a fresh burst of sobbing.

'Is it something is on your mind, Mary Kate?'

'I suppose it is.'

'Would you like to tell it to me?'

'I'd love to,' she said, 'only you'd hate me after.'

'Ah, I'd never hate you,' he replied. 'Whatever you said to me, I'd never think the worse of you for it.'

She was silent for a while, shaken with dry sobs, staring out into the darkness.

'Do you mean that?' she asked.

'I'll never forget what you done for us when my mother was dying, Mary Kate,' he said softly. 'It was the best kindness I ever had of any one, and I'd never forget it.'

Suddenly she bent across him and kissed him anyhow in the darkness. The kiss alighted on his cheek and stung him.

'Phil,' she whispered, 'if 'twas your own sister was dead this minute you'd be sorry for me.'

'What is it?' he asked.

'You know Nick McCormick?'

'Ay,' he replied non-committally to the rhetorical question.

'Well, I'm in love with him.'

He grew very still beside her. His arm slackened its hold.

'I knew,' she whispered quickly. 'I knew you'd hate me for it.'

He took his time about answering.

'I don't hate you for it,' he said thoughtfully, 'but 'tis an awful thing to say. Are you sure you mean it?'

'I do mean it. I mean every word of it. And he's in love with me.'

'Your mother's husband!'

'Ay.'

'That's an awful thing.'

'It is.'

'And I suppose 'tis all my fault,' said Phil, his overburdened conscience staggering like an old ass mounting a hill. 'I ought never have advised you to go up to that place at all, at all.'

''Tis not your fault,' she exclaimed, clutching him with a hand that was wet and sticky with tears. 'It was me thinking it would be such a lovely thing if only I had a father, and when I went to Dublin I was ready to go through hell-fire for him.'

'You didn't think so much of him, for all,' said Phil gloomily.

'I didn't at first. You don't remember your father, so I suppose you don't know what I was expecting in him. It was something different, and I couldn't get accustomed to him at first, or the queer feeling I had with him, and it never dawned on me until last night when you hit him.'

Phil shuddered.

'I don't know under Heaven how I did that, Mary Kate.'

'No more do I,' she admitted in the tactlessness of grief. 'If it was any one else you hit——'

'Mary Kate,' said Phil firmly, 'you must talk to the priest about it.'

'Sure, I know that,' she said almost impatiently.

'And you must try to master yourself. You must try and use your will power.'

'Will power isn't much use when you're in my state.'

'Will power is the most wonderful gift Almighty God gave us,' said Phil emphatically. 'I heard of a university student, and he developed his will power so far he could sit out in the back yard the coldest night that ever came and will his right leg to get warm. And he could make it that warm it was like an oven.'

'On a cold night,' sniffed Mary Kate, ''twouldn't be much use if that was all he could warm.'

'Everybody,' said Eternal Boy as though he had not heard her, and quite unaware of the wan little smile Eternal Woman gave him in the darkness, 'has some passion that eats him up, and his will power is the only weapon he have against it. I haven't a strong will power, and I never had, but bad as it is it's all that stands between me and a shocking life.'

'I don't believe you have any passion like that, Phil,' she said.

'I wouldn't like to tell you what passion I have,' he said gravely.

'Tell me, Phil,' she coaxed.

He was silent, and the itch of curiosity made her suddenly forgetful of grief.

'I'm not ashamed to tell you things I wouldn't tell another soul,' she continued gently.

'If you want to know, then,' he replied between his teeth, ''tis lust.'

Mary Kate suppressed a chuckle that seemed to force its way up through her grief like a mermaid's head rising above the waters and sunning itself in sudden light. She sighed, laid her head upon Phil's shoulder, and lay silent, happier than she had been for any of the twenty-four hours that had gone before.

XIX

SHE was wakened by Phil's hand gently pressing her arm. She heard him breathing softly beside her and put her head back on his shoulder where it had nestled. Then she started, and again he pressed her arm with warning fingers. There was the sound of footsteps on the road outside.

Startled, she listened with all her senses. She heard voices. The catch of the gate was noisily lifted and the footsteps, slow and dragging, came nearer. The voices spoke in whispers, but the feet dragged heavily as if the owners were too old or too weak to lift them. Her body grew cold as the footsteps stopped outside the door and a hand fumbled for the hasp.

'Don't open your lips,' whispered Phil as she clutched him despairingly.

The door was pushed in, inch by inch. Suddenly a voice that was not his spoke in a raucous whisper to the darkness.

'Is there any one there?'

She stiffened every muscle lest a straw should stir beneath her. The raucous country voice spoke again, this time more loudly.

'Is there any one there, I say?'

'Strike a match,' whispered a woman's voice from behind.

'I will not strike a match,' the man's voice replied impatiently, and he stamped in, kicking up the straw with his heavy boots.

'Ay, then, ay, ay,' he called soothingly, ''tis only friends. Is there any one at all there?'

'There isn't,' answered the woman's voice tensely.

'There isn't,' said the man's.

'Bring him in,' she said, 'bring him in for God's sake, and let us begone out of this place before any one would come.'

'No one will come,' the man grumbled with exasperation. 'Can't you be quiet, woman?'

When she spoke again there was hysteria in her voice.

'Bad luck to you,' she half-cried, 'and 'twas you brought it on us! You struck me, but 'twas you brought it on us, 'twas you brought it on us! If you ever dare to rise your hand to me again——'

There was the sound of a scuffle. The man pushed her off and she staggered towards the door.

'Are you at it again?' he cried. 'Are you? Are you at it again? I told you I struck you because you wouldn't keep quiet, and I'll strike you now if you open that divil's mouth of yours again. Do you want the parish in on top of us, do you?'

''Twas you brought it on us,' she hissed once more. 'Only for you I'd have drove him apast the door. You were so grand, you were! You were so fond of company, you were!'

The man stepped nearer to her, and she retreated before him. His voice when he spoke had grown cold and tired.

'And hadn't I reason?' he asked at last. 'Was there

ever an hour's fun or jollification in that barracks of a
house since the day you thrown your shadow on the
thrashel? Was there?'

'That's right. Blame it on me! Do!'

'Was there ever the sound of a melodion or a fiddle
heard in it since the night you come home to it? Was
there ever anything but the clink of coppers in it? You
with your screwing and scraping for what you'll never
leave to chick nor child of your own!'

'Oh, God help me!' the woman's voice cried. ''Tis
the hour he taunts me!'

'Ay, taunt you,' he said. 'By Chrisht, woman, I'd
rather one little child would be wetting me pants than
all the money you ever had or hoarded.'

'Oh, listen to him, Sweet Lord!' she cried.

'Here,' his voice was harsh with bitterness, 'stop
your old gab and help me to bring him in.'

The steps retreated once more past the threshold
and Mary Kate and Phil looked at one another in the
darkness. They heard a sigh as the two outside bent
to their load, they heard the heavy dragging steps
resumed, and in a moment the man tottered into the
cottage, panting and fumbling behind him with his
heels.

'Lay him in this corner,' he said.

They laid down their burden and stood for a
minute or two in silence. Phil and Mary Kate were
startled when he spoke again.

'I'll maybe always regret what I done,' he said.

''Tis your own doing,' said the woman.

'Ay,' he said bitterly, ''tis all my own doing. I was
a fool that ever listened to you.'

'You'd rather dip your hand in your pocket,' she

whispered. 'You that hadn't enough to pay the priest the day I married you.'

'I'd rather,' he replied, with mounting rage, 'I'd rather that man a corpse in the house than you a live woman in it.'

'You mean,' she corrected, 'you'd rather him alive in it and me stretched.'

He did not contradict her, but by his heavy breathing it was easy to see he was keeping a strong check on himself.

'Go on with you now,' he said.

She turned and went swiftly out the door. He followed her slowly. At the threshold he turned and seemed to be looking back. His wife had disappeared.

'Good-bye, little man,' he said softly. 'With the help of God, they'll find you in the morning. And don't blame me to Him, little man, for all.'

He closed the door gently behind him. As he did so, Phil disengaged his arm from about Mary Kate and rose.

'Oh, Phil,' she cried, 'what is it? What is it?'

'Let me look,' he said dully.

He struck a match and moved carefully towards the corner in which the pair had deposited their uncanny bundle. As he reached it the match flared up suddenly and showed the bluey-white face of an old man whose little yellow beard pointed straight up at him. The head was sagging backwards over the left shoulder, the knees were lifted, the eyes stared widely and questioningly at him. Mary Kate screamed and Phil dropped the match. It was the first time, since his mother's death so long ago, that he had looked into the eyes of death, whose look no language had ever described, and the shock penetrated deep into his bowels. Fear, indignation, and pity surged through him in alternate hot and cold waves.

'Oh, Phil, Phil, Phil,' cried Mary Kate, 'take me out of this, take me out of this, quick!'

Phil's only answer was to plunge his hand into his pocket, take out the matchbox, and strike a fresh light. He lit the candle.

'I don't want to see him!' cried Mary Kate. 'Take me away!'

Phil bent down and touched the little man's hand. It was almost cold. He rose slowly, the fascination of the pathetic face drawing his eyes.

'He's dead all right. God have mercy on his soul,' he said gravely.

Mary Kate clutched his arm.

'Phil, come on away, come on away before anybody would find us.'

He turned his face to hers and she saw that one side was distorted with emotion. He was crying, and pushed her off rudely.

'You'd like,' he said, hiding his face in his sleeve, 'if he was your own father, you'd like him to be thrown out like an old dead dog, wouldn't you?'

Immediately the springs of fear dried up in her. Phil, kneeling down beside the body, sobbed unrestrainedly, his back trembling with the fierce emotion that shook him, his boyish head with its tousled mop of brown hair lit by the candle that flickered crazily on the edge of the mantelpiece. It was a new Phil she saw, and she knew better than to interrupt him. She knelt beside him, but with as little intention of prayer. At last the storm of tears blew itself over. Phil shivered, wiped his eyes with the sleeve of his coat, and set himself, almost mechanically, the task of straightening the dead man's limbs and giving his poor skeleton body the appearance of repose.

The breeches had sagged to the knees, obviously pulled on the still warm corpse in haste, and the old grey military shirt hung out above it. Phil called on Mary Kate to lift the body with him while he drew them up. She did so without question. As he opened the ragged old coat to pull down the braces a penny whistle dropped out. He picked it up and looked at it, his eyes glittering like fields after rain, and the cheap brightness seemed to answer him and tell him what he wished to know. It had an abashed and frightened look, as at finding itself in immediate proximity with the terrible thing called death. Phil laid it down on the straw. Mary Kate thought he was going to cry again, but he was beyond tears.

'If Almighty God doesn't throw them out at the last day,' he said coldly, 'there's as little justice in heaven as on earth.'

He made an attempt that was only partly successful at closing the staring eyes. He laid two pennies on them, and the pennies stared back like eye-sockets, dark and cold. He forced the hands together, dipped in his pockets again, and twined his own rosary beads about them.

'Before the candle goes out,' he said, 'we'll say the rosary.'

He gave out the rosary. Mary Kate responded. Then he said as many of the last prayers as he could remember, making up in simple words what memory failed to supply. The candle flickered for the last time and went out.

'Eternal rest grant unto him, O Lord,' he said.

'And let perpetual light shine upon him,' responded Mary Kate, thrilled by the omen of the sudden darkness.

XX

THEY lay for a long time side by side, his arm about her, in silence. She had made one more feeble request that they should leave, knowing well that he would refuse, and now each lay with different thoughts. Somehow all their fear had gone. No death-house was ever less tormented by evil spirits than this in which the old musician had been thrown, when his last tune was played and his last copper gathered. Something pure in the gall of old age and poverty, something pure in the honey of unworldly youth, kept evil spirits at bay.

It had been long years since Phil's mind was besieged by so many turbulent thoughts. He had lived in a vacuum, entering it in turbulence and emerging in turbulence. He made no attempt to master it. Again and again, as if by clockwork, his mind reverted to the hour of that golden summer evening when the little musician had come that way. Did he know he was dying? Did he deliberately conceal it and play and sing in the hope that he would not die by the roadside? What good company did he make of his poor perishing body that induced the slave of the farmhouse to let him stay? And how did they discover his condition? Did the slave remember some good story or some old song and come to his bedside? Was he dead then or only dying? Was he even dead when they dressed him and dragged him out? And were the stars above him the last things he saw? What were his last thoughts? Had he ever known wife or child and were these in his mind, or did he search back past a lonely and struggling existence to his home and the graveyard where his parents lay and he would never lie? And each time his mind reverted to the musician's coming it was exhausted by anguish and fury. Tears came to his eyes and glazed them without falling.

While Mary Kate was imagining herself in the place of that childless miser. If only *she* had been the mistress of that house, and the tramp had come to her, how she would have tended him, how she would have watched by his bed all night, so that the image of her face would be the last that he would carry out of the world before the throne of God! God! She sometimes wondered vaguely, like Mrs. Verschoyle, whether there was a God at all, that unwashed old men with white beards should die homeless.

But the end of that eventful night had not come for Phil and Mary Kate. Just before dawn, when a cold wind was blowing across the midland plains, two women banged open the gate and stumbled up to the door. This time Phil was on his feet and at the door before them. But before he was noticed, he heard the clamour of an old woman's voice:

'Aisy, aisy, now, *a leanbh*,[1] and you'll soon be at rest. Isn't the pain any better, *a leanbh*?'

'It is not,' the other woman muttered behind her in the darkness, ''tis bad now. O Jesus!' Her teeth were rattling with the cold and she spoke in shivers.

'Sweet Heart of God look down on me this night!'

[1] *a leanbh* = child.

the wheezy voice went on. 'And on all like me. Whisht now, whisht now, whisht, *a laogh liom*,[1] and you'll see the lovely place I brought you to.'

The sighs the first woman gave were almost mechanical. Phil faced her in the doorway, and had to look down at her. A tiny creature he could barely imagine a woman, she of the wheezy voice; she was only a silhouette against the doorway, with her dark shawl gathered about her head and little wispy locks blowing about it wildly. When she saw Phil she gave a terrified screech and staggered back as though she had been struck.

'Jesus, Mary, and Joseph,' she squealed, 'the fetch, the fetch! Eh, Bridie, Jackie the Lantern have me! Run, Bridie, run, for the love of God!'

She grabbed wildly at Bridie, who only stumbled and moaned.

'Oh, ooah! Keep away from me!' bawled the old woman, her eyes averted.

'Don't shout!' said Phil in a fierce whisper; 'you've nothing to be afraid of.'

'Keep away from me!' she cried, with a vague memory of exorcism. 'Whoever thou art, and whether thou art from heaven or hell, or whatever have thee out of thy bloody grave this night, keep away from me, in the name of the Father, the Son, and the Holy Ghost. From all evil spirits and such as walk in the darkness, good Lord deliver us!'

One hand sweeping up the old shawl across her face, she sketched a wide cross over Phil.

'Is he gone yet, Bridie?' she called from behind the blanketing shawl.

---

[1] *a laogh liom* = my calf.

'I'm not a ghost,' said Phil indignantly. 'Come in, if you want to; only I warn you there's a dead man inside.'

His words acted like magic on the old woman, who tremblingly lowered the shawl and looked round at him, as if expecting that at any moment he would don horns or tail.

'O God,' she said unsteadily, 'and I thinking you were a fetch! Oh, oh, oh, and the heart jumping like jalap inside in me! Listen to it,' she said, one hand fumbling beneath her shawl, the other dragging up the cowl about her poll. 'Oh, listen to it, you Eternal God, going like a traction engine inside me!'

'Come in and lie down if you want to,' said Phil. 'There's nobody but myself and a girl, and the little man.'

'And my daughter,' squealed the old vagabond, her voice rising again resentfully as her natural state of suffering reasserted itself, 'my daughter that's on her feet this livelong day, and I dunno will she ever see the sun rise again, the creature. Come in, Bridie,' she called magisterially, and proceeded to waddle towards the door, her diminutive frame rolling from side to side like a sailor's on a stormy night. Bridie followed her, staggering. As she reached the door she fell clean over into Phil's arms, moaning and shivering. He staggered, too, and the old crone gave one of her shrieks, to which Phil was now growing accustomed.

'It's all right,' he said gruffly; 'she's a bit weak. I'll bring her in.'

He brought her in and laid her in the straw beside the door. The crone shrieked again; this time she had stumbled across the body of the little musician.

'Come over here out of the way,' called Phil in exasperation.

'What's wrong with him?' she asked stupidly. 'He's drunk. Tell me he's drunk, like a kind Christian young man!'

'He's not drunk,' replied Phil, 'he's dead.'

'Dead? You're draming, *a chuisle*![1] How would he get dead?'

'He died in a farmhouse over the way, and they didn't want the trouble of him, so they thrown him in here.'

'Dead? Dead?' called a feeble voice from the straw. 'I wish I was dead too.'

Phil and Mary Kate started as though this time they had really heard a ghost. The stifled voice of the sick girl set their exasperated nerves a-tingle, and its effect on the crone was even worse.

'That the Lord God may wither them!' she cried. 'That the Lord God Almighty may wither them!'

'Don't curse!' said Phil, horrified at the tone in which the words were said.

'I'll curse them, living and dead,' squealed the half-animal voice, 'I'll curse them, waking and sleeping, that grudged my child the shelter of an old barn. I'll curse them they get and them that got them. Hold me up,' she cried, and Phil heard her fall heavily upon her knees. 'Hold me up till I curse them!'

'Come up ou' that,' he said angrily, fumbling his way towards her and grabbing her by the shoulder. But she was too heavy to lift, and against his will he found himself supporting the tiny frame that rocked to and fro upon its knees in an ecstasy of malevolent

[1] *a chuisle* = pulse (of the heart).

animal violence. The ceremony began in Irish with a long invocation of the Deity, under all the beautiful names and kennings of the folk's invention. Then she broke into a torrent of English:

'Oh, Lamp of Light in the Well of Divinity, my heavy curse, and my double curse, on all them that wouldn't give a man and two poor women shelter this night. And the curse of the Lord God and of the holy Angels and Archangels on the three that chased us with hayforks out of the barn we were sleeping in. May bad luck folly them in everything they do; and if they are single, may a woman never rest beside them; and if they are married, may they never see their child's face; and if they have children, may the children rot before their eyes; and if their children are grown, may all the bad luck I wish for them light on their children as well. I beg rock to crush them and water to drown them and lightning to strike them; drink to poison them, food to choke them, heaven to be shut on them, and the red flames of hell to burn them. I beg disease and death never to leave their house, and the body of God never to enter it. All them that persecutes me, all them that belies me and mine, and most of all, O Lord, the three that took pitch-forks to a girl after giving birth to her child. A bad luck and a bad end to them all! Amen.'

Phil shuddered and let her go; she fell face foremost in the straw, and squealed and twisted like a cat in her efforts to rise. She found her way on all-fours into the corner where the sick girl lay, and bent above her, tossing back the wild hair from her eyes.

'Are you better now, *a leanbh*?' she asked, with an astonishing change of tone; Phil could scarcely believe her high, cracked voice could, after such an outburst, express such compassion and tenderness. The girl said something, her mother bending one ear to her flaming face.

'She's cold,' she squealed up at Phil's shadow. 'Jesus help us, she's cold, and the poor head lighting on her wid the fever!'

'What's up with her?' asked Mary Kate.

''Tis the fever, child. Come here and put your hand to her.'

Trembling, Mary Kate fumbled her way into the corner; the old woman reached up, caught her cold hand, and approached it to the face of the sick girl. She had spoken truly; it was raging with fever.

'A child she had,' she squealed on, 'the first, and she never overed it proper. And them bloody divils was saying 'twas some fellow got at her. That I may be killed if she wasn't as much married as yourself, child, to a blackguard that left her on my hands; and never a step did she step out of her way for a man besides. And they called her all the names they could think of, as if she was a public character. Pitchforks they took to her in her labour, the creature! Pitchforks they took to her and her child!'

She was screaming again, but it was futile to interrupt her.

'What happened the poor child?' asked Phil.

'What happened him?' A curious tone crept into the voice, which immediately dropped to a normal pitch. 'What would happen him, the angel? Sure, you wouldn't expect him to live after that, would you? Five minutes he lived, the creature, and with my own hands I thrown the drop of wather on his head.'

'As soon as there's light,' said Phil, 'I'll go for the priest and doctor.'

'Ah, you're a good boy,' she said. 'Who's that poor creature over there, or do I know him at all?'

'A small man with a beard,' he answered; 'he used to be playing the penny whistle.'

'Wisha, for God's sake, is it Batt Galvin?' she cried.

'Come over and look at him,' he said. She clung to his hand, keeping him between her and the body. He struck a match.

''Tis, 'tis, 'tis,' she screamed instantly, ''tis him; wouldn't I know him by the dooshy beard? Oh, Batt, Batt, and is that the way I find you after all your travellings? . . . Hold up the light. . . . Batt Galvin from Mitchelstown, 'ithout song nor story from him, and he wid his two poor shrivelled stumps like a robin-een's legs. Oh, my handsome man, you that had the heart of a hundred, did I ever think I'd live to see you with the wind gone out of you for to blow us a reel on your little flute? Oh, Batt, Batt, the last roof is over you and the last bed is under you, and there's no one but Nodge Coholan to cry a neighbourly tear. . . . Strike another match, decent boy, till I look at him.'

She did not cease to put Phil between her and the body, but looked round him at it, crouching, her bony little hand gripping his, while she pressed the other, tightly clenched, against her mouth. She gave a sniff or two. As he struck another match—a difficult operation because of her hold on him—she raised her wail afresh, violently beating her face and head with her fist.

'Oh, Batt Galvin, may the angels make your bed in

heaven this night, and the Son of God look down on you and console you for all the slights the world ever put on you! 'Twas you were the gay man, and the good man, and the kindly man, and what little you had you scattered to them that needed it. May purgatory fire never burn one grey hair on your head, Batt, for all the good turns you done for old Nodge Coholan, and she begging her bit on the roads of Ireland! I could cry my two eyes down for you, you creature, and you so lonely and so far from home. Among strangers and deceivers, Batt, among liars and traitors, you poor shabby corpse so far from home!'

There was no doubting the intensity with which she delivered her oration by the light of Phil's two matches, but the celerity with which she passed from it was comic.

'Help me to my corner, decent boy,' she exhorted, and Phil put her sitting down again beside her daughter.

'Are you feeling better now, *a stór*[1]?' she demanded with the same compassion as before. 'What's that you're saying, *a ghile*[2]?'

Her daughter answered with a dry, inarticulate babble, to which the woman listened in rapt attention.

'What does she want?' asked Mary Kate.

''Tisn't anything she wants at all, *'inghean ó*.[3] 'Tis the poor wits that wanders on her. Listen to her now, and she babbling away like one demented.'

Sure enough, the girl was raving in the height of fever. It was possible only to understand her when something excited her terribly, for then the dry, mono-

---

[1] *a stór* = O treasure. [2] *a ghile* = O brightness.
[3] *'inghean ó* = daughter.

tonous babble gave place to a few words that were shrill and clear-cut. Over and over again the listeners heard her call 'baby'; once, with atrocious distinctness, the word 'water'. The old wanderer crowed complacently in the darkness.

''Tis that is in her mind, the poor child. She was in dread he'd die on her without he being baptised. Water, that was all she was thinking of.'

'Where would I get a priest and doctor?' asked Phil between his teeth.

'You won't get them nearer than the town, and that's four long miles away.'

'I'll go now,' said Phil.

'I'll go with you,' said Mary Kate hurriedly.

'Eh, what use would that be when you don't know your way and you haven't light enough to travel by?' demanded the old tramp. 'And do you think them divils in hell will get out of their own warm beds for the sake of a poor sick girleen?'

The girl called out something incoherent, which her mother chose to interpret after her own fashion.

'He's in heaven, *a ghrá*[1],' she shouted. 'I'm telling the young man we have no one now to put our trust in but the Almighty God. Be sure He won't see us wronged and your innocent child praying for us before His holy throne.'

They sat back to await the full light of day. Phil glanced at his watch. It was half-past three. The old woman opened a cloth bag and spread the contents before her; they were pieces of bread, some buttered, some unbuttered, some mere crusts. She offered some to Mary Kate, who refused, but Phil, who had an

[1] *a ghrá* = love.

exquisite sense of courtesy, accepted. She picked him
out a thick chunk of buttered bread.

'Take that, *a leanbh*,' she said. 'There's a lovely
morsel of yesterday's bread with prints of butter
on it.'

They fell into silence, eating. Grey bars of light
pierced the boarded window and splintered into red,
blue, and green. Mary Kate felt intolerably sleepy.
She woke after a fantastic doze that mingled motor-
cars, flights, pursuits, and dead men to hear the crone's
shrill, exasperating voice raised at Phil, who lay wake-
ful beside her.

'Ah, indeed, but 'tis true for you, young man, there's
wrongs and bitter wrongs put upon the likes of us,
and there's no one but the poor knows what the poor
suffers. Twenty-four years I'm on the road since
before my daughter was born, and what I didn't see
in them long years, leave it to the reader.'

'And no way out!' said Phil dryly.

'No way out at all, my son, but the two ways, the
workhouse and the big hole.'

'I'd blame no one,' said Phil, 'that wouldn't go to
the workhouse.'

'Is it blame them?' She gave a shrill cackle. 'I'd
rather you thrown me live and lovely in a pit of quick-
lime than go into one of them. I seen a man and he had
such a dread of the workhouse he'd never go within
ten miles of one. Yes, so, *a vic*.[1] Down the seacoast I
seen him go, not to go next, nigh, or near the workhouse
of Rathdrum. And, for all, didn't the poor man die
outside Cork city, and didn't they bring him up to the
workhouse there, and one night didn't they shove his

---

[1] *a vic* = son.

carcass on an ould butt and off wid him to the college? They did, my dear, and they took my handsome Jo Ryan insunder as if he was an ould clock.'

'Did they?' asked Phil, startled. 'Did they do that to him?'

'They did then. Because he had ne'er a one in the world to claim his bones.'

'My God!' said Phil. 'There's a deal of badness in the world.'

'My fine Christian gentlemen!' the old woman crowed at the highest pitch of her voice. 'My fine Christian gentlemen that skinned him in life and skinned him in death, and they with their smart coffins and their vaults. What'll he do on the Resurrection Day? What'll he do when the trumpet sounds, with his head in Bantry and his heels in Cork?'

This problem in applied theology staggered even Phil. It rounded off with the last touch of the grotesque his experience of the night that had driven him from dismay to bitterness. He had forgotten completely that he was the youth who had struck Nick McCormick. All that was only a detail to the things he had begun to see about him. No better listener could have been found for the old hag's tirade against the kind Christian gentlemen. But Phil had heard what it is death to the soul to hear.

At last he rose stiffly and tiptoed to the door. When he opened it he was dazzled by the radiance outside. At the same moment Mary Kate sprang to her feet and rushed to him, catching his arm in a vice-like grip.

'Oh, Phil, Phil,' she cried, 'leave us be going now!'

The dawn wind had died away and the sun was

rising. All the sky above them was smeared with the rose-tipped remnants of defeated night. The dark host was like an army retreating by the light of a burning city. The trees were still and glistening to their leaf-tips with dew; all the countryside was still, as if it were a dreamer sunk back into that primal repose from which all visions spring.

'You wouldn't be afraid if we left you alone now?' asked Phil, turning undecidedly, half his face to the morning, the other half to the night.

'Erra, what would I be afraid of?' the old woman cackled with daft humour. She rose and hobbled to the doorway, letting the shawl drop loose from her tiny knot of bedraggled white hair. Her bronzed face was even more a miniature than her body. It seemed to be broken in two, for where the nose should have been was only a hollow from which half a knuckle's length of noselet projected horizontally; and above and below this hollow, forehead and ivory chin jutted outwards, the bones shining whitely beneath them in the clear light. Dazzled, she looked up at the sky.

'Praise be to You, God, isn't the morning lovely?' she cried in ecstasy.

'We wouldn't leave you at all, only we have to be home before night,' said Mary Kate timidly. Though she would not have admitted it for worlds, she believed far more in the supernatural powers of the woman than in those of the corpse.

'And ye will, *a leanbh*, ye will,' she replied. 'Sure, any one would be glad to give the likes of ye a lift. Ye're a grand pair, God increase ye! and 'tis your husband have the picture to be looking at.'

The picture said nothing, but the husband put his

hand in his pocket and produced two half-crowns. He reddened with shyness.

'I'd be ashamed to offer you that.' he said non-committally, but, as he spoke, her two skinny paws swooped upon the money and incidentally upon his hand, which she wrung with all the might of her fragile arms.

'That the Lord may spare you and give you a happy death and a throne in glory!' she bawled. 'And that He may have mercy on the souls of all that's dead belonging to you! My handsome boy, till the hour of my death I'll remember you in my prayers.'

'We'll be going now, Phil,' said Mary Kate hastily, half in dread lest an excess of good wishes might induce him to part with still more of their little treasure.

'One moment,' he said. He took off his cap and knelt for a moment in the straw. Mary Kate would never forget him as he appeared at that moment, mistily lit, his head just touched with an aureole of grey light, beside the dead man, whose clenched fists and raised knees belied the repose suggested by Phil's rosary beads.

'Ye didn't search him?' whispered the old woman fiercely, beckoning and whispering in extravagant regard for the sanctity of Phil's orisons. At Mary Kate's shocked reply she smiled and nodded with great satisfaction.

She directed them down the road, and they set off stiffly, endeavouring with exercise to drive the numbness from their limbs. All the fences were bright and still, and the fields lay deserted for miles about them. Suddenly a lark shot up out of the grass, and rising at a sharp angle began to unwind his tiny spool of

song. He changed his course to a spiral and chugged
up over their heads like a motorist climbing a stiff
hill. They could see him trembling with effort, his
wings fluttering wildly, his melody streaming behind
him like a slender silver ribbon. At last he paused, a
faint speck in the milky light, rocking as though upon
an invisible wind-stirred bough, and screaming with
rapture, shot himself headlong towards the east. He
paused again, turning at a perilous angle like a skater,
singing gaily alone in the sky. Then, with the sudden
shyness of a child taking fright before a shadow, he
dropped dead from his height.

XXI

In the town, Phil called on priest and doctor, and though these walking devils showed no great reluctance to go to the aid of the tramp woman and her daughter, there was a notable stiffening in Phil's bearing, an air of aloofness which it would have been impossible to find in him previously. For the old Phil had that complete disregard of worldly appearance which belongs to the saint.

Something of his new sense of differences was illustrated by his conversation with Mary Kate over the breakfast table.

She came downstairs, having washed the sleep from her eyes, but looking haggard and pale. Phil, who had merely drenched himself under the pump and appeared with a dripping shirt-front, looked uncommonly well in spite of his pensiveness. His normally neat clothes had fallen into disarray, one day's sun had browned out his pallor, and with his drenched and glittering black hair plastered flat on his head, his deep-sunk dark eyes, and his sombre boyish features, he looked like a young soldier. He was examining the prints which graced the back-shop, in which four crazily creaking tables and a dozen of ancient cane chairs were set. The print which now attracted his attention was one of those that seem to survive only in Irish country towns. It represented two very bashful children, the foremost in a gigantic hat; it was dedicated to H.R.H. Prince Albert of Saxe-Gotha; it was dated 1841, and bore—in Irish and English—the title 'The Young Mendicants' Noviciate'.

'That's a massive piece,' he said, pointing to it.

Mary Kate blinked nonchalantly and admitted that she didn't care for pictures that were not in colours.

When hunger was half assuaged with bread and butter, and, in Mary Kate's case, with a boiled egg, Phil approached the subject from a new angle.

'We ought to be thankful for what happened us last night,' he remarked gravely.

'For what?' asked Mary Kate, with a cross expression.

'For giving us a chance to see what life is like.'

'Don't we see enough of that at home?' she asked, with a start.

'For all we notice of it, we do not.'

She made no reply to this, and he went on. 'The way I look at it is this. 'Twould seem as if 'twas done for a purpose. I mean me finding out about— *him*' (Phil stammered over the word), 'and our not having enough money to come by train——'

'He gave me two pounds,' she said quickly, 'but I wouldn't take it.'

Phil flushed with pleasure.

'That was fine, Mary Kate,' he said; the taciturn Phil so chary of praise disappearing for the moment. 'But look how all that fits in. You not taking the money, and the pair of us being dropped next door to that house. Even then we might have spent the night there and no one come near us. Or after the little man —God rest him—was put in, we might never have met that nice woman and her daughter and never know what sort of a man he was.'

'We don't know now either,' said Mary Kate, buttering herself another round of bread, 'only what she told us.'

'Well, she knew him.'

'I don't know whether she did or not. I know she told you a heap of lies, and you swallowed them.'

'Now, Mary Kate, you shouldn't say things like that,' he protested.

'She told you a heap of lies,' Mary Kate repeated, her voice rising. 'She told you her daughter was married. And she said that the child died.'

He looked up, startled.

'And what do you know about it?'

'I know she wasn't married, and I know that old devil destroyed the child.'

'Destroyed it?'

'Drowned it.'

Mary Kate went pale, and then reddened from brow to chin, eating all the time with lowered eyes. He looked at her for a few moments and went on with his breakfast.

'I'm glad, all the same,' he said.

And he was. For the first time for years, life was coursing into him from the roots of his being, and, as in a numbed body, causing him at once anguish and delight. He was tasting in innocence the joy of discovery. He was tasting it through a sordid adventure only because he had barred his soul to approach from any other side. He was, in fact, as genuinely inspired by his adventure as another would have been by his first experience of courtship or soldiering.

Everything pleased him: the garishly papered room; the colourless morning light on wall and ceiling; the slattern, with the face that resembled the blade of an oar, who served them; and Mary Kate, her tam-o'-shanter tossed aside and her dark hair framing those features so full of the craftsman's sensitiveness. Features from which time would steal slowly and never entirely plunder, each lit with an inner brightness. It has been already remarked that her face gave the impression of having been drawn at more than life-size and reduced in the model to less, in order to achieve its fineness; and this was very clear in the white light that pursued its contours and exposed the minute network of lines that gave the brown eyes their humour. Perhaps, too, it was more obvious for the weariness that stilled it.

They strolled out into the sunlit street. There was a fair in progress, and they passed up and down, reviewing with a cityfied wonder the parade of creels and ass-carts in the midst of which frightened animals reared and plunged. The farmers, freed from their womenfolk for the day, shouted and gesticulated their bargaining in excitement that made the whole dingy street brilliant with life. Bargaining with Saint Peter for admission into heaven they could hardly have been more extravagant in their display of emotion. Oaths, curses, and shouts were raised, sticks were brandished, and mobile faces performed prodigies of distortion. Little groups thronged the public-houses. It was Phil who paid most attention, he who first commented upon the difference between town and city. There was 'Rich. Henecy's Drapery, Hardware, Grocery, and Funeral Establishment', which sold newspapers,

tobacco, and cooked-meat besides. This gave them
both a laugh, their first that day, and it seemed to call
for others, so that, in increasing good humour, they
joked and jostled through the crowd, up and down,
not caring to be gone. The farmers cracked jokes
at Mary Kate's good looks, and she responded
gamely.

But their greatest amusement was derived from a
gigantic negro who was engaged in the sale of patent
medicine. Surrounded by a throng of watchful faces,
lit with doubt and laughter, he stood on a soap-box, his
coat off and his white shirt sleeves rolled up to expose
his great gleaming muscles. In one hand he held a
quart bottle.

'A few days ago,' he shouted in a rich voice that
filled the whole street, 'I was lecturing to a large
gathering in London. A girl come up to me, and she
say: "I heard you announce, mister, that you cure a
certain disease. Well, mister, I am suffering from dat
disease," and she show me, ladies and gentlemen,
she show me a bottle—dat size' (he held up his little
finger). ' "Tell me," she said to me, "tell me if dis
bottle, which my doctor give me, is good for dat
disease." Ladies and gentlemen, I look at dat bottle
—for I am an honest man, and I do not tell lies—I
look at dat bottle and I say, "Miss," I say, "I do
not scandalise medicine." '

'One minit now,' a voice bawled as the negro paused
and with a white handkerchief wiped his streaming
brown face, 'one minit till I show ye, ma'am. Absolutely unbreakable. Yew can dance a fourhand reel on
that plate and it won't crack. A family heirlewm tew
be handed down from generation to generation.'

A plate flew in the air and landed on a large packing-case without accident.

'Three bob the set.'

'I say I do not scandalise medicine,' boomed the negro indignantly, and immediately the Dublin voice was lost in a rich torrent of sound. Phil and Mary Kate looked round sympathetically. A pair of wrathful eyes glowered at the invader while the voice trickled on, discouraged and resentful, addressing now an audience of three—Phil, Mary Kate, and a tramp, dressed in a shabby navy blue suit, who sat on the kerbstone, a switch between his knees, eating a piece of dry bread out of his hand and watching the comedy with gloomy, meditative gusto.

'My God!' bawled the seller of hardware, 'is there ne'er a one at all will give me one tew shillings for a half-dozen of lovely willow plates yew could ride an express train over? Is there? Tew shillings. One and sixpence. Yes, one shilling and six pennies. Or is there any one in Ireland that ever had the misfortune tew break a cup or a saucer?'

Apparently there was not.

'But my friend who scandalises medicine,' boomed the negro, 'my friend say to her, "Dat bottle, miss, contains noting but water with brown sugar and a pinch of bread soda." And dat bottle, ladies and gentlemen, cost the young lady four shillings and sixpence. Now what I sell you is not medicine . . .'

'The divil suffocate you with your own medicine,' snarled the dealer. 'Here,' he called to the tramp, 'mind them and the old car till I get one drink inside me. I feel as if I swallied a gallon of his sheep drench already.'

The tramp took his place at the packing-case. He was a small man, grey-haired and toothless. His neck was like a reed with a gigantic Adam's apple. His eyes were a cold grey like winter skies at sunset, and they had a knowing look, a look of supreme irony. He winked at Phil and Mary Kate. Then he took two cups from the improvised counter and proceeded to juggle with them listlessly. They flew high in the air while he, nonchalant and almost abstracted, kept them spinning. Some of the crowd looked round and nudged others in front of them who also looked round and gaped. For a moment the negro was in eclipse. But the tramp seemed unaware of the effect he was creating and continued his juggling. His skill seemed to be of the most elementary kind, but the crowd was in a mood for spectacle, and spectacle it would have.

'Hey, what are ye selling the plates for, mister?' bawled a wag.

The tramp gave his cups a farewell spin and collected them carelessly.

'I'm not selling plates,' he retorted. 'I'm selling egg-cups.'

'Who do you think is going to buy them?' the wag asked again.

'Mugs,' responded the tramp gravely; and there was a roar of laughter from the crowd.

'And they'll want them,' he continued as the mirth subsided. He lifted an egg-cup and surveyed it from every angle with a quizzical look and a toothless smile. 'This,' he said, 'is the only article ever known to stand the shock of a black man's mixture.'

There was a renewed outburst of joviality. The negro glared about him, the whites of his eyes showing, and then went on to recount in a still louder voice, broken with sobs, how his dear old mammy had raised him on herbs, and how he could never think of the old lady without, as it were, his eyes filling with tears of gratitude. 'What my dear old mammy was to me, let me be to you, my friends!' he boomed.

'Did I ever tell ye the story of the German submarine that tried to torpedo one of them soup plates?' demanded the tramp, without a smile.

He had won. The crowd's interest was now centred in him alone. Within ten minutes he had sold more than the dealer in the whole morning, and though his prices had a tendency to wobble, they left even to an outsider's eye a clear margin of profit. The driver, when he returned to his deserted stall, opened his eyes wide with astonishment as he saw the little heap of silver that had accumulated in his absence. He was rather drunk.

The tramp continued his banter. You learned that his name was Peter John Cross and that he did not live so very far from the Dolls' House. Phil and Mary Kate listened with delight, and when at last he retired gracefully and left the conquered field to his friend the dealer, they made their way to his side and quickly introduced themselves.

.'Are you going home?' asked Phil.

'I am, I suppose.'

'We are too. Will you be down with us.'

'I left my car in Dublin,' said Peter John Cross, with a grin.

'We got a lift from Dublin,' said Mary Kate proudly.

'Oh, you might get a lift.' He eyed them curiously, and then placed his thumbs in the sleeve-holes of his waistcoat, throwing open his ragged blue coat and exposing a torn and filthy shirt. 'Though to tell you the truth,' he added in a whisper, 'I was watching the sod with the crockery. He's going as far as Charleville. Will I ask him for a lift for you?'

'Oh, do,' said Phil enthusiastically.

They watched their new friend sidle through the crowd towards the dealer. He had a true quay-side swagger, adjusting his pants without removing his hands from the pockets, and swinging himself upon his hips. He came back after a moment, a secretive look on his face.

'Bob down,' he whispered, at the same time looking away over their heads. 'That'll be all right. Only as far as Kilmallock. You and me will have to travel in the crockery,' he added to Phil.

'That's grand,' said Phil unaffectedly. He liked the tramp with his conspiratorial airs.

'Leave us get out of this place, anyway,' said Peter. 'I'm sitting by that car since eight o'clock seeing would I get a chance of softening him.' He went over and spoke to the driver again; Phil noticed that he spoke into the man's ear.

'He'll meet us out the road,' he whispered as he returned. 'And I only hope he gets there alive. He stinks of whiskey.'

The three strolled off together; Peter, as if ashamed of identifying himself too closely with the others, walking several feet to the right of Mary Kate, swinging his stick and answering questions without once looking at her. She wondered what his age might be. His close-cropped hair was perfectly grey, but in gait and manner he was still a young man.

Before they left the town Phil went into a little shop
and bought cigarettes and matches. Mary Kate experienced a fresh shock. The potentialities of Phil's
extraordinary character left her somewhat alienated.
He offered the open packet to Peter, who took a cigarette and lit it, promptly putting a reasonable diplo-
matic distance between himself and the donor. At last
he looked up in surprise.

'Aren't you smoking?' he asked suspiciously.

'Ah, when the fit takes me,' said Phil, smiling, and
giving no sign of the careful preparation to which he
had subjected his casuistic reply.

'I'll smoke, Phil,' said Mary Kate nonchalantly.
But, as ever, he gave no sign either of surprise or
disapproval. He lit her cigarette.

By what was, for Phil, a subtle process of explanation and silence, Peter was at last induced to speak
about himself. He explained that he was coming from
Dublin where he had had a few weeks' work, doing
messages, and was making his way home.

His method was to walk as far as he could, ten
miles or twelve, and then stop at some town and do a
few days' cobbling for no more than it cost him to
travel. He had no tools but an awl and some thread,
and had to borrow a hammer and last, sometimes
making the heaters of a box iron do for both hammer
and last. He did not make much by it—no more than
one and sixpence a day—but then his lodgings cost
him only about a shilling. It might take him anything from three weeks to two months to do the
journey, as luck or mood decided. Once it had taken
over three months.

''Tis as good we're getting a lift,' he said, cutting

short his confidences abruptly. 'It'll rain before night. Look at the Galtees.'

Rain was slowly driving up from the south, across the wide plains of russet grass, and the mists of heat were being washed from the blue face of the Galtees by the invisible waves of moisture that flooded them. Grey castles stood up in the air, almost from the horizon, storey upon storey of them, all lit with creamy light, and languorously drifted away above their heads, shadowing a quarter mile of country as they passed. Swallows flew flat along the wide road like drunken motorists, careering from side to side, and almost colliding with them before they flashed across the hedges and made off among the fields. There was a heavy scent of hawthorn in the air. Whenever the sun clouded for a moment a moist wind sprang up and stilled the hawthorn scent.

Peter tramped on a little ahead of them, swinging his stick, his red face lifted expressionlessly to the sky, turning from airt to airt; a curious, melancholy face on its slender elastic neck, the sockets of the wintry-cold eyes red and sore.

An hour later the lorry caught up on them. Mary Kate would have liked to get in at the back with the other two, but courtesy forbade. She felt that Phil was attracted by Peter, and was herself attracted accordingly. She mounted in the cab with a sigh. The driver was rather more drunk than before.

As she had guessed, Phil and Peter talked more freely when they were alone. Not that any one could say the tramp spoke freely. Phil noticed that his excitement of the morning was wearing off and that he was growing more gloomy, while his manner

became more and more secretive. Phil could not understand why he spoke in whispers, as though there were
some one listening.

'Sometimes,' he confided, 'you'd get a couple of
days or a week at proper work like sawing timber,
and you'd be a fool not to take it; sometimes you'd get
sick of travelling and stop in a place because you'd
have a horror of the roads.'

He shivered as he said this, and looked at Phil from
under his eyes.

'Did you ever feel like that?' he asked.

'No,' replied Phil.

'It's the sky,' said Peter. 'Just like being in a cell in
jail. You'd get the horrors just to think of it, and if
you had only a bit of a corner in a stable you'd hate
to go out from under the roof.'

'Were you in jail?' asked Phil. He noticed the start
tha. Peter gave.

'Not for what you think.'

'But you were in jail?'

Peter winked.

'Were you in the fighting?' Phil asked.

The tramp winked again.

'Then why don't you stay at home? Why don't you
settle down somewhere? You could get regular work
if you wanted it.'

'I'll tell you what I'm going back for now,' Peter
said in a voice that had suddenly grown excited. 'A
man I knew in the old days, a man that knows the
good turns I did for Ireland, every six months he
sends me a bit of money. He sends it to a house in
Blarney Lane. I have to go back for it when the time
comes. That's what's bringing me home now.'

'But,' persisted Phil, 'when you get it, can't you settle down? Can't you get work at home?'

Peter did not answer. Instead, he began to speak of something else. Yet in that brief conversation he and Phil seemed to have come very close together.

Which was more than Mary Kate could have said of herself and the driver.

'Brian Boru,' he said, as he turned his dewy eyes on her, 'Brian Boru won the battle of Clontarf.' He paused to let this sink in. 'Did you know that, young woman?'

'I did,' said Mary Kate patiently.

'And who did he beat, tell me?'

'He beat the English,' said Mary Kate promptly. She shared the traditional Irish assumption that a battle which may be referred to invariably resulted in the defeat of the English.

'He did not beat the English,' said the driver crossly, scowling darkly at her. 'Did they never teach you history at school? He beat the Danes. And what did he beat the Danes for?'

'I don't know, I'm sure,' she responded flippantly. 'I suppose it was because he had nothing better to do.'

'It was not because he had nothing better to do. It was the bloody Danes sticking their bloody noses in where they weren't wanted.'

'Oh, law!' exclaimed Mary Kate.

'And tell me this. What do you think Brian Boru would say if he come back and seen the country over-run by black men?'

'He'd get a bit of a shock,' suggested Mary Kate.

'He'd get sick in his bloody stomach,' replied the driver despairingly.

'That's what I'll do myself if you don't open that window,' said Mary Kate.

Late that evening the three friends arrived, footsore and weary, in a little village on the borders of Cork county. It had rained and cleared, rained and cleared again, and now a vast arm of cloud stretched from the zenith to a peak of the Galtees that had drunk all the evening's rain and stood out against the horizon with an eerie, blue-filled distinctness. The cloud with its faint curve and its pointed prow looked like the right arm of God the Father in Michelangelo's fresco, outstretched to touch the finger-tip of the sleeping Adam, only now it seemed to touch an awakened Adam back to sleep. Dark under their load of raindrops the trees spattered showers about them; a plump blackbird silhouetted upon a dripping branch sang for them with deep, mellow, contralto notes; lights gleamed below them in the little village, where men and women passed to and fro like ghosts.

Here they parted, for, as luck had it, a lorry laden with butter and eggs for the city stood outside the local creamery. There were seats for two beside the driver.

They parted with many promises of a future meeting, and as the lorry moved off, Phil murmured to Mary Kate, 'That's a grand little man, Mary Kate. And he's so poor. Mary Kate, I wish we could do something for him.'

'Chariots and roads for chariots,' said the Indian sage.

XXII

IT is to be noted on behalf of Life that its best touches pass almost unobserved. That Nick McCormick, when he saw the two pounds where he had left it, should promptly sit down and write to his wife was one of these touches. For whatever Nick said, and whether or not he told Babe the truth, she grew into a belated alarm and took the letter to Mary Verschoyle.

Now Mary Verschoyle had already cut Mary Kate off, and ignored the picture post card (of the pier, Dunleary) which the latter had sent her; but with a passionately kind if cranky heart she united a passionate lust for interfering in what did not concern her. And though Phil and Mary Kate had been but two days from home, they found themselves already reported to the police as missing.

This had no immediate judicial consequences, but it had the effect of inducing Mary Verschoyle to call at the Dolls' House. This time she did not shout her way up the stairs, and arrived quite unexpectedly to find Mary Kate lying on her own bed in tears, while her mother from the big bed and her aunt from the hearth regarded her in stupefaction.

'Such nonsense!' exclaimed Dinah, throwing her hands to heaven a minute or two before Mrs. Verschoyle came. 'Did any one ever in all their life before hear of a girl carrying on about her own father?'

'He's not my father,' said Mary Kate.

'Don't contradict me, you slut! He is your father when I say he is.'

'And what are you going to do with yourself now?' asked her mother.

'I know what she's going to do,' said Auntie Dinah. 'She's going to take my place to-morrow with that old Maggie Counihan. I'm not going to be slaving my heart out to keep the likes of this young lady in idleness. Mark me, you'll go out to work to-morrow morning, girl!'

'I will,' said Mary Kate, 'and I'll never come back.'

'What's that you say?' demanded her mother. 'Now I want none of your crossackling, madam! There has never been any scandal about this family, and there won't be now either. I want no more of your talk, only settle down and do a bit of work and help to feed your little orphan brothers.'

'I don't care what you say,' said Mary Kate, casting a despairing glance about the room. 'I won't stay here; not if you paid me to.'

It was at this moment that Mary Verschoyle made her appearance. She knocked and looked in, then she slowly opened the door, keeping her eyes fixed on Mary Kate all the while.

'Well, well,' she said oracularly, 'this is a nice home-coming.'

'Oh, Mrs. Verschoyle,' said Babe, with a sigh, 'I'm glad you come. This girl have the heart played out of me.'

'And when did you arrive, Mary Kate?' asked Mary Verschoyle.

'Dry your eyes and speak to the lady, you little fool!' shouted Babe.

'Ah, Mary Kate, I warned you; I distinctly warned you,' the other said solemnly.

'She didn't give us a wink of sleep last nightm,' squeaked Dinah, hopping about and dusting chairs. 'Speak to herm, do; the girl have us distracted talking about drownding herself, and the Lord knows what wicked nonsense besides.'

'Now, Miss Matthews, would you for goodness' sake hold your tongue!' said Mrs. Verschoyle alarmingly.

'Yesm,' said Dinah.

'Don't you see the child is tired out and ought to be in bed?'

'There's more than her is tired out,' said her mother, rolling herself up disgustedly in the blankets. 'Here am I with the two eyes dropping out of me for want of a bit of sleep, and I have to listen to her goings on.'

'What brought her back?' asked Mrs. Verschoyle.

There was a heavy silence, broken at last by Dinah.

'It seems she wasn't getting on with her fatherm,' she explained lamely.

'I thought so,' said Mrs. Verschoyle. 'Drink?'

'Something like thatm.'

'I thought so.—Mary Kate, put on your hat and coat and come up to my house until you're all right again.'

Drawing her arm across her eyes, Mary Kate rose and got her outdoor clothes. The invitation was a relief to every one: to Mary Verschoyle, who vaguely felt that there was a great deal still to be learned; to Babe and Dinah, who would have less difficulty in explain-

ing Mary Kate away at a distance; and to Mary Kate
herself, who now hated with an abandonment of hatred
her old quarters in the Dolls' House. Everything
seemed smaller, dirtier, smellier than even she had
imagined it. She had arrived after dark when there
was no one about, and Phil and she had crept upstairs
on tiptoe, he to his room, she to her attic. The children
were in bed, but her mother and aunt were sitting by
the fire. At first she was excited and pleased; they had
made tea, and all at once when she had finished her
meal the fit of nostalgia had come upon her, and had
lasted until this moment.

'Bring her up a drop of water,' said Mrs. Verschoyle. 'Her eyes are all red.'

There were clothes steeping in the wash basin, so
Dinah ran down with a pudding basin which she
filled at the tap on the second landing, and with the
aid of this inadequate vessel Mary Kate succeeded in
making herself presentable. As she went downstairs
with the older woman she was already feeling brighter;
Scrap and Dona Nobis and the others seeming almost
a pleasure in store for her. It was an autumnal day,
half shine, half shower, and the little city under its
white tower was dirty and merry with its leaning walls
and broken windows, its shrill musical voices and
muddy roadways.

Phil's home-coming was very different.

His notice 'Away in Dublin, Back in a Few Days,'
scrawled with pencil marks, a copy of his words in
another hand, and a drawing of a soldier with a rifle,
seemed to come to him not from a few days before but
from ages back. The cold of the room chilled him, and
when he struck a match and lit the lamp the first thing

he saw was an enlargement of his mother's picture that hung above the mantelpiece. It had been taken when she was little more than a girl, and the fading of age and the indistinctness of the enlargement made it seem still more impersonal. But he wondered when he saw it what she would think of him now. He was astonished that he had ever remained in this room instead of going into lodgings.

A vague restlessness kept him from lying down. The milk he had in was sour, so he could not make himself tea. He took out a dry crust of bread and chewed it pensively. Then he turned the glass about and looked at himself in it. He was very brown from his two days' exposure to the open air. He turned its face to the wall again. Then he threw up the window and sat on the sill, looking out at the river and quays. Under the gas lamps on the opposite quay a drunken man walked home, unsteadily but stealthily appearing and disappearing beneath the trees. Some one was playing a concertina somewhere. A last tram clanked distantly downhill on its worn flanges. A heavy shower blew down from the west, and amid all the nightly noises of the little city, mounted on its hills like a child's box of bricks, came the buzz and scurry of the falling rain. He saw it streaking across the river and alighting in tiny bubbles of darkness where the gas lamps shone, and the river seemed to run faster. Then a splash touched the window; he drew in his head and watched it stream silently down the pane. At the same moment some one came out of a house at the opposite side and went up the quay in silence, and for some reason the two phenomena made a simultaneous impression upon his mind, the man on rubber soles and the silent trickle of rain. Restlessness, restlessness, restlessness!

He sat on a chair by the window and began to read a chapter of *The Imitation*. But he had to force himself to finish it. Then he looked for the booklet that contained those lines of Saint Teresa's which he knew so well. He opened it and read aloud:

> *Let nothing disturb thee,*
> *Nothing affright thee,*
> *Everything passes,*
> *God is unchanging;*
> *He who has patience,*
> *Everything comes to him;*
> *He who has God,*
> *He lacks for nothing,*
> *God, only, suffices.*

But for some reason the familiar words brought him no peace. A loneliness filled the room that did not come from the night outside, but from the night within himself, as though there were reaches of his nature that he had never known of or walked in; they suggested themselves to his imagination as dark fields with dark, silent streams dividing them. For once he would have wished for company. The old woman of the night before; how full of energy she had been! Or Peter. He wished now he had spoken more freely to Peter when he had had the chance. But then he had had nothing to say. All this had seemed to begin but a moment before. He was alone. Alone—how strange that sounded.

> *He who has God,*
> *He lacks for nothing,*
> *God, only, suffices.*

Then he must be suffering from deprivation of his

communion with God. God had cut him adrift. The thought startled him from his inanition. He rose with a bound and quenched the lamp. Then with a hand unsteady with excitement he lit the tiny floating wick that burned naked before the picture of the Sacred Heart. It shone ghostlily out at him from the darkness, like a little stage lit with a greenish light. He knelt before it and prayed, prayed desperately for peace and light. Then he wound the alarm clock and got into bed. He was dazed with weariness and depression, and almost immediately fell asleep.

He woke, if waking it could be called, to feel his mother's arm about his shoulder, just as in the old days he would wake to find her over his pillow, kiss her hand as it drew the clothes about him, and fall asleep with the feel of her lips on cheek or forehead. Never since her death had she come to him like this. Often indeed she had called out to him or spoken a few words—for it does not need death to leave so clear a memory of tone that it substantiates itself when our minds are distraught—and when this had occurred he had started up in bed and spoken to her lovingly, only to find that the ghost voice faded as his mind filled with thought, even as visions fade in broad daylight.

But there was no doubting this physical reality of her, and he did not question, did not startle. He lay perfectly still, as often he had lain when a child to deceive her, all his unutterable yearning now transforming itself into wile. This was she. His body was transfigured at her touch, become a thing of radiance and lightness like a dewdrop on a leaf. Her lips bent to his face. They brushed him softly and whispered as they did so one word. Her embrace relaxed, her hand drew the clothes more snugly about him; then he could resist the temptation no longer. He must, must, must see her; he turned his head, and there she was as she had been in life. She was smiling with a melancholy tenderness that was infinitely wise and infinitely remote. But everything was uncertain in the dim yellow light. His eyes burned their way into the cloud of light in which her face had been, and now it was not that she seemed to fade, but that she seemed never to have been there. There was a faint sweetness in the room.

He rose, shivering with delight, tears of delight and exultation streaming from his eyes. In the darkness he fished out his pants from beneath the mattress, his boots from under the bed, and hurried them on.

He fumbled his way on tiptoe down the long dark creaking stairs. He opened the door and went briskly up the quay, crossed the bridge, and climbed Blarney Lane, all strangely savage and deserted in a darkness tinged with grey. Before dawn he found himself on the hills over the city. The fences rustled dryly at each side, cows coughed away in the fields. He walked fast without hurrying. At last he climbed a wall and picked his way through stones and tall grass to the edge of a hill. Here he threw himself down, the uncut grass drenching his knees.

He saw the dawn forming in a cloud above the distant city, not a rosy dawn as on the day before, but a grey, furtive, rainy dawn that seemed as though it were coming for the first time to light a depeopled earth. The river, winding its snake-like coil along miles of valley, gleamed faintly beneath him between its old time-scarred trees, melancholy alders and bowed elms and willows that trailed their leaves in the water. The stones and crosses about him showed more clearly now, faintly derisive, as it were night's monument set in the coming day. The graveyard was full of queer sounds, rustlings, creakings, and droppings. But to all this he gave no heed. When the sun rose he removed some of the wet leaves and sops that clung to him and went back as he had come, meeting no one but an old man and his son, who with a shovel and pick on their shoulders passed him at the top of Blarney Lane. They looked after him curiously.

Then he went back to the Dolls' House.

As he reached the foot of the stairs he saw Dona Nobis come out of his room with a cup and saucer in her hand. Clearly in doubt whether or not it was he, she stood waiting for him at the head of the stairs.

'Well, well, well,' she said—her usual greeting—'is that yourself! A nice fright you're after giving me! I was bringing you in a cup of tea.'

'How did you know I was home?' he asked. 'It was too late when I got back last night or I'd have dropped in to you.'

If he had said 'darling' he could scarcely have conveyed more of his love for her.

'I heard the old alarmer ringing for further orders, so I thought you must be dead tired not to get up and stop it. Come on and drink this cup of tea before it gets cold on you.'

As he took it from her she gave a little squeal.

'Child of grace,' she cried, 'you look as if you were on a batter. Come here till I have a look at you.'

Peering at his face, she glaumed him roughly all over.

'You're drenched to the skin! Come in to the fire this instant, and take off them things till I dry them for you.'

She pushed him into the room before her, protesting.

'I'll be late for mass, Miss Daly,' he complained, shivering.

'I'll engage you'll be late for more than one if I don't get them clothes dry in time,' she said firmly. 'You and your mass! If you got a fine big cold out of it, church, chapel, or meeting wouldn't see you for a while.'

She put him seated on an old rocking-chair before the fire and cheerfully heaped on more coal. Then talking indignantly to herself she fetched him an old coat of her own.

'Give us a call when you're out of them,' she said. 'And take off your singlet and your drawers as well. Lord knows, what a notion you took to go swimming! A big boy like you, one'd think you'd have more sense.'

A bedraggled figure, shyly endeavouring to hide his long neck, hung with scapulars, Agnus deis, and medals, in the fur collar and his dirty legs under the chair, he called her in. Singing a hymn in her cracked voice, she loaded two chairs with his wet clothes and set herself to prepare his breakfast. As she knelt at one corner of the fire making toast she looked up at him through the steam of his clothes and smiled.

'On my soul,' she said, 'you're a picture! You are indeed! Put your toes in there to the fire and don't be getting your death on me. Now what notion overtook you to go rambling at that hour of the morning?'

'It was my mother, Miss Daly,' he said shyly.

'What about your mother?'

'I saw her last night.'

She took the news quietly, only turning her eyes to the fire not to appear as though she were watching him.

'And where did you go?'

'I went up to the cemetery.'

'Thought you'd like a bit of a promenade.' She laughed girlishly to hide her surprise and embarrassment.

'I did not, then,' he replied gravely. 'I wanted to be near her.'

'Bad cess to it for a fire,' she said testily, scraping the toast.

'Did she look what you might call uneasy?' she asked a moment later.

'No,' he said thoughtfully, 'I wouldn't say she looked uneasy, Miss Daly, only sad.'

'All the same, Phil, I'd have a mass said for her in Melleray if I was you.'

'Why?' he asked. 'Do you think it's that?'

She shrugged her shoulders.

''Tis hard saying if the likes of us don't get our purgatory over us in this life, but, sure, not judging her, isn't it better to be sure than sorry?'

'If it was that I'd have known before,' he said. 'She wouldn't have waited so long without letting me know.'

'God's clocks aren't our clocks,' she replied. 'What's a lifetime to us is only a second to Him.'

He shook his head.

'All the same, I don't think it was the way she wanted prayers, Miss Daly. I'd have known it.'

'What was it, then?'

He looked at her, reddening.

'I think she's uneasy about me.'

'About you?'

'Yes!'

He covered his face with his hands.

'She have a deal to worry her,' said Dona Nobis stoutly. 'I never flattered man or mortal, Phil Dinan, but if I was your mother, God rest her, 'twould take an earthquake to shift me out of my comfortable grave.'

He shook his head again, shivering and brushing back with his hands the skin of his temples.

'I don't know. I was very restless in myself last night, Miss Daly.'

'And what's being restless, would you tell me? Aren't we all restless one time or another? When you're my age and seen what I seen, Phil, a fit of restlessness won't worry you. Take it from me, it was only being tired made you like that, and a good sleep and a dose of salts is all you need. By your colour you had enough outing to air a week's laundry. Pull your chair in to the table now and take your breakfast. I'm sorry I haven't something tasty for you, but I didn't know when you'd be home.'

'I wish I thought you were right,' he said, meekly obeying her.

'Of course I'm right.'

She was imagining something now, he knew. Like every one else she took it for granted that he was in love with Mary Kate. It was extraordinary how every one connected him immediately with her, even Dona Nobis who ought to have known better than to confuse his admiration for Mary Kate with true Christian love which bound two souls together here and in the world to come. People's blindness, he concluded, was astonishing.

'Almighty God, honour and praise to His holy name,' continued Dona Nobis firmly, 'may take us from one state and put us into another for His own wise ends, and so long as we have a good conscience wouldn't we be fools to quarrel with what He has in store for us?'

'I don't know,' he replied, ravenously attacking the fresh toast. 'If we could be certain that He wanted it—but how are we to know it mightn't be a temptation?'

'Ah, go to Jericho with your temptations!' she exclaimed testily. 'As if He had nothing better to do with His time than make hares of us! I'm telling you, Phil Dinan, there's such a thing as being too conscientious, and I know some who lost every tack of grace they had, crossackling with their consciences. . . . Now finish your breakfast and tell me how Mary Kate is getting on.'

'She's at home,' said Phil, his mouth full.

'Mary Kate?' she cried, starting to her feet.

He nodded.

'She came back with you?'

'Last night.'

'Well! Of all the elopements! How did ye get back?'

'Lifts,' he replied laconically.

'Ye did!'

He nodded again, enjoying her astonishment with boyish pleasure.

'We footed some of the way too.'

Dona Nobis broke into a cackle of pleased mirth.

'Well, of all I ever heard of! She couldn't remain behind you?'

'It wasn't that either. I'll tell you, Miss Daly, because I know you won't tell any one. It was the way the man they let on to be her father—he wasn't her father at all.'

There was a long silence.

Dona Nobis nodded three or four times at the fire. 'Well, well, well, well! Oughtn't that Babe Matthews one be burned? Oh, believe me, wait till I lay me hands on her! No wonder you're blind and stupid, you poor boy. And Mary Kate the innocent girl, and she so proud of herself and all! Well, well, well!'

'It was an awful thing right enough,' said Phil. 'Because the way it was, Mary Kate was after getting fond of him.'

'Ah, rubbish!' said Dona Nobis impatiently.

'Oh, she was!'

'Rubbish!' she said again. 'Have sense! Mary Kate is that age when you couldn't trust her alone with a babe in arms, not to mind an old man. It's not that I'm thinking of, but what that bitch—God forgive me for calling her out of her name—was exposing her own daughter to. Only for the mercy of the Lord that sent you up there.'

'It opened my eyes,' said Phil gravely.

'It did,' said Dona Nobis. 'It made a man of you.'

Phil finished his breakfast, dressed, and heard ten o'clock mass at Saint Augustine's. Then he went reluctantly to the shop. Gregory was sitting disconsolate there, on a bench, his hat on the back of his head. He was smoking his old pipe and the floor about him was aflow with spits.

'Thanks be to the good goodness you're back,' he exclaimed in a hollow voice. 'Such a three days of it I never put down.'

'You weren't in form?' suggested Phil.

'Form? I was not then, in form. And such work! There's a half a dozen tables alone for you to cart home, and as many more if I could only put my hand to them. I dunno what misfortune is on me these days.' He shot out the sooluck from his pipe and looked up despairingly at Phil, his eyes suspiciously moist and bloodshot. 'He didn't as much as leave one sharp or serviceable tool in the place,' he whispered poignantly.

'He's getting busy,' said Phil light-heartedly.

'Now let me alone! Before, if he came for a morning 'twas as much as you were likely to see of him, but now he's here night, noon, and morning, and for days on end.'

Phil began his day's work by carting home the recently sold furniture on his little hand-cart. He splashed through mud, holding the shafts as if they were plough handles. And in the main street he met Mary Kate with Mrs. Verschoyle. He raised his cap to them and trudged on.

'Who was that nice young man?' asked Mary Verschoyle, looking after him.

'That's Phil I came back with,' said Mary Kate.

'Goodness! You might have introduced him.'

'He wouldn't like me to do that.'

'And why not, may I ask? Is it because he's pushing a barrow?'

Mary Verschoyle was always roused by a suggestion of social inequality as applied to people she was interested in.

'Oh, no,' exclaimed Mary Kate quite truthfully, 'that wouldn't worry him,' but she wilted at the thought of explaining just *why* Phil would not care to have been introduced.

'Ask him up to tea to-morrow evening.'

'He wouldn't come.'

'I'll ask him, then. And you'll see whether he won't come, young woman.'

Mary Verschoyle snapped her jaws determinedly.

Phil, luckily for his own peace of mind, was unaware of this new danger, and completed the three or four journeys that were to be his morning's work. He was glad of the opportunity of being alone and in the open air. Already the immediate effect of his vision had worn off like that of a dream, but even as the course of our day is set by the invisible Captain in sleep, so Phil's waking mind even when most distracted was dominated by the feeling of his mother's nearness to him. It was subdued to an almost melting tenderness verging upon rapture. The commonest things drew his attention. For the first time in years he loved the people about him, regardless of whether they were saints or sinners; he liked the hang and dash of the women's shawls, the screaming of dirty children, the indolent grouping of men's relaxed faces at the mouths of tunnel-like alleys, the splash and roll of carts in the muddy thoroughfares. Mixed with this tenderness was awe, awe before the transitoriness of it all. He had been a helpless child about these streets; at this little shop with the crowded window his mother, one Christmas Eve, had bought him a toy train out of the four shillings she had collected as Christmas box. To the white church on the opposite side of the river she had

brought him next day, that he might give his toy to the
Infant Jesus to play with in the manger, and coming
away they had passed through a drunken, blasphemous
crowd. Yet even this crowd was gone. All the screaming, turbulent, intense life that had been here when he
was a child seemed beautiful now, yet it was gone.

The women to whom he delivered the furniture were
glad to open conversation with him, and for once he
did not hold himself back. Dark and simple and
attractive, he sat in their kitchens, hands in the pockets
of his overalls, legs outstretched. At the last house he
visited the housekeeper made tea for him and herself;
he sat in to table and drank it, all the while in some
inexplicable way trembling with eagerness to please
her, to say amusing, kind, and flattering things to her.
He talked fast, describing as he had described twice
already—it seemed the thing they liked best to hear—
the fair at Coolboy, the big nigger with his gleaming
muscles, the Dubliner with the willow pattern unbreakable crockery, and Peter with his jokes that
caused them all such delight. While an older, darker,
wiser Phil gloomed threateningly over his shoulder
and said mockingly, 'That's right, that's right! Make
a proper idiot of yourself as you're about it.'

Outside he cursed himself for a fool. He had made
a promise, or half a promise, to return, only half in-
tending to keep it. All the things he had ever avoided
doing he seemed to be doing now. Where was his
bluntness, his taciturnity, his inward peace? Dispersed
into the things and people about him with his shy,
boyish smile. And indignation with himself increased
until it dropped into reverie.

XXIII

NEXT morning he went off to work in gloomy mood, all the excitement of the previous day worn off. On the evening before he had made his round of the city churches as usual, visiting this time the little chapel on the road to Curraghkippane graveyard, but crushing down the temptation to go near it, a temptation that became so acute as he walked in twilight up the road he had travelled in the morning that it almost suffocated him. Turning his back on the graveyard, he spoke to his mother, telling her passionately that he would, he must, think of her not in that way, but in the way of the spirit. She was in heaven, not there, and he was a soul travelling after her not into the earth, but to heaven. And this denial, while he made it, gave him peace.

Then had come hours of intense spiritual dryness. He had struggled, and the struggle hurt him physically. It seemed to leave an ache in his side. He argued at length with himself, but argument only sank him deeper into despair, because he did not know what it was that he wished to argue out of himself. There was no change in him that he could see, nor was there any change in his circumstances. Quite coldly he asked himself could he have been in love with Mary Kate, and was the pain he had felt when she told him of her love for Nick McCormick pain at losing her; and quite coldly answered himself that he was not in the least in love with her.

He was in no humour to welcome Mary Verschoyle, whose tumultuous entry frightened even that sly sprite Selim so much that his presence in the workshop could scarcely be apprehended. Phil was shy and angry, Mrs. Verschoyle was obstinate and amused, old Gregory was exalted as if his visitor had been an angel suddenly dropped at him through the ceiling, and to all Phil's objections that he couldn't go out to tea, that he had no clothes, that he had other appointments, the old man replied with snorts, taunts, and cajolery. Spinning round Phil and Mary Verschoyle, squatting on his hunkers to look up into Phil's face of alarm, he bombarded him with speeches calculated to impress the lady.

'Shy he is, ma'am,' he sniggered, 'shy he is. Yourself and your work! Sure, what work do you do here? Didn't I get on without you for three mortal days while you went pegging all over the country after a bit of a petticoat? Didn't I? Didn't I? A lot you thought about your work then! Skirts you were thinking about, damsels you were thinking about, you sanctimonious young blackguard!—Don't mind one thing he tells you, ma'am; you couldn't believe daylight from that fellow. Too much of a lady's man he is. Still waters! Still waters! And his pretty little red cheeks like a girl's!—Ahadie, let on you're not blushing now, will you? Now, now, Phil boy, don't be cross! . . . He have no clothes, do you hear that, ma'am? Now isn't he the dead spit of one of the young lords you'd see on the papers? Isn't he?'

Against attack like this, coupled as it was with Mary Verschoyle's shrill jokes, it would have been folly to fight, and Phil, politely, though with an inward sense of violation, surrendered. Then Gregory showed Mary Verschoyle about the workshop. He adopted a lordly air, and to display his contempt for the sort of work he was compelled to do, and which his finer nature rebelled against, scornfully gave chairs and tables alike a series of resounding kicks.

'Look at that old crock of a table now,' he said; 'that's the sort of work a man like me has to do for a living. To compete with machines, that's what they're driving us to. Well, you see, ma'am, the lower classes, the common people, as you might say, have no taste. Any sort of old dirt will do for them so long as they get it cheap. Cheapness, that's all they think about, and meantime a man that has a soul for higher things has to be a slave to them. Sometimes I lie awake and think of the beautiful things I could be making only for that scum. Scum, ma'am, scum, that's what they are.'

When he had escorted Mrs. Verschoyle to the road, he came back wiping his brow with a dirty old handkerchief. He was aglow. He lit his pipe afresh with trembling hands.

'What do you think of that, boy? What do you think of that? Who said Gregory Mahon doesn't know how to talk round a lady? You'll see, Philip Dinan'—this with a great smack on Phil's shoulder-blades—'you'll see the effect my words will have. And you, you—you—cold monster, refusing to go up to her house. My God, you were near throwing away the chance of a lifetime.'

He loosened his collar with mortal anguish.

'God above, if I wasn't here to look after you, look what you'd have done! That woman could make your fortune. Instead of Tim and Patch you could be working for all the swanks of Montenotte. And you'd spend your life making old tables and chairs, dirty, insignificant, contemptible little articles, instead of making lovely nicknacks for Sir John and Lady Goldsmith. I can see them, inlay—I never showed you how that's done—cabinets, tallboys, bedroom suites, upholstery. We could have three hands and ten apprentices working in this shop. Ten apprentices, and charge them twenty pounds apiece! Two hundred pounds! I'd make you my partner and leave you to bring in the trade. You need never do a stroke of work again.'

'Ah, you're crazy,' said Phil testily.

'Crazy? I'm crazy?' Old Gregory grew almost apoplectic with excitement. His fists clenched, he pounded out a furious tattoo on the work bench and rolled his eyes to heaven in frenzy. 'Listen to him, You God, correcting me that's old enough to be his grandfather! I tell you again you're mad! Mad, that's what you are. You don't know what a woman like that would do for you if she took a fancy to you. She'd introduce you to every toff in Montenotte, and how do you know if you handled her right but she'd find you a wife with a stocking? . . . Listen to me, Phil, my own lovely boy! Phil, I always admired you. I was the first man that ever saw what was in you. I prophesied you'd be a Rothschild, didn't I? Don't deny it, I prophesied that.'

'You did,' said Phil timidly. He was almost afraid of the anguish in Gregory's eyes, and fully convinced that in a moment the old man would launch himself about his neck.

'I did. And now, Phil, I never asked anything of you before, but at this moment I beg and beseech you —be nice to her. Don't let her see the black strake in you. I implore you, Phil; I'll go down on me two bended knees to you, only don't cross her. Whatever she asks you to do, Phil boy, do it with a smile.'

'All right, all right,' said Phil crossly, the dark suggestion implicit in this going by him, 'leave us get on with that couple of chairs.'

'Chairs? I will not go on with any old dirty chairs. There's a lovely bit of American oak somewhere, if only I could lay my hands on it. Have a look round for it, Phil, till I see could I make anything out of it. A little present now would——'

'You threw that out six months ago.'

'Did I? Did I? As sure as fate I did? . . . Never mind, Phil, never mind, boy. Go on with that old dirt and I'll do a couple of little drawings that will take the sight out of your eyes. You'll see what I can do when I'm roused.'

That evening found Phil at Verschoyle's. He had not changed out of his working clothes; had done nothing, in fact, but wash under the cold tap in the yard. His hair was untidy and streaked with water, and deliberately he was far from being Phil at his best. But he showed no embarrassment. That was what impressed Mary Verschoyle about him, as, in a different way, it impressed Mary Kate. His bearing gave the impression of a compulsory family visit, and the compulsion did not alter the fact that he was quite at ease.

His hostess knew as much as Mary Kate had chosen to tell of the reason for Phil's lightning visit to Dublin, and had had described to her the way in which McCormick had struck Phil ('The dirty unscrupulous bully,' said Mrs. Verschoyle), and the way Phil had replied by up and giving him a crack with the poker; of this initiative she was highly enamoured, almost as much as of Phil's reputed sanctity. She resolutely endeavoured to keep the conversation on Nick McCormick, and as resolutely Phil, with one eye on Mary Kate, side-tracked it. He knew that Mary Kate must be suffering agonies at the thunders loosed on the head of Nick, 'that debauched and conscienceless rascal' as the other woman called him. Of course, in this defective version of the story Phil was made doubly to shine, and a mild glory was reflected from him on to Mrs. Verschoyle, who had seen it all coming.

'It's absurd for a young man like you,' she said at last, 'to waste his time at the sort of work you're doing. You should be in a responsible position where you'd have scope for your initiative.'

'That's what I told him,' chimed in Mary Kate with relief. 'I told you you were wasting your time, Phil.'

'You did,' he replied coolly, draining his second cup; 'and I told you that was what I wanted.'

'You'd rather be a carpenter?' asked Mary Verschoyle in consternation.

Phil nodded, and at that moment she pounced.

'Well, you won't even be a carpenter, take that from me. Your boss is a dolt.'

'He's an idiot,' added Mary Kate with enjoyment.

'He has no more idea of carpentry than I have of'—

she paused to choose a subject of which she need not
be too ashamed to confess her ignorance—'of astro-
nomy.' She laughed a gay, infectious laugh, coloured
with an infinite complacency. 'You needn't think I
was taken in by his ravings; I wasn't; not a bit.' She
paused and with trembling fingers lit a cigarette, her
eyes half shut, her brows puckered seriously over it,
then she laughed once more and blew a gay wreath
of smoke towards the ceiling. 'Not a bit,' she repeated
with gusto. 'There wasn't a thing that he showed me
that was fit for the lunatic ward of a workhouse hospital. I know a thing or two about furniture' (What is
it I don't know something about? she seemed to ask).
'Besides . . . I always distrust people who run down the
lower classes. Take it from me'—she pushed the open
packet of cigarettes towards him—'take it from me,
your boss is a fool.'

'He's not a fool,' said Phil.

'I distrust people who run down the lower classes,'
repeated Mary Verschoyle with rigid emphasis, grind-
ing the used match into the ash-tray and tapping out a
tentative rhythm with her finger tips.

'He didn't mean to,' said Phil.

'Of course he didn't. He only said it because he
thought that, being a Protestant, I'd be fool enough to
like it.'

'That's it,' admitted Phil quickly, impressed in spite
of himself by her unfeminine acuteness.

'Of course it is. Well, I don't like it. I don't like it
a bit. And I warn you that whatever he tells you, you'll
never learn anything from him.'

'My goodness,' said Phil, almost hurt that she
should have such a low opinion of his intelligence, 'I

know that quite well. I'm a better carpenter than he is myself.'

She was taken aback.

'And still you stay on there?'

'I stay on there,' said Phil, roused to retaliation by her domineering tone, 'because it suits me to stay on.'

'And you have no wish to get on? You have no ambition at all?'

'I have ambition.'

'And you think you'll have scope for it in that—that hole?'

'I do.'

'And that other filthy den you live in, that even Mary Kate can't stick?'

'It's the only place I would have scope.'

'I don't believe one word of it,' she answered shrilly, whirling sideways in her chair with wrath; 'not one word of it.'

'Because you don't know what I mean.'

'I know perfectly well what you mean,' she retorted, her voice rising still higher. 'Thank God I've still my wits about me, boy. And if you think you can be a saint or anything else in that stinking garret you're very much mistaken. You'll rot there, body and soul. You're rotting already, only you don't know it. You're too perverse to see yourself.'

Phil sat silent under this last accusation. Then she swept the cigarettes towards her and rose, smiling.

'Come out into the garden,' she said, 'and bring a chair with you.'

Phil realised after a few minutes that she was not dependent upon the garden for her inspiration, but carried her surroundings about somewhere inside her;

that neither garden nor flowers distracted her from her original intention of flattening him into surrender. Her passion for interference was like a logician's pursuit of an idea, and it absorbed her utterly, even giving her a certain nobility by its very abstractness. To his dismay he found that he was slowly surrendering, not indeed his belief—that was unthinkable—but his prejudice against Protestants generally, above all, against this particular Protestant who smoked, dabbled in spiritualism, was more than half an atheist, and had deliberately tried to sap Mary Kate's faith.

'Mind,' she said, in the tone of a sibylline oracle, 'I'm warning you solemnly, as I warned Mary Kate, you'll regret this.' She pointed a minatory finger at him. 'You'll leave that shop. You'll leave it whether you like it or not. And what's more, you'll leave that wretched garret of yours.'

Then he laughed. For a moment she looked at him in surprise. Suddenly she laughed too.

XXIV

PHIL'S reaction was not long in coming. For a few
hours he was pleased, diverted, giving way to a feeling
of amused tenderness for this strange woman. All this
he revealed to Dona Nobis, sitting by her fire that
night. A strange figure she looked too, brooding, head
and shoulders forward, hands on lap in the half darkness, her prominent mouth set out from the rest of her
face by the thick lips and the one great tooth. One
realised she was growing older, and the older the more
like a sibyl, much as the poet has described her, 'high
and hollow and burnt out'.

'What did I tell you?' she nodded. 'Didn't I always
tell you not to be running down the Protestants until
you knew them. Believe you me, you'd get better turns
from them than you'd get from your own.'

'Still,' he said, 'they're not our own.'

'Nobody says they are, child, but aren't they as the
good God made them?'

'They've all cold, snibby faces.'

'Well, they didn't make their faces either, did they?
And if I was depending on looks to keep the life in me
I wouldn't be long outside the poorhouse walls.'

Phil remembered that though Dona Nobis vigorously denounced Protestant errors with copious refer-
ences to abstruse theological tracts, and knew to a

nicety the number of Catholics burned or hanged under 'that bloody jade Eliza', she could never think of the little pension that stood between herself and the workhouse without rising for the defence. So he did not answer her. But she was not to be diverted.

'Are you getting that mass said for your poor mother?' she asked.

'I am.'

'Did you send the money to Mount Melleray?'

'No, to the Franciscans.'

'You might have sent it to Melleray,' she said reproachfully. 'God knows them poor little Trappists, 'tis the least they deserve.'

''Tis all the same.'

'It is *not* all the same, Phil Dinan. I'm very fond of the Franciscans, but it's enough to drive a creature mad to see them old serpents of cheating huxters— God forgive me for saying it!—them rrrrreptiles that would rob an orphan of a penny, leaving hundreds of pounds to fat parish priests, when there isn't ten shillings to stand between the likes of your unfortunate mother and starvation.'

'That's true,' said Phil, moved by the memory of the old musician's dead face.

'It is true,' she cried hotly. 'No wonder the Protestants do be laughing up their sleeves at us half their time. As Miss Littleton said when she seen the six priests after Jackie Roche's coffin, "Bridie, the likes of that scoundrel would need six more."' Her voice suddenly became fierce and pensive. 'He would, and sixty-six, and a hundred and sixty-six on top of that, and the deepest pit of hell wouldn't be hot enough for him after they were finished! 'Tis a shame and a disgrace,

Phil Dinan, and an insult to Almighty God, and I say, as solemnly as if I was standing before His holy throne at this minute, that I don't believe one mass, nor two masses, nor three masses, nor a hundred masses is worth that much to them.'

She snapped her fingers wrathfully. She had suddenly flared up as her way was into a towering biblical rage, which was as clearly evidenced by her tendency to rise in arithmetical progressions as by the energy with which she thumped the bed beside her.

'Ahaha!' she cried, her face flushing up red and wrathful in the firelight, ''tisn't Bridie Daly they're talking to. Not one see of my few ha'pence will they see, and if every one else done what I do it wouldn't be long before the priests came back for their living to the poor. 'Twould be more charity to give a ha'penny to a poor man than to give a pound to one of them. No wonder the Protestants laugh at us! No wonder at all!'

It was some time before Phil got her off her angry Pegasus and back to earth. At last he induced her to sing the *Ave Maris Stella*, and went off to bed, not wholly satisfied with himself or with her. He did not deny that the old charm was wearing thin, that she could no longer be the keeper of his conscience as he had been the keeper of Mary Kate's. At times he envied her. She could work everything off in a towering passion, and then with the best will in the world towards her enemies, settle comfortably down to sing hymns or read a chapter of the *Imitation*. But he could not do that. And his mood of depression grew, accompanied by the same restlessness and the same spiritual dryness as he had experienced two nights before on his return.

He should not have gone to Verschoyle's, he told himself, that was clear. The woman had upset him afresh with her notions. But why was it that he could not be like other people, that even the least break in his routine, the merest visit and friendly talk, should thrust him out of his paradise? He could no longer be satisfied with telling himself that nothing was different; something was, terribly different, and it was inside himself. He had lived in a vacuum, and now, whatever had taken him out of it, he could no more help noticing Mary Verschoyle's abstractness than he could noticing Dona Nobis's childishness, and the mere noting them fed his restlessness.

The next few days produced a terrific effort at concentration. He saw nobody, spoke to nobody, not even to Dona Nobis, went to Holy Communion each morning and performed his round of the city churches each evening. And always he prayed for peace.

Peace seemed to be with him when the terrible thing happened.

One day, just as the angelus rang, the thought came into his mind, 'If mother was before me when I went home!' He passed it off, smiling at his own inconsequence. A quarter of an hour later it returned, but this time as a brazen suggestion. And this time it was a voice that spoke—coldly, clearly. 'Suppose she's there already?' A cold sweat broke out through him. What was this terrible idea that insisted on returning? Of one thing he felt sure: it was temptation in its most insidious form. Now he did not try any longer to lose himself in his work, but prayed hard. At last he found he could contemplate his surroundings afresh. They seemed to push out from him and grew smaller and clearer. The temperature dropped. The window brightened. Everything was bathed in a hard material light that picked out coldly the clean white shirt of old Gregory as he bent above a plank. Phil stood and watched him for a while, and nothing was to be heard but the squeal of the saw and the old man's chesty puffing as he ground his knee into the plank. A blast of cool air swept in and rustled among the shavings. Gregory looked up.

Thank God, thought Phil, it was gone again. And now he envied Dona Nobis her ear for music. He felt he would be all right if like her he could sing when the black thoughts came.

Just as he was putting on his coat at lunch time the voice returned. 'She's there, she's there,' it said. For that moment he could picture her quite clearly, waiting for him in the little upstairs room, sitting at the window, hands in her lap, trying to peer round at the clock face of Shandon. He went pale and shivered.

Gregory looked curiously at him. 'What's wrong with you, Phil?' he asked in a voice of pathetic tenderness.

'Nothing,' said Phil mechanically, but the old man had caught the curious dead set in his eyes as though they had suddenly lost the power of motion.

'What's wrong with you? What's wrong with you, boy?' he shouted, and Phil started awake with the old man's big hands gripping his arms and shaking him violently. He shivered again and came to himself, fixed in resolution.

'I'm all right, Mr. Mahon,' he answered, shaking himself free. 'A bit of a weakness, I think. I won't go home. Would you mind if I made my dinner here?'

'Mind? Why would I mind? Didn't you often make it here before? Take your dinner, and go for a walk to study you. Aisy, a minute,' he added, 'till I get a drop of whiskey for you.'

But Phil was master of himself once more.

'I won't drink whiskey,' he protested. 'I'll go out and get myself a couple of eggs.'

Gregory looked after him with doubt and compassion.

The task of preparing his dinner diverted him once more. He ignored Gregory's suggestion that he should go for a walk. He continued with his work, but when the voice came again about three o'clock, louder and more insistent, it terrified him so much that he immediately began to sing. His queer, loud, tuneless wail made the old man jump, and Phil trailed off as he saw the grey eyes levelled at him. There was silence for a few moments, and then Phil smiled weakly. Gregory dropped the plane with a crash on the work bench.

''Tis a great mind for gaiety you have,' he said.

'Keening the woman next door called it,' Phil replied.

'The first time I ever heard you rise a stave,' the old man continued, with an uneasy laugh. But he kept talking in a purposely loud voice, forcing Phil to reply. About Mary Kate, how she liked being back in Cork, whether she was still staying with the Verschoyles, and what her new job was like.

Phil wondered what made him so curious about her.

He was not troubled again until he opened the front door and found himself in the street. It was a calm evening, misty, cloudy, and still, but for him it was like a hurricane. An invisible current swept him along the quay in the direction of the Dolls' House, swept him along in spite of himself and at twice his usual speed. At the bridge he stopped and clung to an iron railing on the quay wall. It was a desperate effort to regain control of himself. He realised quite clearly that this was an obsession, and realised too that, obsession or no obsession, if he went in now and she were not there he would go out of his mind. He looked up the quay at the cracked gable of the Dolls' House, bulging with its content of human suffering. No, he could not go back there now. He must, must, must beat this thing, wear it out of himself at any cost. With the small quick step of a dipsomaniac passing a familiar public-house he crossed the bridge and made off up the hills.

At the same moment Gregory was knocking at the side door of the large and fashionable drapery shop in which Mary Kate was now employed. She came down to him from her tea, red-cheeked, all in a flurry. For a moment he scarcely recognised her in her tight-fitting black dress with the high collar.

'That boy of yours,' he said at last, gripping her by the shoulder, 'that boy of yours, girl; there's something wrong with him.'

'What boy?' she asked in stupefaction.

'Ah, what boy? How many have you? That boy, Phil Dinan. He's going mad.'

'Phil?' She laughed, and continued laughing into his excited face.

'Do you know what, girl,' he whispered fiercely, 'if you don't stop your giggling I'll give you a clatter about the gob that'll send you staggering.'

On the instant she became serious.

'Now listen to me, girl. That boy is going mad.'

'We're all going mad,' she replied in the endeavour to say something. She was by now convinced that it was old Gregory who was going mad.

'We are,' he agreed with horrible gusto, 'we are, but this is religious madness, and thanks be to the good God we're not all as holy as that yet. Girl, do what I tell you, and go over to the house after him before he'll do himself some harm. Does he shave?'

'He does.'

'Well, put away the razor.'

'You're not serious,' she said, impressed in spite of herself. 'Our Phil? Why, he's a rock of sense.'

'He's no model for sense now, then. Do you think I don't know what 'tis like and my own brother up in the asylum with it?' He drew the skin down from his eye. 'In there I look for it; in there.'

She looked into his dreary red-rimmed eye and began to be frightened.

'All right, so, I'll go across.'

'Do, and hurry, let you!'

She dressed in haste and hurried up the quays to the house. That Phil was going mad she did not believe, but she was afraid lest something else should be wrong. She no longer wholly distrusted Mahon's judgment. On the steps she caught up on Dona Nobis, with an old coat about her returning with a small loaf and a pennorth of milk.

'Did you see Phil, Bridie?' she asked breathlessly.

'I didn't see sight nor light of him these three or four days,' said Dona Nobis. 'He's dodging us all.'

'Oh, Bridie!' cried Mary Kate, with a catch of dismay in her voice.

'What's up with you, child?'

Mary Kate stood on the stairs and held her back with one hand.

'That old idiot Mahon was into the shop to me,' she whispered. 'He says Phil is going dotty.'

'Ah, cock him up with his dotty!' said Dona Nobis coarsely. 'Up in the madhouse he should be himself if the loonies had their rights.'

'He gave me an awful start, all the same,' said Mary Kate, one glove pressed against her mouth.

'See if the boy is in his room, and put them foolish notions out of your head.'

Mary Kate gave the door handle a shake.

'He is not.'

'Would he be inside all the same? You're taller than I am. See is the key on the ledge.'

Mary Kate felt the woodwork above the door.

'It is.'

'Then come in and have a cup of tea and wait for him.'

Mary Kate sat on a chair beside the door, fumbling nervously with her umbrella and gloves while Dona Nobis wet the tea.

'Oh, Bridie, he ought to be back from work long ago. 'Tis a quarter of an hour since old Greg was in with me, and he was gone home then.'

'Ah, for goodness' sake, child, have sense! He probably went into Peter and Paul's on his way back. You're as bad as old Greg yourself.'

'Oh, Bridie!' wailed Mary Kate, 'you're just as frightened as I am. Why did you think he'd lock the door on himself?'

Dona Nobis grunted and got out a fresh cup and saucer from the cupboard in the wall.

'Did you notice anything queer in him?' she asked.

'I didn't see him since the day at Ma Verschoyle's, and he was grand then.'

'That's the night I saw him last.'

'He wasn't queer with you?'

'He wasn't queer, but he was a bit uneasy.'

'It was nothing about me, Bridie?'

'It wasn't anything about you, though indeed, Mary Kate, now that you mention it'—a baleful look reached her from Dona Nobis's lowered eyes—'between you and me and the wall, you ought to be bloody well ashamed of yourself.'

'I know that, Bridie,' said Mary Kate meekly.

'It was about his mother,' said Dona Nobis in the softened voice she always adopted after she had pulled some sinner down a peg. 'He saw her the night he came back.'

'Oh!' The exclamation came in a long-drawn wail from the girl.

'So I told him he ought to get a mass said for her at Melleray.'

'But that's awful!' cried Mary Kate pitiably. 'And you never told us a word about it, Bridie.'

'Set in to the table. . . . I don't see that there's anything awful about it, and it was no business of mine to tell you if he didn't tell you himself.'

'But that's old Greg's words out!'

'Oh, no, Mary Kate.' Dona Nobis laughed with cool appreciation of the joke and cut herself a slice of bread. 'Oh, no, that doesn't follow. As the theologians say, that's a *non sequitur*. I seen a few spirits in my own time, but I wouldn't like any one to say I was dotty. God forbid! At that very table I seen my own father standing on one leg with a Child of Mary Manual in his hand.'

Mary Kate shook her head. She had little faith in the good sense of people who either saw or heard spirits.

'I dunno, Bridie, a ghost isn't a thing I'd like any one belonged to me to see, God between us and all harm!'

'Unfortunately, Mary Kate, we have no choice in the matter.'

She went on about spirits, and Mary Kate listened, the cup in her hand, her little red mouth relaxed into a rosy cave of doubt and dissatisfaction.

'Anyway,' concluded Dona Nobis, ''tis no use shaking hands with the devil before you meet him. Wait'll Phil comes in and we'll see whether he's as bad as you say.'

But she cleared away the tea things and still there was no sign of Phil. Then Mary Kate went upstairs to see her mother and Aunt Dinah. She left the landing door open and listened with ears alert for his step. At half-past eight he had not yet come in. She went down to Dona Nobis again. Even she was now showing signs of the anxiety that had been gnawing her all along. Nine o'clock struck and Mary Kate sank into a brooding silence, shaken with little shivering fits. Dona Nobis sat by the window with her Key of Heaven. She was reading 'Prayers for Certain Eventualities'.

Half an hour passed before they heard Phil's footsteps coming up the stairs. Mary Kate looked at Dona

Nobis, who nodded, looking up over her glasses. They listened, trying to read his mood into the steps. They were slow and heavy. Mary Kate rose, and Dona Nobis motioned her to her chair again.

'Leave him alone for a few minutes,' she said quietly.

They heard him fumble for the key and unlock the door. He went in. Mary Kate tiptoed to the door of Bridie's room and listened. There was no sound.

'You'd better go now,' said Dona Nobis at last.

Very softly Mary Kate opened the door, crossed the landing, and turned the handle of Phil's door. She pushed it in and saw him lying on the bed, his two hands under his head for a pillow. She smiled weakly, her eyes brimming with tears.

'Well, Phil?' she said.

'Well, Mary Kate?'

She closed the door behind her, crossed the room, and put her hand on his forehead. It was fiery hot.

'Tired, Phil?'

'Yes, I am tired,' he said slowly.

She put the candlestick on the mantelpiece and sat on the chair beside his bed.

'What is it, Phil boy?'

He was silent for a moment, and then sighed. She ran her hand gently through his thick dark hair that was dry and wiry as a brush.

'There's something on your mind.'

'There is.'

'And won't you tell me?'

One hand rose from under his head and caught hers.

'I'm afraid I'm going mad, Mary Kate,' he said dryly. She too was silent for a little, then she rose and began to unlace his boots. While she removed them he looked up at her, a look that was pitiful only in its tearlessness. She took off her wide straw hat and put it on the table, fluffing out her hair.

'I'll go and make you a cup of tea,' she said.

Though it was too dark for Dona Nobis to be reading as she sat beside the window, she looked up over her glasses as the girl entered, and Mary Kate responded with a helpless shrug. She rinsed out the teapot into the slop bucket. Dona Nobis scratched her nose and rose slowly, put her spectacles on the mantelpiece beside her prayer-book, and took up the kettle. She filled it outside at the landing tap. Mary Kate put on fresh coal. Then she went back to Phil's room and brought out a loaf and butter. She took one slice of bread and Dona Nobis a second. Once the latter said, "'Tis a bad fire for toasting,' poked it, and a few minutes later rose and lit the lamp. They divided the labour silently between them. Again Dona Nobis said, 'Bad cess to that Vaughan woman! Wouldn't she give you a headache the way she rocks that child?' as she slashed the toast and cut it into neat fingers. Mary Kate wet the tea and boiled an egg.

'Sit up and eat this, boy,' she said cheerfully as she brought in Phil's meal. The room was in darkness. From outside came the faint green light of a gas lamp, the red and blue of a hoarding, the shine of the white quay walls and the glint of a seagull's wing. She lit the bracketed oil lamp and hung from two hooks on the window the bit of bagging that served for a curtain.

As she did so Phil sat up and swung his stockinged feet over the edge of the bed. She filled him out his

tea and put the plate of toast beside him on the quilt.
She sat in her old place near him, nervously fumbling
with her cheap rings. She took back the egg-cup from
him and put it on the mantelpiece beside her, then
took his cup and filled it afresh. When he had finished
she put them all away on the table, and Phil buried
his face in his hands.

'Is the light too strong for you?' she asked.

'You may as well out it,' he said in a half voice.

She quenched the lamp and took down the bagging
again. He lay back on the bed.

'Take off your clothes now and lie down properly,'
she commanded.

'I'm all right.'

'You won't go into work to-morrow.'

'I'll have to. 'Twould be better for me than moping.'

She knew he was right.

'I'll come and take you out for a long walk to-
morrow night,' she said.

He murmured something she did not catch.

'Would you be all right if I left you now, Phil?'

'I'll be all right, Mary Kate.'

'I'll be killed when I get back to the shop. You
won't be uneasy?'

'I'm dropping asleep already.'

'I'll turn my back, Phil love, and let you get into
bed properly before I go. I won't sleep a wink if I
have to leave you like this. Come on now like a good
boy, and I'll help you off with your coat and vest.'

Half joking, half caressing, she lifted him up in the
bed and obediently he let her help him off with his
coat and vest. She heard him fumbling with his collar
and tie, and knew by his heavy breathing and his

helpless, half-dazed manner that he was drugged with sleep. She pulled the braces down from his shoulders and took off his stockings. She stood at the window while he got off his pants. She tried to adjust her hat looking into the dark window-pane. She heard him get into bed and stretch himself with a sigh of content. Then she bent over him, drew the blanket up about him, kissed him on the forehead, and went quietly away. Dona Nobis was standing on the dark landing and startled Mary Kate with the hand she laid on her arm.

'Did you get him into bed?' she whispered.

'I did. I think he'll go asleep all right now.'

'Thanks be to God! You're a great little woman, Mary Kate. 'Tis the best thing for him.'

''Tis.'

''Tis so. He might sleep it over.'

'He might.'

'Are you going now, Mary Kate?'

'I am. I'll be killed.'

'Never fear. I'll keep an eye to him for you.'

Twice that night Phil woke to find some one bending above him and drawing the clothes securely about his shoulders and feet. But he knew it was not his mother, because the face in the candlelight was the face of Dona Nobis. He will scarcely ever know how many times she came unnoticed by him, though not indeed by the neighbours, who judged that Phil was unwell, and said, 'God knows, it was astonishing the nature that old regulator had for him, and she without chick, child, or cherub belonging to her.'

XXV

HE woke late next morning to see a rainy sky. He looked at the alarm clock, which alone in that greyness preserved its pert and shining face. It was nearly nine o'clock; he had forgotten to wind the alarm and had slept it out. His first impulse was to jump out of bed, but a deeper impulse fixed him there. It was an impulse that sprang from the memory of Dona Nobis's face in the candlelight and Mary Kate's in the twilight, two women's faces palely swimming before his eyes in anxiety and affection. Then it all came back to him. He had been going mad, and had walked and walked until he was well beyond the city. Then he had begun to run. He had beaten that fit, but not altogether. Within him, for all his exhaustion, a spark of it had lingered as he climbed the stairs, and the opening of the door on his deserted room had plunged him into utter melancholy. He was better now, the melancholy had gone, but the fear of it had not; a new necessity had arisen in him, the necessity for being still.

Dona Nobis came in with his breakfast on a tray. Her face was shining with joviality.

'Ahadie!' she cried girlishly, 'he's still there.'

'I slept it out, Miss Daly,' he said weakly. 'I'm ashamed of myself.'

'You should read what Saint Teresa have to say

273

about sleeping it out!' she cried. 'That'd open your eyes for you. I can tell you that one was no believer in early hours.'

'I'm a plague to you,' he said, lifting himself in the bed. 'You were in with me during the night.'

'I was sure, and 'twas a great trial of me. Mary Kate said you'd a bit of a cold, and I was in dread like all boys you'd leave yourself uncovered.'

As always, he took such a statement literally.

'I had not a cold,' he said, frowning. 'It was the way I was taking leave of my senses.'

'Taking leave of your senses?' She laughed harshly, throwing back her head. 'Well, well, God give you more sense and me more money! Wait till you're my age and 'twill be time enough to talk of that. 'Twas nothing but a fit of depression, Phil Dinan. Maybe 'tis the way you're taking influenza depression, like I had the time they said I was going dotty and wanted to put me up in the Big House. You take my advice, child, and rest yourself, and don't worry your innocent head about what don't concern you, and you'll find and see 'twill pass.'

She took her stand at the foot of his bed, lecturing him while he ate, her left hand gripping the bedrail and shaking it to and fro, her right going like a windmill. And he was so guileless that even this did not cause him to suspect that while he lay sleeping Dona Nobis had been consulting her oracles.

''Tis a fact well known to saints and theologians,' she declaimed, 'that spiritual depression is a sign we're forcing our nature to do something we're not able for, and Saint John of the Cross and Saint Teresa and all reliable authorities agree that we must wait till we're strong enough before we begin to fight it. As Saint John says, a soul like that must face old Nick on a full belly, and 'tis on this very point Saint Teresa is laying down the law when she advises the soul not to mind a bit of mortal weakness like sleeping it out of a morning. And as I often told you before now, Phil, she was never one to speak without consulting a theologian, though she was no poll-parrot herself, by the same token.'

It is doubtful whether any advice to one in spiritual anguish is of any use whatever. When Phil rose and went to late mass and later turned in to work there was a voice in him that warned him far more clearly than the voice of Dona Nobis what course he must take. Something inside himself, some instinct that was free of his will, slackened his motions, deadened his usually purposeful step, and stilled even the fervour of his prayer. And he was aware of this, and whatever Saint Teresa or Saint John of the Cross might say in palliation, the knowledge caused him intense grief. It was as if he saw all the years of effort, of concentration, slipping away from his powerless hands. The years of adolescence and young manhood were passing into nothing, and he realised all too clearly that if the process continued, a few months would see him spiritually a child again.

How many of us, even when most we rhapsodise of childhood, would be prepared to become children once more, and begin once more the endless succession of trials—foolish joys and equally foolish sorrows —by which we have become men? Not one. Bad as our state may be now, the chances of our reaching even this state again seem infinitely remote. A miracle, or many miracles, made us men; in submitting our-selves to the humiliation of rejuvenescence we cannot count on miracles.

This was what Phil tried to explain, that same even-ing, to Mary Kate, a good listener, though her methods of reasoning were dubious and incalculable. Fear had for once shaken him out of his silence. There had been a long argument before they started out. Phil had wanted a road with chapels, and Mary Kate, schooled by Dona Nobis, would have none of them.

And so they wandered up the hills like any young courting couple. The rain had all but stopped and a last flash of sun came out, but there was a high wind blowing. Autumn was on them almost before they knew it. The city glowed beneath them, its thousand roofs a steely glitter, its river a dull ribbon of slate and brown; spires washed, everything clear cut like a child's drawing, from the bars on the cell windows of the jail to the grey thread that spanned the river and carried an insect-like procession of vehicles and figures. The steep lanes they followed ran quick with sand-coloured streamlets, and the fences, tossed by the wind, splashed them without mercy. Mary Kate walked doubled up against the wind, hands in the pockets of her mackintosh holding down her dress.

'God knows,' she said with heathen gusto, 'I don't know from Adam what grudge you have against the world.'

'I have no grudge against the world,' he answered patiently, his lowered eyes seeking hers. 'I have so little grudge against it that I want to live in it.'

'Well, *do* live in it! You hate the world. You hate the

people in it. One'd think by the way you talk that there was no release for you until you got out of it.'

'I don't hate the world, Mary Kate. If I did I'd have no dread of living in it. What's wrong with me is, I'd become too fond of it if I left myself.'

'There's a deal of fear!'

'There is fear. Here I am, after all the trouble I had getting a grip of myself, seeing it all go for nothing.'

'You're damned altogether going walking with the likes of me,' she shouted gaily.

'It isn't that, Mary Kate.'

'Well, 'tis uncommonly like it,' she screamed again, running a step or two ahead of him, and facing back to walk on tiptoe, leaning on the wind. At this her dress made a frantic attempt to blow about her waist, and she laughed recklessly as she tried to keep it in place and talk to him at the same time. Her face was aflame and sprinkled with shower drops as if with tears. His own face was crimson as he turned away his eyes.

'I can never make out why you have to live like that, Phil. Denying yourself every little thing you'd have a liking for. Can't you live well without an alarm clock? Even Dona Nobis hasn't one. Sure, if we all lived like you what sort of a world would it be? . . . Ah, damn you, you idiot, keep down!' she chuckled gaily to her insubordinate attire.

He quickened his pace till he was level with her. Then she staggered with pretended weariness and clung to his arm, letting him guide her backwards up the hill. She went on tiptoe, looking down at the bright flooded city between its hills.

'It isn't necessary for some people,' he explained gravely. 'It isn't necessary for Miss Daly, because she never had a bad thought in her life; and it isn't necessary for you, because you're good without it. I don't believe you ever did a really wrong thing as long as I know you, and you don't understand the danger there is for the likes of me.'

Mary Kate drew in a deep breath and giggled fiercely deep down in herself. Honestly, she said to herself, was there any end to the simplicity of men? She raised a laughing face to the tormented sky.

'You're a caution!' she said inconsequentially. And then with a change of tone, 'Don't you want to run against that wind?'

'I do not.'

'Well, I do, and I'm going to. I'll run you to the corner.' She caught at his sleeve. 'Come on, come on, you melancholy lump.'

Laughing, she dragged him by the elbow until he began to run with her. Then she flew off from him, doubled up against the blast, her dress blowing, her long thin legs covering the ground like a greyhound's. Phil increased his speed. At that moment he didn't want to let her beat him. He was in better training than she. She screamed when she heard him close behind her; next moment he was passing her out. She made a grab at his coat tails, but he turned and loosened her grasp on him. He was at the corner long before her, but by that time she had ceased to run.

'What do I have to give you for that?' she asked tauntingly.

He was silent and she was silent. They were over the hill and on the slope of a wide valley stretching up to Blarney. It was filling with shadows, and the white gateposts that dotted the fields beneath were like fresh headstones. Phil pointed them out to her. They were all so white they must belong to the same farmer.

'I know the sort of farmer,' she replied scornfully.

Her mood had changed suddenly with the change of scene from city to countryside. Darkness crept in about them. She lengthened her strides and went ahead silently. A chill seemed to have fallen between them. Phil, as always, acutely sensitive, noticed it instantly.

The chill was partly dissipated by Peter, who was sitting in Dona Nobis's room waiting for Phil to return. He had already become fast friends with her because of the intransigence of her political opinions.

Dona Nobis's republicanism was of an unusual and characteristic kind. She disapproved of the Free State Government because (a) the late Michael Collins was from West Cork, and as the whole world knew, you could trust a West Cork man just as far as you could fling him; and (b) because Eamonn de Valera was a Spaniard or half a Spaniard, and Spain was a decent Catholic country that had produced, among other desirable types, Saint Teresa, John of the Cross, and Ignatius Loyola. But what her opinions lacked in clarity they made up in heat, and during the civil war you might have seen Dona Nobis in women's meetings and processions, saying her rosary with the rest (though indeed, as she confessed herself, 'it was black rosaries she was saying half her time, and sixty of them wouldn't be near as satisfying as getting in one good clout at some pup of a sentry'). This had bred bad blood in the Dolls' House, which had given many of its sons to the regular army.

It was good to see Peter's skeleton face and close-cropped head again. Phil sent Mary Kate out for milk, cakes, and jam, and all four settled down to a spread. The political discussion continued, rather above the heads of Phil and Mary Kate, who had been too young to know the passions of the civil war, but they enjoyed the disagreements of the other couple. Dona Nobis, still impassioned, had lost none of her faith. Peter was bitterly disillusioned.

'Ach, I dunno,' he said at last, 'weren't we all fools to go breaking our hearts over what didn't concern us? Wouldn't it be just the same if the republicans won? Wouldn't it? Wouldn't the same old moneybags be running the country?'

'No, they would not,' said Dona Nobis, jamming her last slice of bread. 'We'd have driven them into the sea like Saint Patrick did with the snakes.'

'Or Brian Boru with the Danes,' added Mary Kate helpfully.

'Better for us we had snakes or Danes or Dutchmen any day,' said Peter despondently, taking out a very worn pack of cards. 'Come on and we'll have a game of forty-five.'

'I don't know how to play,' said Phil.

'Nor I,' added Dona Nobis.

'I do, Peter,' said Mary Kate.

'We'll teach them, then.' Wetting his thumb, he shuffled, cut, and dealt. 'What do you say, Phil? Wouldn't we be better with the snakes?'

Phil laughed and coloured, looking blankly at his cards.

'I don't know anything about it,' he replied, 'but I'm for the poor people against the rich.'

'Hear, hear!' said Mary Kate. 'Do I lead, Peter?'

'You lead, Mary Kate.—Highest in reds and lowest in blacks, Phil. There's an eight of clubs down.'

They played amid much chaffing from Peter and Mary Kate.

'What would you do for us if you'd your way, Phil?' asked Peter banteringly, pushing the cards towards him.

'I'd ease the rich of some of their money and give it to those that want it.'

'You're a communist,' said Peter.

'I don't know what a communist is.'

'He's right, anyway,' said Dona Nobis.

'Of course he is,' said Mary Kate.

They played on silently, each with his own thoughts of some better world in which there would be a more equal distribution of things. And the thoughts of each were very different.

''Twould be a great thing, sure enough,' sighed Peter at last. 'But I suppose the likes of us will never see it.'

'Why not?' asked Phil.

'I suppose because we're so ignorant, and they keep us so ignorant. When we fight we fight some one else's battles, about an oath or a treaty or a boundary that doesn't mean a ha'penny difference to us. And when they're done with us they send us to die in the poor-house.'

'What do I do now?' asked Phil.

'Have you a red card left?'

'I have not.'

'Then play the worst black you have. A ten or a nine or something.'

'Education,' said Dona Nobis firmly, 'is a wonderful thing. Often I wished and wished I had education enough and I'd open my mind to the general public about some of the blackguarding I see going on about me. I assure you, Mr. Cross, I'd open some people's eyes.'

'A king,' said Peter as she played.

'The divil sweep all kings!' she retorted.

'Ay,' said Mary Kate, ''tis a great thing to have education.'

And again they were silent, and again each imagined a world in which it would be possible to speak with an angel's tongue about that which most occupied his mind.

Phil accompanied Peter to the door. Shandon chimed ten, but the quays were already half deserted.

'Was that letter waiting for you all right?' he asked gently.

'No,' replied Peter hesitantly, 'it wasn't.'

'There's no time lost, though.'

'No. Sometimes it doesn't go easy with himself to send it, and I hang round for a few weeks until it comes. But he'll send it, never fear.'

He left Phil to a more restful night than that which had gone before. Yet it was not altogether restful, for the image of Mary Kate haunted his mind, flashing up before him now and again as when she had linked him, walking backwards, her face to the sky. He groaned. This was what came of taking things easy. But that which troubled his conscience least was that which most troubled his mind—Peter's future. That a few pounds should stand between a man and his own self-respect was a maddening thought, and none the less maddening because he had spoken so freely about taking from the rich.

Phil did not know the wise saying of the Indian sage that in the heaven world there are no chariots or roads for chariots, for the soul creates them in itself, nor did he know that other saying that when men fall from sanctity they think of goodness to their neighbour. Perhaps it was as well.

XXVI

PETER lived in a dosshouse in Blarney Street. In the
memory of the oldest inhabitant there was never a
time when it was not being condemned as dangerous
and insanitary, and there was never a time when it
was not full. It was presided over by the McCarthys.
The McCarthys were: Michael McCarthy, tall, thin,
sandy, and consumptive, who called every man 'sir' by
force of habit, acquired heaven knows where; Mary
McCarthy, who spent most of her day sitting on the
doorstep with an unwashed and squealing child in her
arms; and innumerable Charlie, Billy, Dolly, and
Babsy McCarthys who entered and departed the
world at irregular intervals, to the great vexation or
relief of their parents, according as to whether they
came or went, but quite unnoted by the world beside.
The neighbours declared that Michael was so stupefied by nature's exertions on his behalf that he never
knew exactly whether he was a subject for congratula-
tion or sympathy, and had even gone so far as to don
a crêpe band to attend the christening of one of his
children. This was probably untrue, or he may have
so misbehaved under the influence of drink. But it is
certain that he took pleasure in introducing his off-
spring *en masse* with the words, 'Meet the family; here
to-day and gone to-morrow.' His wife had a doleful,

sing-song voice. She drank too, but was scarcely likely to mistake a christening for a wake even after twenty years of it. 'But what can I do?' she would ask plaintively of a mixed assembly. 'When a poor creature have a drop taken sure any one can take advantage of her.' If her husband's motto in family life was, as he said, 'Aisy come, aisy go,' hers, delivered in a quite indescribable southern drawl, was, 'Sure, 'tis de will of de Almiiighty Gaaaawd.' He was extravagant, she was mean; he was gay, she melancholic.

They harboured five or six well-known characters, one answering to the name of Born Drunk, the other to that of Seldom Sober; these were lodgers of old standing who had certain recognised privileges, such as a stool beside the fire. There was also Hit the Deck or Hoppy, a wizened ex-navy man with a wooden leg, his assistant Toby of doubtful sex, and a noisy old beggar-woman, best known as Faith and Fatherland. The household was always in an uproar as one kitchen served all these and others, and quarrels over frying-pans and saucepans, and particularly over mugs, knives, forks, and spoons, were so frequent that one was always either brewing, raging, or subsiding.

It was to this house that Phil and Mary Kate called one night when they were seeking Peter. Though they had met regularly since the evening on Gurraneabraher, the coldness between them had never actually disappeared. Mary Kate blamed herself for it; Phil blamed himself for it, but self-accusation was no help. So they were glad of Peter when they met him, which was not often. He was said to be drinking.

They were welcomed uproariously. At their knock a half-naked child ran out and was so astonished at their appearance that it promptly crashed to the ground and after a moment's meditation set up a fiendish yell. Mary Kate reluctantly took the child in her arms, where it continued to yell to the accompaniment of a mild conversation in the kitchen. To end it she walked in and faced a battery of eyes. Within two minutes she and Phil were settled in the seats normally occupied by Born Drunk and Seldom Sober, and apparently settled for the evening. Peter was not there. Poor man, said Michael sympathetically, he was very disappointed in a bit of money he was expecting that hadn't yet turned up.

'No, indeed,' wailed his wife, 'and he owing us for three weeks' lodgings, and everything so dear and the cost of the child's funeral and all.'

'Ah, be quiet, woman,' said her husband impatiently. 'Didn't we get over more than that? Sure, 'tis for poor little Peter I'm sorry.'

'Oh, ay,' she retorted scornfully, ''tis for him you're sorry, and nothing at aall about your poor drag of a wife. . . . Men are aall the same'—she was addressing Mary Kate—'filling their guts and never bothering where 'twould come from, but if they were left without it you'd never hear the end of it. . . .'

'You'd pity him,' said Michael, ignoring his wife. 'Such a decent little man!'

'Why doesn't he settle down?' asked Phil.

Michael shook his head.

'He wouldn't be contented.'

'Why not?'

'He wouldn't.'

'Frightened he does be,' added his wife.

'Frightened?'

'Since the fighting,' Michael explained. 'He was never the same after.'

'He was an inquiry man,' explained his wife.

'That's queer,' said Phil.

'He can't rest under the one roof. It was the strain.'

'The man in America must know that, then?'

'To be sure he knows it. But Peter is afraid the money would be cut off.'

Phil nodded.

'Between you and me, he thinks they're plotting against him.'

'Who are?'

'The Government.'

Phil laughed, and Michael laughed with him, but for politeness' sake. To him there was nothing strange in the idea.

'He thinks they might take it away in the post office,' said his wife questioningly.

The upshot of it was that Phil and Mary Kate were invited to a party. The McCarthys gave parties on the slightest provocation, and sometimes on no provocation but the whim of a moment. Their wakes and funerals all turned into parties; their christenings turned into parties. Parties were talked of in the same way as fights, and required as little preparation. As soon as the teas of the household were over, messengers were sent out to the four quarters of heaven for all the necessities—mugs, glasses, candlesticks, and the rest. A train of McCarthy children, all with red hair, looking like an Egyptian wall painting, would trail into the house each carrying something. One with the horn of a gramophone, another with the gramophone itself, a third with three or four records, a fourth with

more records, a fifth with a melodion, a sixth with a
chair, and a seventh with a tumbler in each hand and
a corkscrew stuck dagger-like in his braces of twine. So
the procession would go on until the house was ready,
and by noon next day it would be stripped bare again.

On the night of the party Mary Kate called for Phil
about half-past eight. He was sitting by the window
looking out on the quay. They went along among the
squealing children in silence. At the foot of Shandon
Street she suddenly stopped and said, 'Phil, aren't
we getting terribly out with one another?'

He grew crimson, but continued walking.

'I suppose we are.'

They did not turn up Blarney Street, but walked
ahead until they came to a little arched laneway. They
stood in here. Nothing was to be seen at the end of
the misty tunnel but a patch of sloping field and a
sandstone campanile dark against the deepening blue.
Mary Kate looked round.

'I'd hate to think there was anything between us,
Phil,' she said.

'I'd hate it too,' he admitted heavily.

'Because I'm very fond of you, Phil.'

He thought over that for a moment. She wished in
her heart of hearts he would say, 'I'm fond of you too,'
and be done with it. When the thought of Nick
McCormick came to her mind she could have beaten
herself for a fool. Oughtn't she have known it was
madness to tell Phil anything about that? Oughtn't
she have known every man was inhuman? Dona
Nobis's 'You should be bloody well ashamed of yourself' was human, but a man's kindness was always
tied up with something abstract and cruel. Her

thoughts grew bitter as the silence was prolonged, but a faint hope still lingered. If only he would say something, anything, with a bit of human nature in it. The hope was crushed by his reply, given in a choked voice.

'It's all my fault, Mary Kate.'

She groaned.

'Oh, what's the use of talking? 'Tisn't any one's fault. We might as well go on.'

'But it is, Mary Kate.' His arm detained her. 'I was a fool.'

She smiled wanly. Was he going to say something sensible at last?

'That dread I had on me—about going mad—that was childish, Mary Kate.'

'I know that, Phil,' she said meekly.

'It was a temptation,' he said in a strong voice with an iron ring of determination in it, 'and I gave in to it. It was the devil trying to frighten me. And he did. I was frightened and restless. I was thinking of what that Verschoyle woman said. And I was thinking of other things as well.'

'Yes.'

'I was thinking of you.'

'Yes,' she said again, a chill touching her heart.

'I was thinking of nothing else,' he continued with a sort of suppressed passion. 'That's what brought the coolness between us.'

'It was not,' she whispered.

'It was, Mary Kate. Anything good there was in me is gone, and now I'll have to start all over again. When you came in to-night I was thinking it out. I see I'll have to start where I started before.'

She shivered. It was as if she was talking to a shadow of the Phil she knew. There was nothing, nothing, between them, nothing she could call on now. Then she looked at him for a moment with grave unwavering eyes.

'Did it strike you that that was what your mother wanted?'

He gave her back glance for glance.

'Yes, that struck me too. I know now she wouldn't be happy to think I was giving up a chance of getting on in the world. She'd have been on Mrs. Verschoyle's side.'

'And on mine,' she added with passion.

He looked hard at her, thinking it over.

'That's my loss,' he said at last, and she started at something in his voice, something graver and deeper that woke suspense and anguish in her. 'I see now I was in love with you all the time, only I wasn't honest enough to admit it.'

A sudden feeling of the unreality of it all overcame her. It had happened before when she had thought long and hard about something, when she had found herself moved for the twentieth time about something, that quite suddenly it ceased to be of importance; she and all concerned became wisps of disembodied stuff mouthing words into the void. Phil's declaration affected her like this, and she laughed harshly. She found herself unable to answer otherwise.

'And what are you going to do now?' she asked in a changed voice, a voice that suddenly had caught the overtone of weariness.

'I don't know,' he replied humbly. 'I'm praying hard for light.'

At that moment she noticed that his hair was growing wild from under his cap and that he had not shaved
for some time; a fine white down covered his cheeks
and chin. She laughed again, this time a little hysterically. He looked up in surprise.

'What is it, Mary Kate?'

'Your hair,' she laughed back, though her eyes were
very bright.   'How long is it since you got it cut?'

Immediately he reddened.

'Our Lord wore his hair long,' he said shamefastly.

'And is that why you didn't shave?' she asked.

'Yes,' he said harshly, and moved as if to go. Then
he saw her face as if it were for the first time, and
suddenly remembered with a stab of anguish the day
of his mother's funeral, when she had begun to cry;
he remembered his mother, the first days of her illness,
and then everything seemed to come back to him.
Mary Kate's slim figure, emerging from awkward
girlhood, moving silently about the little room; the
look that had come in her face that day when there
was no money to pay for food, her face when she had
bent over him in the church that far-away morning and
whispered him to come out, her face the first evening
when they had gone to pray in the Friars' church in
Liberty Street. He remembered even what she had
looked like when he came in from school and saw her
by his mother's bed that very first day, her shy,
startled air. And each picture brought its own atmosphere, still blue mornings, evenings of stars, summer
days with the scent of hawthorn on the hedges, but all
translated to a bewildering intensity, so that he found
himself shaken with superhuman longing. Never had
he imagined that his mind remembered all these

things in such a way. He did not trust himself to speak. He could not. But he heard her speaking.

'Phil,' she said, 'some day you'll be sorry.'

She merely whispered it and that was all. But it was enough—more than enough. He had to steel himself not to catch her arm and press it fiercely to his side. The world seemed to hollow out before him and leave him standing on the edge of the pit. They walked on in silence.

The party was in full swing when they arrived.

Peter was not there. He had been out all day, Michael said, no doubt drinking again.

Seldom Sober had already reduced himself to a state of coma, and Born Drunk was showing him off to the assembled guests. It always happened that when one of them was drunk, the other on the instant became quite sober and took advantage of him. They were like a swing—if one fell the other rose.

'He's from Donoughmore,' said Born Drunk, pointing out the poor wretch beside the fire. 'Donoughmore, I dread you.—You are from Donoughmore, aren't you? Speak up, you ignorant country lout, and tell the lady where you're from!'

'Let him alone,' said Mary Kate wearily.

'Tell the lady where you're from,' repeated Born Drunk, with a shout. 'He comes from beyond the lamps—don't you, you clown?'

'Donoughmore,' said Seldom Sober, 'is not beyond the lamps. There are lamps in Donoughmore.' He pointed a disdainful, wavering finger at Born Drunk. 'As good as in your old dirty Quarry Lane, anyway. Pfooh!' He spat and traced designs with it on the point of his shoe. 'Dirty, ignorant Quarry Lane.'

'They're not Christians at all in Donoughmore,' bawled Born Drunk, winking at Mary Kate. 'What do they pray to in Donoughmore, Seldom Sober? Tell the lady what they pray to in Donoughmore.'

Some one gave a glass of wine to Mary Kate. She drank it. She talked for a while to the two men, and then her head began to reel. She saw through a mist the two old men by the fire and the circle of faces about her. She tasted whiskey in the port wine. Hit the Deck sang a song. He had a deep bass voice. There was great applause when he finished. He sat down and wiped his palms on his knees.

'There's no weakness about that voice,' he said proudly, clearing his throat and caressing his Adam's apple. 'There's fellows going round singing now, and they pretend not to have any voice at all so that you'd think they were dying with the hunger. That's a dirty, contemptible way of cheating the public and cutting the throats of honest men.'

Mary Kate drank more of the wine and began to laugh immoderately without reason. She seemed to be very far away, and listened with great joy to the sound of her own voice, which seemed to her remarkably sweet. She saw those around her doing funny things, and realised that they were drunk. When she saw Hit the Deck's hand tremble she knew he was drunk. Michael McCarthy staggered—he was drunk. She knew by the way everybody smiled at her—so stupidly —that they too were drunk. The kitchen swam in smoke. Toby sang; he had a voice like a girl, and kept his cupped hand to his ear as though he were listening to himself singing.

Then she noticed that Phil was nowhere to be seen.

She suddenly got very angry and stood up. Michael McCarthy was standing by the door. She crossed to him and told him she was not going to be treated in this way. If a fellow took a girl out to a party he should wait to see her home. To her own surprise she heard herself call Phil a great many names. He had treated her outrageously, and she wouldn't put up with it any longer. Then she noticed that Mary McCarthy was there and that she and her husband seemed to be carrying on a dispute of their own. This made her really angry. With a dignified and slightly unsteady step she left them and went down Blarney Street. Toby followed her and said Phil had told him to see her home. She shouted at him to go back and called him outrageous names.

There was a moon shining somewhere and Shandon was reflecting it on one of its white walls. A cold wind blew, but she felt hot and sick. People moved around her silently and white faces were turned on her, but she ignored them. There was great dignity about the way she chose her steps. She could not forget that she did not really belong to these people at all. Her father lived in a castle. When Phil spoke to her again she would fling something in his face. He didn't know when he was dealing with a lady.

She crossed the bridge. There was a crowd on the quay. She went in the direction of the crowd. It swayed this way and that. Angular crags of slate projected from the roof-tops with a milky whiteness. That was the moon. The moon was shining in the water, broken up by an unusual trembling. Its image formed and dissolved, formed and dissolved again. Then she noticed two men in a boat. Near the crowd was a shining track of water that led from the footpath across the street to a public house. She followed the track and went into the public house. No one stopped her. There was a policeman inside and he was talking to Phil. She affected not to see Phil, and walked by him with her head in the air. Then she stopped and screamed. Phil turned round and saw her. He grabbed at her immediately and dragged her away. The policeman took her arm and held her with her face to the door.

Phil was explaining to the policeman that they had been at a party and some blackguard had put whiskey in her drink. They took her outside and the policeman beckoned to a young man. She heard him whisper to the young man that he must take the lady home. She suddenly saw Phil's face appear from the shadow into the moonlight, his long black hair tossed over his face, his eyes gleaming strangely and whitely, and wanted to go home with him. She had forgotten that he had insulted her. He was strange and handsome, and she wanted to go with him.

But the young man led her gently away. All the way home she had the feeling that something terrible had happened, and was shaken with little shivering fits. The moon seemed sinister, the houses seemed sinister. But when she tried to recollect what had happened her memory of it was like the moon's reflection in the water, momentarily forming and dissolving.

XXVII

. . . to let you know how every one at home is getting on. You will, I am sure, be sorry to hear your old friend Greg Mahon died shortly after you left. I did a bit of nursing there, as you may imagine, and like yourself he always liked me to sing for him, though he had no smack for the hymns at all, and was always at me to be singing 'A Cottage by the Sea', and he hated the sound of 'Daily, daily Sing to Mary' so much he once got up in the bed and flung it at me, and my shoes were drowned; but believe me after that he heard hymns and nothing but hymns, except the night before he died, when I sang 'A Cottage by the Sea' and 'After the Ball was Over' for him. I was so sorry to see him going. It was a great worry to me I could not reconcile him at the end, though indeed he went resigned enough, saying, which was very wrong of him, and I hope it was not true, that thank GOD he had brought tears to many a woman's eyes, and would die happy. He had some queer notion it was time for him to go, because Someone called Selim was always in the room, and that was a sign. I think he meant the DEVIL, but I would not mind much what a man like him would say. I sprinkled every bit of floor and wall and ceiling with holy water, but it seemed to make no difference at all, and the old ruffian was lying on the bed splitting

XXVII THE SAINT AND MARY KATE 297

his sides laughing at me. I could have killed him there
and then. The doctor could not see anything wrong
with him except imagination, and was surprised
he went so quick, but as I often said to you, Phil,
imagination will kill a man quicker than decline.

He left me what furniture and things was in the
house; it was three tables and a couple of chairs I got
twenty-two shillings for from a dealing woman in the
Coal Quay, so I was very rich and had two masses
said; one for the repose of his soul and the other for
your intention. They wrote me a lovely letter which
I am having framed. Also a whole lot of wood, which
is dry and grand for kindling and will last another six
months. I am keeping the tools for you, as I am sure
you will want them one of these fine days when you
will have a home of your own.

You won't believe who is in your old room now.
Mary Kate's Auntie Dinah. Herself and her sister had
great falling-outs on the head of a bread-van driver
that was gone on her, so at last she left. Babe is trying
to get her back now, but there is a lot of bad blood
between them, and Dinah is a black cow, and I think
myself the bread-van driver will have her. And it is
great nonsense of Babe to say he is beneath her. No
one knows who they are or what they are or where
they came from, and at any rate he is in a steady job,
though very advanced and a bit of a fool (GOD forgive
me for judging him).

Babe is a great vagabone. There is shocking scandal
about her. A lovely fellow she took up with, a Nor-
wegian sailor, she told him she could not marry him
because he was a Lutheran. So he was so fond of her
he got instructed and was received a few weeks back.

Very devout. And then she had to tell him that of course she was married already; and it came out he had given her his savings of three years to keep until they were married, and she had spent it all, the thief of hell. He nearly went out of his mind. Took to drink and had a terrible scene with her in the attic one night. It was Mary Kate who got him away down to my room, and oh, the creature, the two of us cried our eyes down for him. In the excitement he was after forgetting what bit of English he knew, and there he was stretched out on my bed calling to HEAVEN for vengeance on her in his own tongue. It is a sight I will never forget. But if he did not beat her I did, and though I am ashamed to admit it almost, I tore that one's hair out in handfuls. It was the first time ever in my life I did the like of that, so you will understand how put out I was. Mary Kate had a falling-out with her too—it was, of course, a great come down—and now they do not speak at all, though Mary Kate visits me regularly. I hope and trust she will die in the poorhouse, and I never had more satisfaction in my life than to hear her screeching when I laid my hands on her. I am glad to say I left her prostrate.

We made a collection among the neighbours to bury poor little Peter. I went to the republicans and shamed and disgraced them so much that they had to send out a band and give a pound to the funeral. We buried him in the tricolour as he would have liked, and a whole battalion of fellows followed the coffin. I also went to the Franciscans and explained how we had no money and how poor little Peter fought for his country, and they sent out not one but two priests, young men and hot republicans, and I became great friends with them after. They have been very good to me in other ways. They are grand men, and you were right to admire them. I forgot to say the money from America came after.

About Mary Kate, now upon my word I think in some ways you are very stupid and lacking in sense. Though I was never one for saying a flattering thing about anybody, I must say that I do not know a better or more God-fearing girl; and as I told you before, I think you took up wrong whatever little thing she said to you about any one else, for it is my certain conviction, for which I would go to the scaffold in the morning, that she is very fond of yourself. Anyhow, you would hardly know her now, for in many ways she is a different sort of girl, and am sorry to say she is losing a lot of her fun. Though I sometimes think GOD contrived it all for the best, as what we get easy we do not value after, and she will think all the more of a good husband for having to wait for him. Still, I hope she will not have to wait long. One good thing, everybody says she is improving in looks because of it, and turning out a real little lady, though I cannot tell, for the blindness is getting worse on me, though I believe it all. On the other hand, as I often say to her to keep her in her place, that is only by way of inviting worthless blackguards, and enough of them are running after her already, though I must say she does not encourage them from the little I see.

She is very friendly always with the woman Verschoyle, who, I admit, seems a real good class of woman, though a Protestant. I mean a sensible woman. She says to Mary Kate what I said to her from the first, though Mary Kate does not believe either of us, that you will be bound to come home, and what is more, that nothing will stop her getting a good job for you when you do. She is very good to me in a lot of little ways you will understand, though I have only seen her once in passing, and I disapprove *strongly* of her mixing with spirits, which in my humble opinion are all agents of the DEVIL.

I trust you are in Ireland and will get this letter soon. A little beggar-woman called Coholan said she seen you near Fermoy, and you had a bit of a beard and your hair was down your back like a girl's, and you went by her without recognising her, but Mary Kate says she is a great liar and not to be trusted. I also heard, which I hope is not true, that you were very shabby like a tramp. You should look after yourself better.

Now what I think is this, that Peter's death and your own interior troubles were a great shock to you, and that you did right to go away like that and see could you find your own soul away from us all, for I am afraid we were all annoying you. The soul is like that, and that is why people go into monasteries and convents, but it is clear to me that you were not cut out to be a monk, and that when you get some peace you will settle down again in the world, and find out that after a time you can live with your soul and your feelings separate, for I know a great deal about it, having myself at one time fallen into such melancholy that I was nearly being locked up, as I told you, in the Big House.

However, I am sure if you are in Ireland at all you will visit the monastery some day, and I am writing to the superior to have all inquiries made and giving your description and all, and asking him to show this letter on a board so that you can't miss seeing it. And remember I am dying to lay my eyes on you before the sight leaves me altogether. My dear boy.

Mary Kate has just come in. It is long past tea time and I have been hours writing this, so I have asked her to wet the tea while I finish. I am not telling her who it is to, because she would cry herself sick, so you see for all the way you left us we have not forgotten you yet, and we are always thinking of you. Sometimes I think if you do not come home she will go on the tramp too until she finds you. I would not blame her much. I shall never forget the morning after Peter drowned himself when we woke up and found you were gone. I often think too of the night you had the bad turn and the way we waited for you hours and hours, and sometimes I say to her we will hear you coming up the stairs like we did then. I think it would be nice if you came back like that some night the two of us would be together.

I have just told Mary Kate, and, as I thought, she is crying. Too fond of crying that girl is. But as there is room for a line or two yet, I am giving her the pen as a great compliment. I am sure she will write something nice . . .

THE END

OTHER TITLES
from
BLACKSTAFF PRESS

DUTCH INTERIOR
FRANK O'CONNOR

'Moonlight streamed down in a narrow cone and expanded in a corner of the whitewashed wall. Ned tossed restlessly and drew his hands through his hair …
"Bloody old fools!" he whispered savagely. "Fear is the one thing in their lives – fear, fear, fear. Fear of this world or fear of the next. 'What'll become of us?' 'What'll the neighbours say?' 'You can't do this and you can't do that.' " '

Intimate and truthful, Frank O'Connor's portrayal of Irish provincial life has made him one of the most influential and respected of modern writers. But it was this same searching honesty that caused the censorship of his work by the Irish government in the 1940s and 1950s.

Banned on its publication in 1940, *Dutch Interior* is striking for the integrity of its account of the effects of Catholic conservatism and sexual repression on a group of young men and women growing up in Cork city. As they fall in love, marry, emigrate or become trapped by their own pasts, O'Connor traces their changing fortunes with characteristic humour and sensitivity. And in its insight into the 'flash points of human experience', this novel is a forceful reminder of his unique talent.

'Every word has to be read.'
New Republic

'Frank O'Connor is a master of prose.'
Irish Times

198 x 129mm; 304pp; 0-85640-432-2; pb

£4.95

NIGHTFALL

AND OTHER STORIES
DANIEL CORKERY
EDITED BY FRANCIS DOHERTY

'That terrible promiscuity of rock, the little stony fields that only centuries of labour had salvaged from them, the unremitting toil they demanded, the poor return, the niggard scheme of living; and then the ancient face on the pillow, the gathering of greedy descendants – he had known it all before; for years the knowledge of how much of a piece it all was had kept his mind uneasy.'
from 'The Priest'

Passionately committed to the idea of a unique but vulnerable Irish identity, Daniel Corkery was nevertheless clear-eyed and unsentimental in his observation of peasants and poor town-dwellers. Widely recognised as among the finest Irish writing of this century, his masterly short stories, of which twenty are presented here, spring from this tension and from his sense of an unknowable mystery at the heart of common experience.

'The simplicity of the writing at times reminds you of Hemingway, but it has a warmth and passion that Papa rarely showed. Powerful, elemental themes – exile, death, blindness, loss – are dealt with in flexible words that add to the pathos of what is being written about.'
Irish News

198 x 129 mm; 224 pp; 0 85640 414 4; pb
£5.95

THE LAST OF THE NAME
CHARLES MCGLINCHEY

Between evocative, turf-lit pictures of a hard-working, neighbourly peasantry, and matter-of-fact accounts of such shocking practices as rape-marriage, Charles McGlinchey, weaver and tailor, of Inishowen, County Donegal (1861–1954), has bequeathed an astonishingly detailed tapestry of life in the west of Ireland in a period just beyond the grasp of living memory. He describes the clothes, the food, the cures, the story-telling and ceilidhing. And in the same quiet-spoken way, he tells of a vicious landlord who would take the girl of his choice on fair day; of a priest who evicted families to make himself a large farm; of faction fights and poteen-making.

McGlinchey told his memories to schoolmaster Patrick Kavanagh and now Brian Friel has edited them to create a book which will give readers a powerful empathy with our own ancestors, a curious sense of remembering what we cannot possibly have experienced. . .

'*The Last of the Name* represents the life work of two extraordinary Inishowen men, and although it is a posthumous publication, it already feels like a minor classic. By his subtle care for the story which Charles McGlinchey had to tell and for the words in which he told it, Patrick Kavanagh maintained the great tradition of those Irish country schoolmasters who have helped to give voice to the local cultures which they loved and served. This is a book full of emotional truth and the beauty of immediate, trusting speech, overbrimming with folklore of great imaginative richness.'
Seamus Heaney

198 x 129 mm; 152 pp; illus; 0 85640 361 X; pb
£4.50

DECEMBER BRIDE
SAM HANNA BELL

'And what was it ye said? To marry one of the men. To bend and contrive things so that all would be smooth from the outside, like the way a lazy workman finishes a creel.'

Sarah Gomartin, the servant girl on Andrew Echlin's farm, bears a child to one of Andrew's sons. But which one? Her steadfast refusal to 'bend and contrive things' by choosing one of the brothers reverberates through the puritan Ulster community, alienating clergy and neighbours, hastening her mother's death and casting a cold shadow on the life of her son.

'a story of the eternal triangle, held, like the land, by stubborn force'
Fortnight

'a quiet, compassionate story'
New York Times

'stands out as a remarkable novel'
Benedict Kiely, *Irish Times*

'invested with a disquieting and sullen beauty'
Saturday Review of Literature

198 x 129 mm; 304 pp; 0 85640 061 0; pb
£4.95

SOON TO BE AN IMPORTANT FEATURE FILM

NO SURRENDER
ROBERT HARBINSON

'The event was spectacular. Nearly eleven pounds I weighed. "Ya've the muscles of a man," said the district nurse when she congratulated Big 'Ina on having such a brute. My mother never forgot the nurse's remark. The years that followed were to prove that only those muscles would ensure our survival.'

Robert Harbinson's famous account of his Belfast boyhood – the devastating shock of his window-cleaner father's early death, his mother Big 'Ina's unending battles against poverty and tuberculosis ('It' to the little family), his first rapturous encounters with nature, circumscribed as it was by 'the Bog Meadows' marshy steppes' – was enthusiastically received when it was first published in 1960.

'A tough, but never a hard-luck tale Mr Harbinson manages to make his; full of pathos and pride and fresh, hot anger. . . [he] makes us believe in the passions of his childhood.'
Guardian

'He is on all planes at once; humorous, detailed and objective as a Brueghel village scene; quietly indignant over injustices practised by the toffs; puzzled, exploratory, expectant, as a growing boy. . . He writes as one with a true sense of poetry.'
The Times

'. . . crammed with the stuff of life. The raucous cobbled streets, the grimy mission halls and the evening mists that made the Bog Meadows a place of mystery, the bitterness and the passion of the religious and political background – Robert Harbinson conjures them up out of his memory with a sureness of touch that gives authority to every page.'
Irish Independent

First paperback edition

198 x 129 mm; 224 pp; 0 85640 383 0; pb
£4.50

SONG OF ERNE
ROBERT HARBINSON

'My mother's last words, flung through the window as the bus gathered speed, were – "An' keep yer snout clean up there." For her, the country was always "up there", and she was anxious I should forsake the evil ways I had picked up in the city. She wanted me to come back sobered and settled, prepared to face a steady life in the docks. Wild escapades must be at an end, new leaves must be turned, my snout, in fact, kept in an impeccable condition.'

Leaving the tough Belfast life, Robert Harbinson continues his successful autobiographical sequence with the story of his stormy time as a World War II evacuee in the woods, fields and lakes of County Fermanagh. Suspicious, scruffy, sectarian, belligerent, the twelve-year-old Robbie is a terror to the county, rampaging in quick succession through a rectory, a workhouse and a liberal sprinkling of large farms and small cottages before finding at last the perfect 'billet' with Christy and his sister Maggie. The profound joy of his life with them, helping with the farm work, enjoying their kitchen ceilidhs, basking in their uncomplicated love for him – their 'wee cub' – reverberates through these pages, making this book truly a 'Song of Erne'.

'What a gloriously nostalgic picture this is: what a delightful book to read and read again!'
British Books

'a delightful pastoral, timeless, and smelling richly of the deep country: truthful and genuine'
Tablet

First paperback edition

198 x 129 mm; 244 pp; 0 85640 394 6; pb
£4.50

THE ARAN ISLANDS
JOHN M. SYNGE
WITH DRAWINGS BY JACK B. YEATS

In 1898, acting on the advice of W.B. Yeats, J.M. Synge visited the remote Aran Islands in the west of Ireland. The primitive lifestyle and complex ancient culture of the island people had a profound effect on the young writer and his work. The memory of his Aran experiences, brilliantly distilled in this account, was to provide a rich quarry for his great masterpieces *Riders to the Sea* and *The Playboy of the Western World*.

This beautiful new gift presentation, in buckram hardcovers, is a facsimile reproduction of the 1911 Dublin edition, including twelve magnificent line drawings by Jack B. Yeats.

198 x 129 mm; 272 pp; illus; 0 85640 412 8; hb
£9.95

ORDERING BLACKSTAFF BOOKS

All Blackstaff Press books are available through
bookshops. In the case of difficulty, however, orders
can be made directly to the publisher. Indicate clearly
the title and number of copies required and send
order with your name and address to:

CASH SALES

Blackstaff Press Limited
3 Galway Park
Dundonald
Belfast BT16 0AN
Northern Ireland

Please enclose a remittance to the value of the cover
price plus: £1.00 for the first book plus 60p per copy
for each additional book ordered to cover postage and
packing. Payment should be made in sterling by UK
personal cheque, postal order, sterling draft or inter-
national money order, made payable to
Blackstaff Press Limited.

Applicable only in the UK and Republic of Ireland
Full catalogue available on request